Beloved Disciples

Mario Elías

AMBLE PRESS
ANN ARBOR

2026

Amble Press

Print ISBN: 978-1-61294-337-4
Library of Congress Control Number: 22025949548

Amble Press First Edition: May 2026

Printed in the United States of America
on acid-free paper.

Cover & interior designer: TreeHouse Studio
Cover photo & interior etchings: Mario Elías

Amble Press
PO Box 3671
Ann Arbor, MI 48106

www.amblepressbooks.com

Dedication

For my husband, who has believed
in every dream I've dreamt up.
And for my parents, who taught me so much,
even as they were still learning themselves.

Dedication

For my husband, who has believed
in every dream I've dreamt up.
And for my parents, who taught me so much,
even as they were still learning themselves.

Part I

How to Remember

Chapter One
First Love in Perpetual Motion

The night I met Albi, I had a vague thought my old life might end, and some new, truer life had already started forming its spinal column and fingernails.

At the end of a street on the edge of the city, I balanced on the curb, floating inches above the wet pavement, blinking violently. Street lamps sprayed light into the humid air, casting a shadow at my feet that could have belonged to anyone. The ragged palms crunched against each other. A frog chirped nearby. I needed to remember who I was in that moment before I changed.

Lenita clapped her hands in front of my face and pulled my arm as she led me toward the dark house in front of us. Fence posts circled the yard with no proper fence connecting them. Chicken feet and other unrecognizable bones hung from the posts and clacked in a witchy way as the breeze stirred them. Just beyond the sound of rattling bones, the faintest rhythm drummed underground.

"Please welcome to the stage our hostess with the . . . Well . . . with just enough, I guess . . ." Muffled laughter filled the spaces around the introduction. "They say beauty fades, but talent lasts forever. Lucky for her, she doesn't have to worry about either.

Her latest one-star review said, 'Wow, bigger snooze on stage than in bed.' *Cariños*, give it up for Isabel Panocha!"

We heard the introduction as we descended into El Palomar for the first time. The worn wooden steps creaked beneath us, scratches revealing layers of faded color. I imagined the stairs crumbling under a mass exodus, bodies climbing over each other to escape. My pace slowed, but Lenita's grip tightened, a handler guiding her cowardly horse.

The song began while the crowd continued erupting in whoops and whistles. Waves of sound bounced up the staircase around us as her muffled voice clawed its way out of the rumbling din below.

"Hurry up, Simón! The show's already started!" Lenita hissed, quickening her pace and leaving me trembling on the steps. I could feel the heat first in my feet, and as I continued down, it moved up my legs and overtook my body entirely with its tidal weight.

The performer, Isabel, weaved her way through the crowded dance floor, plastic costume jewelry twinkling in the dim light. As the applause subsided, everyone quieted. She continued singing a cappella, the clatter of her bangles the only sound accompanying her husky, smoky voice. It was a song about being a woman like any other, about living with her defects in defiance of what any man thought. Everyone knew the words. Everyone knew what they meant, and I wondered if they understood them the same way I did.

On the steps above, I stood frozen, watching the sea of people sway, singing with her in hushed, reverent tones. Above them, the air hung thick like river water, and we were all being held beneath its surface by this siren. Her hair was piled high, the sides slicked and glued into place. Her gown, simple in silhouette, clung to her curves. Thick layers of makeup carved features into her round face.

Then . . . the illusion clicked.

I had never seen anyone like her before, and my first reaction was to look away. Shame had been tucked into the folds and valleys of my brain, but I immediately defied it. A small ember took hold, once smothered by all the garbage inside me. I might have shaken my head and opened my eyes wider, absorbing more of the sight. I might have cheered as she crescendoed.

I might have wanted to run away.

I might have wept.

Sweat trickled down her chest, carrying trails of makeup from her face, now softened like a reflection in a foggy mirror. And, as she hit the final note, Isabel flung her arms above her towering hair, scattering beads of sweat like holy water.

The crowd erupted in yells and applause, surging toward her. They wanted to touch her, press money into her hands, as if she were a prophet or visiting saint. She slithered through the throng toward the back of the bar, gliding like it was all part of the act.

Bodies rearranged themselves with practiced urgency as the music kicked back in with a merengue brass and scratch punching through the heat.

El Palomar is not a nightclub, but rather a basement where music is played and there's booze to drink. A concrete box. A self-fueled furnace. Tiny, narrow windows line the back wall, drawing fresh air in, while a fan at the front door sucks moist heat out. This method barely suffices on a weekday, let alone a Saturday, when the place is packed full of bodies like plastic bags stuffed with more plastic bags in a kitchen drawer.

Lenita waved me in, and I imagined my new life developing a heartbeat, growing hair. I gathered my resolve, stepping down, level with the crowd. Bodies crashed. The stairs disintegrated behind me. I couldn't swallow. Couldn't breathe. I backed into the wall, my hands dripping with sweat.

The rough concrete was clammy against my palms. I pressed harder into it, settling into the blooming pain while I watched. The dancers had all paired up, hip to hip in the syrupy, semi-opaque air. Women spun, guided by disembodied hands held overhead. Whistles punctuated the music as men swirled and collided with debauched abandon, ducking low to dodge elbows here or a revolving blade of hair there. A singular, hive-like rhythm hummed under the chaos.

Then, I noticed the nudges exchanged between some of the men, the flirtatious glances shared by others. Asses colliding. Crotches brushing against thighs. The lust, the abandon. I could almost taste it in the air. The sweat was sweeter. Tension building below the belt, electricity creeping down legs, pooling at the clavicle, and wrapping its fingers around throats. It teased every follicle, clung to each back rubbing against a bare arm.

I had never seen men express such genuine, unguarded happiness. I took inventory of every face. Mustaches stretched across upper lips. Eyebrows were lifted, not furrowed. Hair glistened with sweat. Clothing stuck to skin.

I was an orphaned anthropologist encountering a tribe he had no idea he belonged to. I felt lied to. Kept out of a secret conversation. I wanted to remember the design of every man's shirt and whether it was tucked in or not. I wanted to remember the girls in high heels and the ones brave enough to dance barefoot.

A group of older men sat around one of the tables flanking

the dance floor. Four women leaned on another. A third table held a gaggle of flamboyant guys around my age, clucking and cawing at each other. Conversations crossed, pinging off one another like a tennis match, a glorious cacophony of insults and laughter peppered with profanity even my cousin Camilo would blush at.

"You wouldn't know good dick if it came with *arroz con leche, maricas*," one of the older men said before swigging his beer and groping himself.

"If that's what you're offering, *cagalitroso*, you can keep it. Sounds like something else has expired besides your dusty brain," one of the younger guys snapped back, flipping invisible locks over his shoulder. Laughter erupted.

And then . . . behind the chaos, like a holy apparition . . . there he was.

Maybe it was the way he stood just beyond the cackles and screams, arms crossed over his broad chest, that struck me dumb. Or maybe it was the veins in those arms, protruding and alive, pumping blood just beneath the surface.

His glowing skin was draped with a fine, translucent blanket of black hair, hovering above the flesh. The hair stopped above his elbows, but the veins and skin carried on, and I ached to touch the parts of his arms I couldn't see.

I looked up to his face and recognized him instantly: the altar boy from my childhood church. His beautiful, strong nose. His honey eyes, dark one moment under a furrowed brow and gleaming the next.

I had stared at him every mass as he carried the cross and placed it next to the altar, cleaned the blood from the gold chalice, swung the thurible with hypnotic precision. While other boys fidgeted and yawned, he moved with purpose, reverence.

I'd watched his hands cradle sacred objects as if they were extensions of his own body, hands that now lay tucked defensively against his chest. I'd dreamed of those hands touching me with the same care, fingertips leaving marks on my skin like the smudges he wiped away from the reflective surfaces.

My gaze hovered around his mouth. A sly twitch of his lip as a smile spread. My eyes met his, and my face caught fire as I darted along the concrete wall, hoping to disappear. A roach scattering at the flick of a switch.

I edged toward the bar. The surface was cluttered with bottles, glasses, and puddles of spilled liquor. People crowded around it in mounds. Some leaned in, jostling to keep their place for drinks, while others simply loitered, shouting over the music.

"Simo! Simón! Over here!" Lenita's voice boomed from inside one of the mounds, and I dove toward it.

"This is insane!" I gasped, wedging myself between people. "I don't want to close my eyes. I don't want it all to disappear." I rubbed one eye and wailed theatrically before wrapping my arm around her, pretending to weep.

"That's so funny 'cause you looked like you were going to make a run for it. I thought we'd lost you for sure." She shoved her elbow into my ribs and nodded toward the altar boy. "I knew you'd love it here," she added, moving her tongue obscenely against the inside of her cheek.

"*Sucia!* You knew what kind of place this was?" I shrieked, louder than intended. "Why didn't you tell me? I would've dressed differently!"

I smoothed one hand over my hair while the other tugged at the hem of my shirt, one size too big and five years too old, fidgeting like a toddler about to piss himself.

"Look around, Simo. Everyone is a sweaty mess. You actually look better than most of these guys in here."

"Actually, huh?" I pushed her backward as she chortled and hit the bar. "Anyway, they looked better than me when they walked in. Imagine how disgusting I'll look when we leave."

Lenita leaned close, her breath hot on my neck. "I've known you since we were six. You're the worst fag I've ever met. You'd have found some excuse to bail." She twisted her hair up and away from her shoulders. "You've gotta pop that little cherry sometime. We're not leaving until you at least kiss a guy."

The memory of our awkward teenage fumbling flashed through my mind: her detached expression as I tried desperately to be good at something that left me completely cold. She'd shrugged afterward and said, "Nothing. I felt nothing at all."

Now, ten years later, I stood in a sea of beautiful men in love with each other, while the only person I'd ever been with was laughing at my discomfort. Twenty-five and still a virgin in all the ways that mattered.

"Okay. Let's do it," I said. "Not you and me. Me and a man. I'm gonna find a man."

"Literally any man!" Leni screamed over the music, and I ducked down again.

A woman came around the corner behind the bar, balancing two bottles in each hand. It was the host who had introduced Isabel Panocha. Tall and elegant, she had an aura that demanded attention, like a leading lady whose unflappable resolve wins everyone over by the end of the film.

She set the bottles down without glancing at the tables, already deep in conversation with two women at the end of the bar. As she poured them drinks from unmarked bottles, she smiled and gave us a casual chin-lift. A cool "What'll it be?"

"Two shots of whatever you're pouring!" The words bumbled out like a caricature of some womanizing beer drinker, and my cheeks flushed. Who was I posing for?

"Two shots, eh?" she mimicked. "Loosen up, *bebé*. This is just water. I think you need something stronger."

She poured three glasses of a dark liquid before ambling over to Leni and me. "It's your first time here, right? Just have fun. Leave that macho bullshit with your *tíos*. These are on me. *Salud*."

We clinked glasses and took the shots.

"I don't want you to get in trouble for giving us stuff for free." I kept my eyes low as I fumbled for my wallet.

"Don't worry. The boss is a bitch, but she can surprise you." She winked.

"I'm Simón, by the way. And this is my best friend, Lenita."

"*Encantada*. I'm Coco." She poured us another round. "Coco Tazo. Now go dance before I give you one." Her hand delivered a light slap to my cheek, playful but firm.

We knocked back the shots, and I folded some cash under an empty glass. Shaking off my awkwardness, I grabbed Leni's hand and pulled her into the crowd, all pivoting to the merengue scratching through the speakers.

In the maelstrom, I saw him again. This time, he was laughing, swiveling and swirling his body with a curvy girl. Her face glistened with sweat, and her hair coiled in on itself like a *buñuelo*. Every movement they made, she controlled, whether he realized it or not.

Smiling over her shoulder, she butted into a nearby conversation. Then, with a glance back at the altar boy, she rolled her substantial ass in a slow, flirtatious circle, hands resting loosely at her waist. There was a savage poetry to the way she moved, a crude etching of self-assured passion. A swipe of ochre. Charcoal on stone. The Venus of Willendorf, hypnotically swaying her hips and clapping her hands to the rhythm.

My gaze then fell to his hips, swirling like a slight breeze to her hurricane. Where the Venus was a demand, he was a quiet wish. An inclination. Undulating fluidly, he moved effortlessly through the pulse of the music, each motion dripping with slight and surprising femininity, with power.

My stomach tensed as I watched him move. I let my body mirror his rhythm, following the curve of his motions. I spun Lenita a little too forcefully and tried to reposition us for better viewing.

"Let's get over there," she said, responding knowingly to my odd behavior.

We moved closer and closer in a frenzied descent. His gravity, so irresistible, sucked me out of my slumberous orbit and catapulted me around him. He burned hot and bright, this newborn star in my galaxy.

He laughed loudly as he dodged some brazen dancers slicing across the floor, then reunited with the Venus, spinning her three times in one direction before darting to avoid a collision with another couple.

Lenita broke away, spinning herself in a circle, bored with my neglect.

He looked at me. Not accidentally in my direction— but at me. His smile grew, and the music swelled in my ears, pounding with my heartbeat.

The Venus whooped.

Lenita clapped her hands.

He glanced again. The smell of smoke and sweat thickened.

His curls traced the shells of his ears, each one perfectly placed, like someone had measured them. The vein in his neck pulsed. His hand gripped around her body.

I imagined that hand on the small of my back . . . leading me through the crowd . . . spinning me and smiling before holding me close again. So close I could smell the rum on his breath. So close I could feel his heartbeat in his thighs, zippered tightly against mine. He could press his chest into mine, and I could breathe in the steam between us.

Leni slapped my shoulder. I'd been holding her too tightly, breathing too hard into her neck.

"Now that I felt," she whispered in my ear, raising an eyebrow and glancing down at my crotch. She gave my ass a slap, turned herself, and suddenly there he was.

We were side by side.

I could lean over and sniff him.

He spun around, and so did the Venus. Her shoulders collided with mine, and she grabbed me, made me twirl her in a circle as Lenita danced next to my altar boy.

His cheeks raised. His teeth sparkled.

I clumsily fumbled the rhythm out with my suddenly numb, cinderblock feet. He looked into my eyes again, and I looked down.

Lenita yelled into the Venus's ear, "*¡Oye, perra!* Let's get a drink. I'm buying." Then she turned to me and the altar boy. "No boys allowed, though. My mother always told me never to take money out in front of a man . . ."

I finished her sentence without looking up. "Yeah, yeah, or he'll never go get his own."

The two women slipped away through the crowd, and when I looked up, he was standing in front of me, blinking expectantly. His eyelashes were long and thick. They could reach for me, pull me in close.

"I've never been here before. Have you?" I yelled over the music, scrambling to say something, anything.

"No, it's the first time for me too," he said, his voice carrying a slight formal precision that hinted at starched collars and sacristies. "That girl I'm with is my neighbor. She asked me to take her dancing, but she's mostly just been flying around the room, yapping and dancing with everyone else." He shrugged, small and controlled. "But that's fine. I'm—I'm doing alright now."

He stood close, arms crossed over his body again. My eyes involuntarily darted down to the layered view of flexed chest behind bicep and then back up to his eyes.

His mouth twitched. He'd noticed my gaze. But instead of backing away, he let his arms fall to his sides, opening himself again.

"Yeah, I saw you standing by yourself earlier," I said, my voice shaky, "and wondered if maybe you were dragged here. If you wanted to get out of here, I could cover for you. You know, if this place wasn't what you expected . . ."

"You're a funny one." His shoulders relaxed. He smiled, slow and easy. "It's not at all what I expected. But if I were to get out of here, I was hoping you might want to come with me."

His words hooked into my stomach and reeled me in. I blinked, wide-eyed, dragged gasping to the surface.

Just then, the older man with the expired balls and brain approached us, looking only at my new companion. "*Ey papito*, let me buy you a beer. I can introduce you to some people around here. What's your name?" He stood at an angle that made it quite clear I was not included in this invitation to the other side of the basement.

"It's Albi. But, actually, me and . . ."

"Simón," I said faster than I've ever spoken.

"We were just headed out." Albi grabbed my hand and pulled me across the dance floor. Lenita sent a piercing whistle into the moist air as we passed her and went up the stairs out of El Palomar.

Outside, the air felt thin and light. The pavement dully reflected the streetlights glowing over our heads. Albi turned around and looked at me. "So . . . I'm not usually that bold." He picked at his cuticles, clearly nervous now that we were alone.

"Me neither," I said. "Not that I did anything bold. I'm not bold either."

Albi stopped fidgeting with his hands and let out a chuckle. "You crack me up. I don't think I've met anyone like you before. Are you always so . . . quirky?"

"I think so." My shoulders slumped, but I built them up quickly again. "Yes. Yes I am."

He smiled, shaking his head and puffing air through his nostrils. "You seem familiar in some way. I just can't figure out from where."

"I went to school at St. Sebas. I saw you every Tuesday and Sunday at mass for, like, four years." I tried to say this coolly and not betray that I did not merely see him twice a week, but that I'd been collecting moments of him for years, a reliquary he'd never known he'd given me.

"Wow." His thumbs scraped at his cuticles again. "Now I feel like an ass for not recognizing you."

"Why would you? I was one of a hundred, and you're, like, one in a million." I felt oddly at ease. All of my nerves had calmed, seeing him squirm.

He laughed, ducking his head to hide his blushing cheeks. "You've been saving that one up, haven't you?" He laughed again. "What a line," he said softly, kicking a rock across the glistening yellow pavement. "You're good."

"That came out cornier than I thought it would." I smiled back. "But it's true. Why would you remember me? We never spoke. The only interaction we had was this one time when I passed out in the pews after all the standing and kneeling for the Stations of the Cross. You and some other kid helped me off the floor."

Albi snapped his fingers. "I do remember that! Wait . . . you would also sit and stare up at the altar and blink really fast." He laughed hard. A little too hard? "I do remember you! Why were you always doing that?"

"I honestly didn't think anyone was ever looking at me." I laughed out loud, joining Albi in my humiliation. "I used to do the blinking thing when I really wanted to remember something. It was my way of cementing a memory, I guess. It sounds dumb. Apparently looks dumb, too."

"It's not dumb. Just funny." He stepped closer, his voice soft. "I guess it was like you were taking pictures of the scene or something. That's kind of cute." He grabbed my hand, ran his thumb over my knuckles, and then let it go. "What were you trying to remember at church then?"

He stood close. His body heat hit me in waves.

"You," I said without hesitation, blinking once. "It was always you."

We walked through the empty town. Aimlessly at first. We

talked and talked. Albi laughed at the way I formed sentences, the strange ideas that popped into my head and flopped out of my mouth. And I couldn't stop smiling.

"Do you always obsessively inspect things like that?" he asked as we walked, catching me checking my back pocket for my wallet for the hundredth time and looking left to right.

"I'm not the only one obsessively inspecting if you noticed me doing it," I said in a huff.

"I don't usually. Maybe you inspire neuroses in me."

"Oh no. The change is happening too fast." I grabbed his arm and shook him. "What monstrosity will you become in a year?"

"I hope to find out," Albi said simply, and I stopped talking for the first time since we'd left El Palomar. Albi knocked his knuckles against mine and laughed.

"I wanna take you somewhere," I said on impulse, taking a sudden right down a street that ran to the bay.

"Don't worry. No one comes here. Not even in the daytime," I told him as we climbed down to my beach. His eyes darted. His hands fiddled. But his smile never faltered.

The sky floated clear above us, the water calm against the shore. The air smelled different there—the towering eucalyptus in the park above, the salt of the sea, the steam rising out of my shirt as we moved through the summer humid heat. The sweetness of the mango trees, miraculously growing in the sandy soil. His hair, vanilla and mint. I breathed it all in deeply, wanting to remember this scent forever, to bottle it and carry it with me.

"My mom used to bring me here when I was super small. She stopped coming with me after a while." I found us a place to sit and watch the water. "She stopped doing a lot of stuff, I guess. But this has always been my secret spot."

"It's beautiful. I can't wait to see the sunrise," Albi said, settling in next to me with a wink.

I told him a few stories, and he told me some too. The clouds started rolling along the crystal sky, but I can't describe any shapes they might have made. I saw them tumbling around his face, floating in the center of it all. All I had to do was turn, and my nose might brush his hair. I could breathe deeply and smell him.

"I imagined dancing with you earlier," I confessed. "Before, when I saw you at El Palomar."

He stood, brushed sand from his pants, and extended his hand. As he pulled me up, he began humming a half-remembered song. He moved to its uneven rhythm, and I followed. His hands found my hips, drawing us closer with each stumbling beat.

He looked like a cat to me, and I looked like a little boy to myself.

Each time I glanced back up, his eyes were already there, waiting. His hand settled into mine as if it had always belonged there. He spun me as he had the woman earlier, keeping me in his orbit. I was spinning with him through a landscape now painted in shades of gold.

I wanted to know how he thought we looked together, to know every thought that had ever crossed his mind. I wanted to know him completely while pretending to know nothing, just so he would tell me everything again—one of those silly feelings when you first fall in love and realize that's precisely what is happening.

His face pressed against mine as we gazed in opposite directions. His body moved mine with each breath. Starlight caught his skin as I imagined lifting him skyward, turning him through the night air, his body reflecting every color an imaginative person could think up. I could see that scene in infinite variations, then and every day after. A stop-motion time lapse of First Love in Perpetual Motion.

Albi shifted closer so that our foreheads almost touched. I could feel the way he hesitated, as if weighing the moment in his hands, afraid to drop it.

His lips brushed mine. So softly at first, I wasn't sure if it had really happened. Then again, more certain. His tongue tasted sweet; his upper lip was salty. Everything was heat and softness and Albi's quiet hum against my mouth.

The mango leaves clattered rhythmically against each other, and the waves crashed in time, while the world rearranged itself around us. New and familiar at once.

I kissed him back with a wild hunger that scared me—when his hands found the small of my back and pulled me closer, when his mouth opened barely enough to breathe me in. I was crazed. I craved to be enough for him, to adore him, to eat his consecrated body. I wanted to place roses at the base of his altar, to make a pilgrimage on his feast day. Kiss his blessed feet and wash them with my hair.

When we finally broke apart, his forehead rested against mine, and he laughed, soft, breathless. "I didn't know it would feel like that," he whispered, brushing his thumb over the pulse in my throat. He guided our bodies onto the sand and kissed me again and again.

"I can never not be like this again, Albi," I said, panting on the sand, not really knowing what I meant by it, but hoping he did.

He said no one had ever spoken to him that way, that it felt like a spell.

Walking back to town, the trees passed their song from one to the next, a subtle trilling, like the tentative burning in your gut after love begins. The naïve hunger to experience every pendulous possibility. The silhouette of imminent pain swinging closely overhead.

His fingers intertwined with mine under the dim rosy light of this new morning, and I followed him back toward a city that suddenly seemed too small to contain what was growing between us.

I try to remember every second exactly as it happened. I want so deeply to go back, travel through time to where the grass meets the sand meets the ocean. I will always hold him up to that starlight. The leaves rustling, the wind whistling the tune as the clouds make their way around him. It was golden, and it was beautiful. My heart. My Albi.

Chapter Two
Capillaries & Arteries

"You're the man, Simón. You need to learn how to act like you're leading," my mother said as she softly placed her right foot forward and used her shin to push my tiny left leg backward as we danced on the porch of that beautiful blue house at the top of the hill. "The lady will always know what to do, but you have a part to play, and that is to make her look good."

A fly buzzes inches above my face and crashes itself into the window. It repeats its violent attempt at freedom again and again. *Thud. Thud. Pfzzzzzthud.*

When my mother was still happy, we would sit on the flat roof of our house and look down the hill as the tide rolled in, striking the seawall, clapping against the stones, shooting a jet of mist into the sky. After the spray settled, the waves seemed to roll backward, away from the city and out into the sea. We lived at the center of the world.

I died three days ago. It seems like three days, but by the looks of things, months might have passed. My body lies there, rotting. Juices seep through the sheets and soak into the mattress. *Thud pfzzzzz.* Maggots might wriggle around, nibbling my innards, while the unwashed plate under the nightstand grows its own ecosystem. The oscillating fan sits unused in the corner, and a stench hangs thick in the unmoving air like a sickly-sweet fog.

The fly bounces erratically. Through its compound eyes, the fragmented world collides with the window. Its tiny, hairy body shudders as the city sprawls beyond the glass in disjointed spasms, like a garbage truck heaving its load down the slope. Just on the other side of these walls, the buildings shift and slam with the movement of the fly's body. The staccato rhythm propels people ambling down streets and churns the waters of the bay that curve into the city's body as the fly's wings make their infinite scoops and rotations.

When my mother was happy, she invented stories to tell me before tucking me in for the night. Climbing into bed, she looked more like herself than she ever did out in the world or when we entertained company. She would let her hair down, curls spilling around her proud shoulders, and her freckles, usually hidden behind makeup the way daylight covers up the stars, were revealed as constellations spreading across her cheeks and nose.

Before my father left, she had an ease about her that no one sees now. She wasn't carefree, but her cares affected her differently, I suppose. Back then, I had a sure place in the world. That version of life sparkled like the glint of her teeth in the morning light as she laughed at an observation I made about the chickens looking like Tía Cachita on her wedding day. "Her third wedding day!" she screamed, and I never felt more proud.

The fly pauses, resting on the sill. Fog drapes over the water and flings its ends across the city like freshly laundered linen. It nestles most mornings in that dark hour before indigo shifts to bruised violet, then to rose and cornflower blue, bringing magic back to the faded paint and complacent people of this stagnant city.

When my mother was happy, she would call me into the kitchen to cup mashed potatoes into my hands and scoop last night's *picadillo* on top. "Your hands are the perfect size for a perfect bite," she would say, and then nuzzle my neck or play bite my hands, which were still cupping the mixture, ready to be folded, breaded and transformed into something new, something different.

I look at myself from above. I'm lying there naked. My skin is stretched over my bones like a thin canvas nailed to its wooden frame. An animal pelt being cured and tanned. The fly continues to concuss itself against the window.

Pfzzz thud, again and again, like the rattle of beads.
Like they're praying the rosary over my corpse. *Thud.*
Hail Mary, full of grace . . . *Thud.*
Holy Mary, mother of . . . *Thud.*
Pray for us sinners. *Pfzzz.*
Each collision, a penance paid.

"Okay, Simón, tonight's story begins in a town that sat on the water, stretching along the coast just like ours. It had hills and buildings of every color. The only real difference was this place was filled with disgusting monsters. They looked like regular people at first, but when they opened their mouths, jagged teeth jutted out everywhere, and the stench—uuuf—*un apeste, muchacho.*" She waved her hand in front of her crinkled nose.

"They hung out of crumbling buildings they'd neglected, tearing through the potholed streets they'd ruined themselves. It would've been a blessing if *Papa Diosito* threw up his hands and slid the whole town into the sea. *Una limpieza así de fácil.*" She clapped her hands twice, wiping her palms clean.

"They dragged their blubberous bodies through the streets, blubbering to each other or to no one at all, slurping slops with every sloppy step," Mamá said over my giggles, snarling cartoonishly and tickling my belly.

"But! There were two others in this town, Simón. Each lived on opposite ends of the street that ran along the sea. They weren't monsters like the rest of them." She squeezed my hand gently and kissed the top of my head. "These two were sweet and sensitive."

"They kept to themselves, sticking to their routines, going to work, and coming home. *Y ya. A mimir solitos.* They found little happinesses where they could, though they knew something was missing. One liked to read, the other wrote rhymes. One knitted, the other tied knots. When one felt music inside, both whistled the tune. They were mirrors of each other, but their paths never crossed. And they were alone until the day they died."

"Mamá! No! Don't kill them!" I cried, clutching her arm. "Why didn't they try to fit in with the monsters? They could've made friends if they tried." I knew very well it wasn't that easy.

"Sometimes, *mijito*, to be different is to be alone. People can't always change who they are like they change their clothes. Imagine I go out with my friends, all of us in new dresses and high heels, looking sharp. And a man walks up to me, asking me to dance, but he's completely naked. I can't dance with him! That's not how it's done." She leaned back, satisfied with the improvisation.

"So, does being different feel like being naked or wearing high heels?" I asked, thinking of myself in her closet.

"Being naked, I suppose. You are who you are, and you can

cover it up with clothes, but it doesn't change you."

"But you and your friends are naked under your clothes too, right?"

"*Ay! No seas comemierda*, Simón. Maybe that wasn't the best example, okay? Can I finish? No more interruptions." She rolled her eyes, squeezing my hand playfully. "Anyway, like I said, both of them are dead . . . But their story's not over. They had unfinished business and were doomed to haunt the years that followed, lonely, whistling their music forever.

"Eventually, the monsters devoured themselves out of slovenly houses and sloppy homes, leaving the town empty for the first time. In the silence, the two ghosts heard a sound echoing off the buildings. A song so familiar, yet slightly different, like it fit perfectly inside the tune they'd been whistling alone for centuries.

"The ghosts traveled along the coast, each moving down the long street they had shared for a lifetime and beyond. One floated from the north, the other from the south. The sun refused to set, the sky glowing gold. As they drew closer, the sun burned brighter, the music swelled louder, and the light swallowed everything. They couldn't see anymore, but they kept moving toward the sound until, suddenly, it stopped."

Mamá grabbed my face and pulled it close to hers.

"Our two ghosts were face-to-face. Inches apart. And they shone brighter than anything you can imagine. Their eyes met, then their hands. And at that very second, they exploded into brilliant colors, melting into each other. The sun wasn't refusing to set. It was their light filling the sky, shining as one star. And the other stars welcomed them into the sky."

She sat up and tucked the blanket, snug, under my chin.

"Their unfinished business was loving each other. Our

two ghosts that were once so alone, whose bodies were dust underground somewhere, found their place in each other's arms, their *media mitad*. And the song they had been whistling all those years kept bouncing off the dark water below."

I can't remember if I stayed awake until the end, or if I drifted off before she finished. Maybe the story wasn't exactly how she told it, but I do remember feeling like a ghost. I remember being scared to be naked in front of everyone. I remember imagining the moment I'd finally feel less different and praying it wouldn't come after I was already dead.

And I remember my mother bending down to kiss my forehead.

"*Te quiero mucho, mijito*," she whispered.

"*Más que mucho*," I murmured, blinking with heavy eyes.

"Wake up, sleepyhead. I picked flowers for you from my garden. I couldn't find a proper vase in this dump, so you'll have to get up and tend to them, Simón." The whisper crawls into my ear.

A familiar voice, smooth and sweet. I can see the motion of the lips and their texture.

A familiar body, thick amber and slick. Both like honey, for different reasons. It floats over mine.

A sigh escapes. It could just be gas. You hear about these things: postmortem spasms, phantom erections, the Lazarus reflex sending limbs flailing, goosebumps forming, farts slipping. A body pretending it's still alive.

The refrigerator door opens. The flat, high whir of the fan snuffs out the silence.

"You can't buy the fruit already cut up, Simón!" Albi's

voice. "It costs twice as much and goes bad ten times faster, stupid."

But there's no light coming from the fridge. It isn't open. There's no fruit in there.

Then it slams into me—the body, not the voice or the fridge. It collides with my lifeless form like the fly hitting the window. Neither of us moves—my body or the one tossed on top.

Another corpse follows.

And another. They pile onto me like I'm the dirt floor of some mass grave. Each one looks like him. One for every time he's ever been here. One body for every time he pressed me into this bed. Most of them are naked. Some are clothed. Some have his smile. Some have his scowl. One is bruised, bloodied and caked with sand. It rumbles and shifts in slow succession, like frames from an old film, crumpled at the top of the pile like a maimed cherry.

"You can't live like this, *habibi*," Albi's voice says, this time inside my head.

Sudden consciousness.

Live.

I'm alive.

Then—a subtle stirring.

The chest seems to rise. Not the bloody one. Not the others. Mine. It falls again under the weight. It might happen once more, a tiny motion anyone could miss unless they stood perfectly still, paying close attention.

The stone rolls back from the tomb, and dust-speckled light warms my corpse. The crust at the corners of my eyes and mouth cracks and flakes off. Somewhere on my street a song plays about a woman feeling like a cat being caught out in the rain.

A photograph sits on the table next to the bed: Albi and me on the beach. My loose brown curls, his tight dark coils. His eyes pinched, squinting against the sun; mine open, looking at him. Next to it, another photo shows my mother making coffee, setting out two small cups on the table, sunlight streaming in through the kitchen window, illuminating the left side of her face. Her mouth is stern, but her eyes glisten. In another, Albi and Lenita eat ice cream at the boardwalk, both glaring at the camera, eyebrows knitted, mouths wide and filled with melting cream. Even with a dirty look on his face, Albi is the most beautiful man I've ever seen.

"I wish I had your green eyes," he said that day, licking ice cream from the back of his hand.

"They're yours," I replied. "But I'll hold on to them for now. It wouldn't be fair. I need at least one redeeming quality."

"Yeah, that's true," he teased, nudging me. Then he sucked the last bit of ice cream from the bottom of the cone and handed me an extra napkin to wipe my hands.

My eyelashes separate and spread. My heart sputters, stomach gurgles. I have limbs, but they lie lifeless, and I'm too scared to move them for some reason. Like they might snap or crumble. My tongue, hot and swollen, peels away from the roof of my mouth like a sweaty thigh from plastic sofa protectors. "I've been sleeping on your side of the bed," I say, cotton-gummed, to the shadows of the studio apartment.

The striated burn radiating through my throat tells me I've spoken aloud for the first time in a long while. I can't remember what I said; the words slip further away each time, like a language I'm unlearning. I try to repeat the sentence, but it feels strange, slippery. The foreign objects tumble around my mouth—rounding the soft ones with my tongue, gritting others like sand between my molars. I count their sides and edges as they click against my teeth and drum against the ridges above. The letters unravel; the meanings evaporate. "I" isn't "I" anymore; it's merely a sound, an unsure interruption in the silence.

There's a knock at the door. Real. Concrete.

"Simón. Open up!" Another knock and a woman's voice, loud and nasal. "It's your Tía Cachita," she continues in a sing-song lilt. "C'mon. I brought food your Mamá made."

Her words hit the door and pile up outside it, clattering as they collect on the floor.

"This isn't a trap. They're leftovers; she doesn't know I'm here." Her high heels clunk against the floorboards as she shuffles in place. "I'm getting my nails done in ten minutes, Simón. I will not suffer unkempt nails because you can't be bothered to put pants on."

"It's open," I scratch out, still unmoving in my bed. The door doesn't lock—one of the small concessions you make for a cheap rental in a shitty part of town.

The door creaks open before Tía Cachita kicks it the rest of the way with her pointy shoe. She's on stiletto stilts and balancing several Tupperware containers as if she were part of a traveling circus. "I don't do manual labor, Simón," she huffs before wobbling down into a crouch to set the food on the table. She stands up, and her face falls as she takes in the state of the apartment. "*COÑO, SIMÓN!* What is that smell? Look at this place. Look at you!" She clicks her tongue and rotates in place. She doesn't touch anything. She just stands there. "Okay, look . . . Your mother needs you. And by the looks of things here, you need her too . . ." Her nose crinkles as she talks. Her toe kicks an empty bottle on the floor. "She'll never say it to you; she'll never say it to me. But she's lonely, and she's taking it out on me and your cousins. I can't take another day. She's been even worse since the whole thing with your . . . friend. Maybe she expected you to lean on her, who knows? What I do know is you can either stay here and shrivel up, or you can go see your mother and save us all." She smooths her skirt and flings her styled hair away from her face before turning for the door. "And *por favor, por Dios*, Simón, take a shower."

I close my eyes and hold my breath until I hear the door close and her footsteps retreat down the hall. They echo against the high ceilings and bounce flatly off the plaster walls.

As I turn my head toward the refrigerator, my eyes roll sluggishly behind the motion of my skull, scanning the space for Albi.

He is everywhere.

I am alive.

I remind myself to blink.

Breathe in. I'm in control.

The bodies are all still here. They're everywhere I look.

I tell myself to blink again, only to realize my eyes aren't open.

"Their unfinished business was loving each other . . ." My mother's voice thrums in my twisted memory, softer now than she might have said it back then. I hold onto the thought, this fleeting memory, an invention like any other.

Breathe out.

"I love you, Simón," the hundreds of Albis say against hundreds of backdrops.

"*Y yo a ti, Albi. Mucho,*" I whisper back, exhaling an unsteady breath.

"*Más que mucho,*" they all sing back to me in unison.

I'm in control.

Water laps around my pillow, creeping into my ears.

Breathe in. I suck the air in as slowly as I can.

So slowly it hurts my chest. My muscles tighten, and my throat feels like it's collapsing in on itself. Heat spreads across my skin, tingling—some nervous system alarm surely, warning me of the lack of oxygen. Cool water wraps around me, tracing a rippling outline like the silhouette of an underwater crime scene.

So slowly, each breath has barely begun before the next is so desperately expected. A fire catching in the trachea ignites a fireworks show of bronchioles, each little air sac erupting into a brief cellular star. I am in control.

So slowly, I become dizzy. Shapes undulating to the rhythm of my heartbeat take over the edges of my vision. My chest is sinking deeper and deeper. My hands tear themselves free, leaving my motionless body behind as they scurry off across the bed. They crawl and grope blindly as the water rises. They scratch and claw, but I stay still. Like a game you play as a child, freezing to remain unseen. My chest is pressed so far down it crushes against the floor. The mattress is as thin as a single sheet of paper by now. I breathe as slowly as it takes to be unnoticeable.

Floating near the ceiling, I watch my submerged body from above. I know I'm not there. I can see that I'm not there at all. Not even a bit. Not how I remember myself.

"You need to open the windows," one of the Albis says underwater. "Let in some fresh air and light."

Light.

So light.

So lightheaded.

I'm headed into the light.

"Turn the lights off!" Coco yelled as she held a match to the candlewicks.

Lenita slapped the light switch, and Albi mumbled under his breath as he fumbled around in the dark with my old camera. "This thing is one click away from falling apart. I should've gotten you a new one of these instead of those dusty books you asked for."

"It's not too late! You can get me both," I said, sitting on the bed, swinging my feet, watching them fuss around me.

Albi wrapped the neck strap around his arm and sat on the floor, finding the perfect position to frame a shot of me blowing out my candles before giving the all-clear for Leni and Coco to start singing. They turned, holding the coconut cake he made, twenty-six candles burning on top. My eyes couldn't stop blinking, over and over, until Albi gave me a "psst" to remind me not to ruin the photo.

The wax trickled onto the frosting as they brought the cake closer. I wondered if my mother might have been thinking of me at that moment and closed my eyes to make a wish. As I blew the candles out, I did it slowly, photogenically, for Albi, so he could get the shot he imagined. I didn't care to be photographed, but I knew he would be hard on himself if he missed the moment.

Leni and Coco cut the cake, and everyone grabbed a slice. Albi sat on my lap to eat since we only had three chairs.

"How was the museum earlier?" Coco asked, lighting a cigarette.

"It was amazing!" I replied, wiping frosting with the back of my hand.

"No, it wasn't. You complained the whole time," Albi said, before mocking me in a nasal trill. "I'm hot. It's too busy. I thought this exhibit was gonna be bigger."

I paused. "Maybe I was paying too much attention to

the wrong things in the moment." I had never realized that something rotten could be good if you just refocused it. Thirteen becomes a lucky number if you simply call it the Lucky Number Thirteen. "I'm sorry I complained," I said into his back. I wrapped a finger around one of his belt loops, and he rubbed his knee against my thigh.

"I guess it was amazing, wasn't it?" Albi said sweetly. He stood and took his plate to the sink.

I grabbed another slice. "The museum, the food, the cake. I don't deserve all of this. Thanks for making today so special, Albi."

He turned from washing dishes and gave me a wink.

"Hey, what about us?" Lenita yelled, with a mouth full of coconut flakes and white frosting.

"And the most beautiful company. I'm a really lucky guy," I said, looking down at my hands. "It's my first birthday in this apartment, and I'm just grateful—" As I teared up, Lenita and Coco heckled me. "Oh, brother!" and "Somebody get him a tissue!" before Leni jumped on me and messed up my hair.

"And it'll be your first birthday working behind the bar. That means big tips, *papito*. I got you a crown to wear." Coco smiled, swiping her finger across the frosting.

"Yeah. I guess I feel bad that I'm not helping my mom out with the tailoring anymore." I enjoyed sewing with my mother. I knew art could never be a career, and besides reading it was the only thing I loved doing. It felt good to be productive, to have something tangible to show at the end of each day.

"Nah, she's doing fine without you. My parents still go to her. She's kinda rude to the customers, but she's so good they don't care," Lenita said as she leaned back and kicked a shoe up on the table. I slapped her foot down and told her to shut up.

"She made decisions she believed in, and so did you," Albi

said matter-of-factly. His white T-shirt darkened with water from the dishes, and my neck flushed as his chest muscles bounced under the fabric. I considered kicking Lenita and Coco out, but a scratching noise at the window pulled my attention.

On the other side of the glass, a set of bright green eyes blinked slowly from the exterior windowsill. "Quick, open the window!" I yelled. "Slowly! He might fall!"

"I can't do it quickly and slowly, Simón," Albi said, inching the window open.

A tiny, brown-striped cat hopped into the apartment and padded across the floor. He trotted up to me and slammed his head against my knee before continuing the caress along his whole body.

"Oh my gosh, he's the most precious little thing," I squealed, squatting slowly. "Should we keep him?"

"I don't know, Simo. He probably has fleas. And what do we know about caring for an animal?" Albi bent down to pet him. "It would be mostly on you. I'm not here full-time." The cat jumped into his arms, smelled his chin and started nuzzling it.

I snatched my camera off the table and snapped a quick photo. "Daddy and Kitty's first cuddle."

Albi rolled his eyes, but shifted so the cat could reach his cheek. I clicked the shutter again.

"He's a street cat," Lenita said. "He can come and go. He knows when he's got it good. He'll probably leave to shit somewhere and come back for the eats and belly rubs."

"Knowing you, you'll probably name him Sapo Verde or something awful," Coco said between sips of wine. The cat jumped down to investigate after hearing her voice, but Coco moved her knees away.

"Oh, now *that* is good. Sapo Verde it is! Best birthday present ever." I picked Sapo up and squeezed him close to my chest. His fur smelled pretty awful, and he probably did have fleas, but I didn't care. He nuzzled into the crux of my arm, began purring, and flexed his paws.

Albi finished cleaning the kitchen. "We gotta go, Simo. You and Coco have to set the bar up, and Lenita has shots to take."

"But what about Sapo? You sure you can't stay with him tonight?" I asked.

"I have eight o'clock mass tomorrow morning. Let's leave the window open a crack and put something to eat on a plate for him." He pushed my hair behind my ear and kissed my head. "He'll come back. He found you once, right?"

"You're gonna make a great priest one day," Lenita said, downing the rest of her wine. "Can you imagine if we had a priest that looked like that growing up?" She motioned up and down at Albi. "Uuf . . . the Lord is my shepherd, I shall not want, okay?!"

"He might become a deacon or something else in the church," I offered, seeing that Albi was shutting down. "Being a priest is a big commitment." He didn't like to discuss his future in the church, especially when the conversation occurred anywhere around me.

We turned off the lights, except the one above the sink. Albi left a bowl of water and a plate of chicken on the floor near the window. I folded towels into a bed. Just in case Sapo wanted to stay.

I wake up, and my eyes are still closed. They begin to open the way a balled-up piece of paper tossed to the ground, unfolds, its fibers springing back into shape. I don't want them to open. I don't care if they do. Maybe they're looking for something. Maybe they don't know there's nothing to find. Peeled like a watchdog's.

Dogs actually don't see very well at all. Humans see detail and color in ways dogs cannot; however, what dogs do well is detect motion. I imagine my body as a dog's body, curled up, nose tip to tail. I imagine my eyes as a dog's eyes. They stare at the wall, waiting for a change, waiting for the bed to shift. I'm waiting for footsteps approaching in a specific pattern that tells me who it is. A sign. Some miracle to prove that he could still be here.

Light shines through the same window it did when Albi was here. The rays don't dance anymore; they lie where they fall and roll across everything as the day moves forward. All I want is to grab the sheets, squeeze them in my fists until the fabric absorbs into my skin, and pull them over my head, but I can't move my hands. They still haven't returned. And I don't close my eyes. They dry out, shriveling into little eyeball-colored raisins, still waiting for change, for the slightest movement.

I had two hands once.

I had a name.

I had it all.

I had him.

I can't tell where the sheets end. I can't tell where all the time went. And I miss my hands, but I miss them for touching him. People talk about heartbreak as if it were a sudden pain you feel. As if it is a quick jolt to your body or a sensation that dulls with time. This doesn't feel that way.

I have this intense burning in my gut, but it feels so very

empty. And my body won't move. I can't make my body move, and a cry can escape my lips, but the searing heat refuses to subside. And my insides are blistering at the smallest memory. It's an infection taking hold of my lungs, making them tender to every breath and ready to burst, but my body lies there, and my eyes stare at the wall.

The warmth in the mattress grows stifling, but I know it is my body heat and not his. We made love. Albi got up to piss, and I rolled into the indent that was the shape of his body and felt the heat that had originated inside of him. I pressed my face against it, and the heat was then in my skin. It was mine. His heat. His body.

Is this what it feels like to truly go mad? Not babbling or drooling, claiming to be God or a reincarnated chicken, but to be hyper-aware of everything all at once. Unable to grasp how any of it matters or what to do with it. Or if it's real in the first place?

We were here in this place together. Albi and me. That is real.

This is the same place. Even if it doesn't feel or sound like it.

There isn't an indent in the mattress that resembles his body anymore. All that's left is mine, and I want to beat it out of the cushion before that shape is all I can remember.

This place doesn't smell like him anymore, either, unless I come home drunk and take my pants off over my shoes, falling face-first into the hardwood floor and imagining so intently that everything is back to the way it was. Black tea and vanilla. Sweat. Soap and shower steam.

"For today's assemblage, we have prepared for you 'Bomba Bliss,' consisting of roughly chopped papaya and rustic dry bread with cheese." Albi sat down cross-legged on the bed and leaned against the wall before passing me a napkin with a pile of leftover food scraps piled on top.

"And the coffee? Service is really taking a nose dive around here," I said.

"Maybe this will wake you up," he said, unleashing a lungful of morning breath onto my face, startling Sapo, who took off, skidding into the bathroom. It was rancid, but it didn't make him any less to me. I pushed him away and popped a chunk of papaya into my equally malodorous mouth. He leaned his head on my shoulder and took a bite, too. Sapo returned and lay on top of Albi's feet.

I bring my nose to that place where he once lay by my side. I can't bring myself to wash the bedding, and the sheets are stiff and pilling.

"Simón, it's not that I don't want to cuddle with you. Your body gets too hot. It makes me feel claustrophobic sometimes. And you sweat a lot," Albi said once, peeling his skin away from mine.

I pounced on him, my damp body glistening on top of his broad, hairy frame. Bestial desire bundled up under his golden skin as he flipped us both over and suffocated me.

Now, my eyes focus on the sheet in front of me, on a dark curl twined into the fabric, ready to wrap itself around my neck.

It's so strange. I knew the world would keep spinning without us. And I would wake up and expect the next day to have started already. That I slept through all of my alarms. That it was only a little cloudier than normal. That the sun just doesn't have it in her to shine like she did before. I thought the world should go on. I thought I would, too. But how can I when my gravitational center is gone? Lost in space, floating aimlessly, no force to propel me through the vacuum.

Loving me was an intimate crime for him in some ways. For both of us, I suppose.

The scenes play over in my head: those moments of love overflowing, and those when love wasn't enough. It's hard to keep it all in order, but it happened all the same. My recall is hectic, spasmodic. It's like an unqualified clerk took over my mind, decided to reorganize everything, and revamp the system, only to take a lunch break and leave halfway through.

My hands have inched their way back to me, inspecting the scene like a family after a house fire. One pauses over the sheet, where the curl rests, caught in the weave.

It comes free with a soft tug, springs into a loose circle between the fingers. A perfect little loop. It looks like something he left behind on purpose. I bring it to my lips. Hold it there. Then place it on my tongue. It tastes like nothing, but I imagine it tastes like the skin of his collarbone. His armpit. I swallow. Slowly. Just to feel something of him move through me.

One hand now circles a nipple while the other slyly moves down to my crotch. They make their greedy solicitations as I stare at the wall.

There is too much wall to look at. Too much time to waste.

Then again, I do sleep very well after jerking off.

I command my hand to leave my crotch so I can spit into it. The viscous spit of a hungry deviant. It slides across my palm as the hand returns to the throbbing, fully erect beneath the sheets. As they glide along my skin, ropes bind my wrists, pulling my arms overhead. My chest lifts; my lower back arches. The hands move freely, roaming my expectant body. One strokes lovingly up and down, while the other plays in and around.

My breathing quickens. Sweat beads and pools.

The scent of it thickens the air as a delirious tightening rises through me. A light blinds me from above. I look up, and the archers all have his face. A quiver descends upon my restrained body. The darts pierce me deliciously, plunging into my abdomen, scattering at my feet. They soar down through the ceiling, the window, the sky—a euphoric fasciotomy.

Then, unceremoniously, the ropes unravel. My arms fall loose. The arrows turn cold and tighten on my skin. I deflate. And as my hands reattach themselves, I wonder what a curious monster I've become.

"At seminary, we're learning what needs to happen before you can become a saint. Martyrs are instantly beatified, but they still have to perform a miracle to be canonized," Albi said, looking over his notes.

"And God said unto him, 'Now prove it, loser,'" I muttered, fleshing out a sketch of the town square I'd started the morning before.

A pillow slammed into the side of my head.

I couldn't have cared less about saints or scripture, yet now I want to clutch these figures and their pain against my chest, grapple them to the floor. I want to hold them like I'd hold him. I want to turn myself into them. I want to turn myself into him, to make a new me in his likeness, spreading the sacred word of his body.

You are me. I was me once, but now I'm you. The words feel like a memory, but I don't know if they're mine or if I ever said them out loud.

The fly still buzzes through the room, zipping over the junk and clutter. Clothes piled on the floor. Canvas and paint in the corner. Turpentine beside a lonely easel. Stacks of books and random empty bottles.

My mother would slap the mouth off my face if she could

see the mess I've made of everything. "Is this how I raised you? To live like a pig? You want me to throw mud on top of you too, *cochino*?" she'd say. "I'll dig a hole in the front yard and roast you for Easter if this isn't cleaned up in two seconds, Simón."

When she was still happy, before devotion overtook her newly broken heart, she'd hold me close. Whether things were wrong or good, it made no difference. She was there, breathing deeply with her cheek pressed to the crown of my head. I could feel my hair swaying toward her nostrils and away again in a rhythm I can't quite remember anymore.

How to remember.

Some things have no equivalent once they're gone and something unrecognizable takes their place. An idealized greeting card. A balled-up thing shoved into a cavity to fill the void. A substitution for the real deal, an artificial replica, a facsimile.

When does devotion to and faith in something unseen eclipse what's standing right in front of you? And once that thing is gone, how do you remember it properly? How do you hold someone in a warped and decaying mind? How can I recall the rhythm of my mother's breathing, now that she refuses to be the mother I once relied on?

I'm going mad.

Tía Cachita is right. I need to see her. I need it as much as she does, if only to remind myself why I left.

My heart beats, and the force feels brand-new. The tireless muscle, grown weary now from being ignored, makes itself known. Capillaries and arteries. Pump the blood. My body waits, poised, anticipating our next movement.

My mother would create herself anew every single morning, even after she hardened. But I don't know who to become. What shape should I mold myself into? Where is this cross I need to bear, and how heavy a cross can I handle?

My tongue throbs, hot and swollen with dehydration, and the raw scrape in my throat hints at having vomited last night. I can't remember the last time I drank anything other than the whiskey from the empty bottle half-tucked under the bed. Still, my bladder aches for release.

I fill my lungs. Ribs feel tight.

I take another breath, deeper this time.

My toes wiggle. My bones creak. Ankles pop. This reanimated corpse—its shell warmed by the sunlight leaking through the paper-covered panes—feels, for a moment, almost alive on the inside.

I swing one leg and then the other over the side of the mattress, bile sloshing audibly in my stomach with the motion. My toe hits the whiskey bottle and sends it deeper under the bed.

Standing slowly, deliberately, the body is propped up, erect. The heart beats again. Capillaries and arteries.

Okay, Simón . . . Lift one foot and then place it down on the floor. Good. This time, lift the foot and move it forward a bit before placing it down.

I remember reading once that bipedal walking is merely maintaining your body in a constant, controlled state of falling forward, so I fall forward a few times, stumbling into the bathroom.

A brief, sharp sting at the tip of my cock, sealed shut from earlier activities, gives way to a forceful stream. The toilet water turns dark orange, and I breathe through my mouth to avoid the pungent smell. I wipe the rim, flush, and turn to face the sink. I'm disgusted with myself. Eyes closed, I hold on to the edges of the basin for a few short seconds. The water runs from the rust- and lime-speckled faucet, and the white noise of the splashing muffles the whirl in my head. Shame. I take a gulp of water and spit it out, then drink again, letting the flow spill over my chin and down my neck. I splash my face, sip once more, and feel the first flicker of calm since my resurrection. One alarm in my brain has stopped sounding, and now another. I can do this.

Leaving the bathroom and seeing the room from this angle feels surreal. The movie set has rotated, but the audience is still seated behind me. What comes next? Will the lines be fed to me, or am I making this up as I go? My eyes blink only once before my cue arrives: a striped little feline figure, perched on the sill behind the closed window. He tilts his head and stares at me with one green eye and one brown, hopping into the apartment as I slide the window open.

"Sapo . . ." I croak, before dropping to the floor and crying into his fur. He lets out a small chirp. A kitty hello. "I'm so sorry, Sapo. I'm sorry." His sandpaper tongue scratches my nostril, then my eyebrow. "I shouldn't have closed the window," I say into his now-damp fur. "I shouldn't have left you alone outside."

Sapo chirps again as I set him on the ground, and he rubs his body against the leg of the table before jumping on top. Through post-cry sniffles, I open a few of the containers Tía Cachita left for me. I glance at him again and feel his belly. He doesn't look like he's missed a meal. He's even gained a little weight since I last saw him. My little survivor was fine all along. Although I'm sure he eats trash in the streets, I rinse the chicken in the sink to remove the spices and grains of rice. He deserves a proper meal while he's here.

Oh God, I am my mother.

"One Sapo Combo! Fresh water and chicken for my

growing boy." I place a bowl and a plate on the window sill. Sapo jumps up, and I prop the window open with a book I have two copies of. *Maurice*. The other was a gift from Albi. "You won't be locked out again, *mijito*. This will always be your home." I bend to kiss his head, but he ducks and slinks to the side. "You're right. Chicken is more important."

While Sapo eats, I take a shower. That's what normal people do. They drink water. They shower. Normal people leave their apartments. They interact with other human beings. But being alone in the shower makes me feel like I could disappear again, so I quickly shut off the water and stand there, dripping. The bed grows cozier in my memory. Closing my eyes becomes the only next step that seems logical. Pulling the sheets over my head makes sense.

Sapo licks my leg, and I snap back into my right mind. His paws press gently on the edge of the shower. His eyes blink slowly.

"You're right, Sapito. I can do this."

After toweling off, I try tidying, picking things off the floor in a random order. I grab the can of paint thinner and open it. The noxious fumes snake into my nostrils and dilate my pupils with the fragrance of pine needles and licorice swimming in a puddle of gasoline. I hold the tin up to my nose and deeply breathe the vapors in. Hold it in. Hold it in.

"Simón, you can make this your life. You're too good for it to be in some corner of your room that you sometimes use. You're a talented artist," Albi said, frozen, posed in bed as I sketched him on a scrap of canvas.

"I'm not an artist. I like to paint. That doesn't mean I deserve a title," I said blandly as I dragged the brush back and forth, remembering my grandmother sitting in her robe, running her knotted fingers over drawings after cleaning and closing the kitchen for the night.

"You're good at sewing, but you're not a tailor anymore. You're good at bartending, but you're not a bartender . . ."

He annoyed me, so I shushed him and told him to get back into the pose. "I never was a tailor. And the bar is temporary."

"Then what's next?" Albi asked.

My eyes water as I drag another gulp into my lungs and hold it there. The room shudders. I exhale slowly. What's next, Simón?

I see my pants on the floor and grab them without thinking. The denim is cold and stiff under my fingertips. The ridges in the fabric feel like mountains. A satisfying crack bounces off the walls as I shake them out, releasing the folds and bunches, and two socks fall out of the legs. Sapo mews and gives a purring mumble.

"I hate that you put your socks on after your pants," an old version of me said to Albi.

"What do you care? Leave me alone." Albi finished putting on his socks and moved on to his shoes.

"It looks uncomfortable. Don't the pants limit your motion? It's easier to do the socks first. I thought everyone did it that way," I said through a mouthful of toothpaste.

"Okay, Pants Police. You gonna tell me how to wipe my ass now, too?" He was leaning back on the bed, waiting for me to finish getting ready.

"Wait, how do you wipe your ass?" I asked, popping my head out of the bathroom.

"Simón, rinse your mouth, and let's go!" Albi collapsed onto the bed.

"I wipe standing up," I said nonchalantly as I turned away.

"How can you wipe standing up?" Shock rippled through this response. "Your cheeks aren't spread anymore. There's no way to clean properly. That's disgusting, Simón. I play around back there, you caveman."

"I don't stand up as if I'm waiting in line, dummy. I put one foot up on the toilet. Cheeks still fully spread. And anyway, you've never complained about the state of the playground before." I stuck my ass out of the bathroom door and wiggled it around.

"You're a monster," Albi muttered through a thick smile. I could hear the soreness in his cheeks from laughing all morning, and I could feel it in mine, too.

The heart beats again.

A wiggle of the toes. I have two feet. Two socks on. The pants slide themselves up my legs, and my feet insert themselves into the near-tattered canvas shoes. My head feels light with the fumes still smothering my senses.

"Wish me luck, Sapo. I'll see you later," I say, springing up to leave before the high wears off and the bed sucks me down into the sheets again.

I turn to the wall where the door has always been, but there is no door.

It's a punch in the mouth. I taste blood. My vision crackles and fizzles.

It was here. It should be here.

I try to conjure the details. The grain of the wood, the metal of the doorknob, the dents and scratches. But they've all gone cloudy.

It was always there, and it opened whenever my fingers wrapped around its cold brass—was it brass?—handle. The latch clicked, the door swung in sync with my step. My body moved. The door moved. The mechanical banality of life.

There really was a door in that exact spot. I know it. I remember.

How to remember . . .

How to sift what's real from what's been ripped up and taped back together.

One memory grips my head like a vise. It forces my eyes open. A past version of myself is summoned to perform the scene: I stood there crying, and Albi walked away. Maybe that me would rather perform something else. Something with tenderness. Or love. But even those memories feel frayed. Dreams, maybe. Made-up images posing as truth long enough to be believed. Stories no one remembers exactly as they happened. Stories like memorial gifts to the dead. To the dead like me. Like Us. Like Albi.

My body still moves toward the wall, and my brain can't see the door.

I am the fly. Slamming itself into the glass.

Again. Again.

There was a door here.

And I fall. Into the sea.

Interlude: Albi

"Bless me, Father, for I have sinned. It has been seven days since my last confession."

In his right hand, Albi held his mother's prayer beads, carved from olive wood and worn smooth from years of her fingers counting blessings on them in Arabic, a language Albi remembered only in fragments. He'd carried these beads with him since he was seven, since she died and left him alone in the world.

"Go ahead, Albi." Father Cordero sounded tired. The night before, Albi had found him asleep at his desk, glasses askew, homily notes scattered across the surface when he came to deliver a second cup of black tea with mint—another remnant of his mother's love.

"I met someone that I need to tell you about."

Father Cordero waited, giving the silence space to breathe.

"His name is Simón." Albi's thumb found the central bead, slightly larger than the others, the one his mother would kiss before beginning prayers. "I met him at El Palomar."

Through the screen, Father Cordero's shadow shifted. When he didn't immediately respond, Albi added, "It's a sort of club on the other side of town."

"I know what El Palomar is, *mijo*." His voice held no

judgment, just a quiet awareness that surprised Albi.

"Yes . . . Well, I went with our neighbor, Verónica. She asked me to go. She wanted to dance." The words arranged themselves with a clunky momentum, building syllable after syllable. "Simón approached me. He knew me from church. He used to go to St. Sebastian." He didn't add how Simón had watched him for years or how that knowledge had sent a current through him, that realization that while he'd been performing sacred rites, someone had been observing him with interest, lust even. "His mother still goes to this parish, I guess. You probably know her . . ."

"Albi, I must ask you to get to the point." Father Cordero shifted his weight, the wooden seat creaking beneath him. "I'm sorry, my son. It has been a long day already."

"Well, we all danced before Simón approached me." The memory materialized with surprising clarity—Simón's mouth near Lenita's ear; the careful distance between their bodies as they moved their partners around the dance floor; the quick, nervous glances in Albi's direction; the tilt of Simón's head when he laughed. "Then we walked to the beach and talked all night."

The silence between them condensed.

"Only Simón and I went to the beach," he added quietly. "There is no polite way to say this, Father." Albi selected each word carefully. "I have developed feelings for him. Feelings that go beyond friendship."

Father Cordero waited once more before responding, giving Albi space to say more. The young man often found himself overwhelmed when it came to revealing his emotions. "Is this the first time you've experienced such feelings?"

The world narrowed to the circular pattern of beads beneath Albi's thumbs. "No." He closed his eyes tightly and tried to keep his voice steady as his stomach lurched and churned. "I thought I could be the son my mother deserved." Albi took in a sputtering breath that didn't seem to fill his lungs. "But . . . I . . . I can't stop thinking about him."

"Albi—" Father Cordero began, but Albi needed to finish before he lost his nerve.

"I thought I could contain it. Structure my life so it wouldn't matter." His heartbeat quickened. "I believed if I served well enough, studied hard enough, if I made you and my mother proud enough . . ."

The confession felt simultaneously weightless and crushing. His mother's face appeared before him—not as she looked in the final days of her illness, but vibrant, standing at the stove stirring lentil soup, singing songs, the windows open to catch the evening breeze.

"My mother sacrificed everything to bring me here. Left her people, her language, the graves of her parents." He couldn't catch his breath, but he couldn't stop now either. "And now I'm . . ." The emotion rose with unexpected force, and his voice caught. "What would she think of me now? She entrusted me to your care. You've both invested so much in me, and I'm failing you."

Father Cordero was quiet for a long moment. Albi heard him remove his glasses, the subtle clink of metal against wood as he set them aside. "When your mother brought you to me," Father Cordero finally said, "do you remember what she told me?"

"That I was afraid of thunderstorms and allergic to shellfish."

"Besides that." Father Cordero's chuckle carried unexpected warmth. "She said, 'This is Albi, my heart. Please help him grow strong.'" His voice softened further, almost to a whisper. "Not 'Make him into something he's not.' Not 'Fix him.' She simply wanted me to help you grow strong."

"But she wouldn't have wanted this for me." The certainty of it ached between his ribs.

An abrupt sound disrupted Albi's thoughts. The confessional door on Father Cordero's side opened. Footsteps, and then his own door opened. He stood there in his simple black clothes, the ones he wore while helping in the garden. Afternoon light caught the silver at his temples, illuminating the network of lines around his eyes.

"Come," Father Cordero extended his hand. "This conversation doesn't belong behind screens."

Albi followed him through the sacristy and out to the garden behind the rectory. Albi's garden. The white roses along the eastern wall needed pruning; he had been putting off the task all week. The afternoon sun filtered through the leaves of a fig tree his mother had planted, creating a pattern of light and shadow across the stone path.

Father Cordero sat on the bench next to the tree and motioned for Albi to join him.

"Your mother would be proud of the man you've become," he said simply. "As am I."

"Even now?" Albi's voice sounded smaller than he intended.

"Especially now." Father Cordero placed his hand on Albi's shoulder, the weight familiar and steadying. "It takes courage to speak the truth, Albi."

Albi studied the roses, mentally planning how he would shape each bush to distract himself with banality, the predictable logic of gardening. He would cut just above outward-facing buds, removing dead growth and crossed branches, and everything would be fine.

"I don't know what to do," he admitted. "When I'm with Simón, I feel . . ." He searched for the right word. Enamored. Lustful. Giddy. Weightless. In love. ". . . unguarded, I guess."

Father Cordero took a deep breath. "When I was about your age, I had a friend named Miguel."

Albi turned, surprised. Father Cordero rarely spoke of his life before ordination.

"We were inseparable for years. He studied literature; I was preparing for seminary." A small smile appeared, then vanished just as quickly. "He wrote poems and made me into characters in his short stories. We were thick as thieves from primary school onward." The revelation settled between them, neither acknowledging its full meaning directly.

"What happened to him?" Albi finally asked, folding his arms over his chest to protect himself from what he knew might be coming.

"Life happened. Last I heard, he was teaching at a university in Madrid." Father Cordero's eyes found Albi's. "I don't regret my vocation. I found my calling. I found love and community. But I understand what it means to stand where you're standing."

The weight of Father Cordero's confession—because that's what this was, a confession from him to Albi—recalibrated something fundamental in Albi's understanding of the world.

"Whatever path you choose, you will not lose me," he said. "I don't speak for the Church or the congregation. I am speaking as a friend, as a . . . Father." He put his arm around Albi's shoulders the way he did in front of his mother's grave all those years ago.

Albi looked at his own hands, strong and calloused. Practical hands. Useful hands. Hands that trembled when Simón's fingers intertwined with his on that moonlit beach.

"Tell me about him," Father Cordero said firmly.

The request caught Albi off guard. He laughed and settled back against the bench, sighing. "He talks constantly. He's very . . . bouncy if that makes sense. Makes connections between things I would never think to connect. He looks at everything sideways."

The corner of Father Cordero's mouth lifted slightly.

"When we danced," Albi continued, "he kept staring at my arms, then looking away when I noticed." The memory warmed his face. "And he has the most beautiful eyes. But he does this crazy blinking thing when he's trying to remember something. It's funny."

"He sounds like a character," Father Cordero said.

"He is." Albi laughed. "He trips all the time and just keeps walking. I feel like I'm constantly aware of how I look to others, hiding what I'm thinking, who I am." Albi paused. "But he acts like we're the only two people on the planet." The recognition felt significant in ways Albi couldn't quite name. "And it made me feel that way too."

Father Cordero pressed his lips together and looked down at the ground. "And that's a rare feeling, Albi," he said with a sigh. "I hope you have cherished it. That is a blessing sent down to you both."

"But he told me a story his mother used to tell him about these two people. They'd searched their whole lives to find each other, but they didn't until hundreds of years after they died." Albi's fingers found the rhythm of prayer on his beads without conscious thought. "I'm scared," Albi admitted. "I don't want to miss my chance, but I don't know if I'm ready. I'm scared that if I follow these feelings and it all falls apart, I'll have nowhere to go from there."

They sat in companionable silence as the shadows from

the fig tree stretched across the garden path. "What do I do now?" Albi asked after a while.

"Now," Father Cordero said, standing and brushing dirt from his pants, "you prune those roses like you've been meaning to do all week."

Albi smiled despite himself. It was such a Cordero response: practical, immediate, focused on the task at hand. "And then?" he asked, rising to join him.

Father Cordero looked at him with eyes that had watched him grow from a frightened child into the man he was now. "Then you listen to your heart and trust it will lead you where you're meant to go."

As Father Cordero walked back to the rectory, Albi remained in the garden. He retrieved the pruning shears from the toolbox and approached the white roses.

With each careful cut, he thought of Simón. How he'd looked at Albi across the dance floor, his gaze unconfident yet unwavering. How his hands moved constantly when he spoke, painting invisible patterns in the air. He thought of the way Simón spoke with such certainty, how he'd leaned his head against Albi's shoulder as dawn approached, how the city sounded in the quiet hours of morning.

"Roses understand things we don't," his mother had told him. "The thorns hurt *us*, but they protect *them*. They keep them safe. It's perfectly fine to look at the beautiful things in life, but we must always account for the danger, for the pain. Both exist side by side, ya albi."

By the time Albi finished with the roses, his hands were dark with dirt and smelled of cut greenery. The angled sunlight cast the garden in amber, transforming ordinary plants into illuminated figures. He gathered the cut stems in a bundle. The evening bells would ring soon, calling him to prepare the altar. He would fold the linens, arrange the hosts, and measure the wine for the cruet.

But first, he took a single white rose—the most perfect bloom from the healthiest bush—and placed it before the small stone marker he had made for his mother beneath the fig tree. "I met someone, Mama," he said to her as he stood. "His name is Simón. And I'm in love with him."

Part II
Sweeter for the Salt

Chapter Three
You are Me; I was Me once

"I would die for you, you know," I had said.

Albi scoffed, exhaling hard through his nose.

"I would! You're so much more to me than I am to myself."
I picked my head up from his chest. His eyes were closed
against the sun, his body dusted with sand. The waves crashed
in time with his heartbeat.

"That doesn't even make sense, Simón . . . And you
really gotta value yourself more." He wiggled closer, a smirk
twitching at the right corner of his mouth.

"I would chop a finger off for every inch it'd bring me
closer to being worthy of you," I spread one palm across his
chest, ready to play the knife game over his heart. "I'd chop my
head off. They'd canonize me in a second."

"The saints didn't mutilate themselves," he said.

"Didn't you tell me about that one who pulled out her
own tongue or something? Or was that the one who got her
chichis cut off? Either way, they died telling stories about the
man they loved. I'd do the same . . ." I shifted closer to him.
"But for you, obviously. No offense, Big Guy," I said, kissing
my hand and looking up to the sky.

He grabbed my hand and buried it with his in the sand.

"You beast. Why do you always have to be so blasphemous?"

Shapes fly past my eyes as if I were squeezing them shut and grinding my knuckles into the sockets. There is no difference when I open or close them, and a slight pressure against my skull turns itself into a hand. The fingers intertwine with my curls. It's a soft caress, a fluid stroking like sliding into bed, cool sheets brushing my naked body. I feel for my own hands to make sure they aren't playing games again, and they touch each other in an animal greeting.

I would. I would die for him, to tell the world about his skin, the dark hairs covering it, the white sand contrasting against it, water beading on it. How the wind whipped his scent up into the dense midday air, bludgeoning my face with that sweet, sweaty fragrance.

The hand on my head becomes two, pulling my head back. One presses my cheek away as the other yanks me forward by my hair. Dragging me along, skipping across the surface like a stone. I don't feel my arms or legs; they should be flailing. Each follicle digs its grip into my scalp, thousands of points howling at once. Where I expect slams, there is silence. Pink and purple flashes come and go, circling my head.

Just as I give in to the tumbling pull of the waves, the pressure shifts. My head feels lighter, detached, floating an inch above my neck. Like a decapitated maiden, hair sprawled in a halo, flowing left to right like seaweed. A self-portrait as St. Christina of Tyre.

Chimes ripple through the water, and I imagine them as birds overhead.

A reflection meets me. As I gasp, bubbles escape my mouth and catch in my hair for a moment, a crown of pearls and flowers. Water forces itself into my nostrils and throat like a biblical flood, my lungs drowned temples. I thought I'd fight, but when our eyes meet in that reflection, there is stillness. I would die for you, you know.

A boat hovers above, surrounded by fish. Albi feeds them, talks to them. I want to be a fish. To swim up and listen. Hear the story of a sad maiden who lost her head and sank to the bottom of the sea. Fisherman Albi dives down, fish following like disciples. I'll be one of them, sprout scales from my flesh, sew my fingers into fins. I will breathe water for him.

He reaches me and caresses my cheek; his hands feel like a warm current.

"Wake up, Simón. My beloved disciple."

Gasping for air, I flail toward what my body insists is up, breaking the surface. My eyes burn as air slides over them, salt clinging to their edges. I hack and sputter, forcing water from my throat. The shore bobs just meters away. I don't remember leaving my apartment. I only remember tying my shoes. Or did I? I remember putting my shoes on. I was so ready to be okay. I had put them on; I know I did. The memory of the stains blending together. The old socks that had another use left. I remember. My toes wiggle in the soggy shoes as I levitate.

Maybe my mind blinked and the world skipped ahead. One moment, I believed I could seize control; now I'm seizing up.

A swell smacks my neck, sending a rush of water into my throat, triggering another coughing fit. I sink and swallow more water before—suddenly—I'm standing on the sand, the waves lapping around my knees. The sun overhead suggests noon, but my sense of time is useless. Before. After. I can't be sure. Everything feels fluid, except the grit of sand anchoring my feet as the water retreats and returns, wave by wave. I was so sure I could be okay.

Turning my back on the beach and on the city clinging to the hills beyond it, I slip off my shirt and face the sea. My vision loosens, the water shimmers and ripples as the sky shoots up and over my head. It's a Rothko effect of blue on blue on blue. Birds float and dip. Climb, climb, climb to dive, dive, dive, weaving invisible stitches into the sky.

Crinkled memories unfold behind me. Dancing with Albi. As a boy, making a crown of leaves and branches, crying after being told to leave the house while my cousin Camilo kissed a girl. My mother climbing down the rocks and laughing when I rushed ahead of her and tripped, falling face-first into the sand. My feet flew skyward, and my body created the letter C. Granules of sand crunched between my teeth for days after that.

The sea pulls my hips forward, then pushes them back toward the shore. Over and over again, like aquatic intercourse. The skin around my shoulders tightens as my upper body dries, sea salt dusted evenly across my arms and my hair. My eyes burn; they ache from fatigue, the salt, the sunlight, from crying. All of it. Dredging up the white sand, my feet shuffle backward, revealing shells, tiny fish, a cigarette butt, but the water remains entirely clear above the plumes of sand that erupt from my heels.

All of the beaches around here have clear water and white sand, but this one has a little extra magic. The breeze glides against your body in a different way. It begs you to stick around, lie in the sand, play in the water, and not worry about how you might look or who might be watching. It's safe, secluded, not a place anyone stumbles upon.

Following the endless grass of Parque La Matancera toward the sea, the *malecón* gives way to a rocky ledge that stretches south along the shoreline. It keeps going and going until it presumably meets the next city's boardwalk, but at one point two large, jagged stones rise a bit higher than the rest, marking the secret entrance to our secret beach. Between these blades, right where the tension screw of this scissor-shaped monument would be, great slabs of pavement blend into the rocks, unevenly strewn down the slope. They trace a pattern suggesting it was once a walkway leading down to our small, isolated section of sand.

People in bygone days always did quaint things for beautiful reasons, no matter how impractical. A promenade to stroll directly into the sea like some sort of parasol-accented elite pastime. It's the stuff of Victorian novels. Bustles and barnacles, and all of that. However, the battering waves and shifting tides have taken their toll. Coupled with a subsequent government's indifference to quaintness, the remnants of that walkway now lie severed and askew, buckling at extreme angles, demanding an awkward scramble to climb down and around.

Apart from its isolation, this beach has one more secret: a small grove of mango trees. Nestled in a tiny plot of earth against the rocks right before the sand and endless water. Where the grass meets the pavement meets the sea.

"These trees here are miracles, *mijo*," my mother had said to me as we sat under one for shade on a lichen-covered lump, once a stone bench hidden behind the trees. "When I was your age, your *abuelita* brought me down here. She told me each tree is one of God's mysteries." She'd reached up and grabbed a fruit hanging just above our heads. "Mango trees need clay in their soil, something for their little rooty fingers to wrap around and latch on to. Not all this sand. And all this salt water that crashes up here and sprays them all day and night. They shouldn't be able to survive. They take all that beating and still bring beauty into the world." She bit into the mango like an apple and peeled back some of the skin for me to have a bite, too. "Taste that? It's sweeter for the salt."

My feet slosh their way out of the water in that sucking, plodding way, carrying my body onto shore. As I walk up the hot midday sand, my wet clothes and shoes feel heavier with every step I take.

My pants squelch as I sit on the cool green stone of the bench, the wet fabric tightening around my bending legs. Mangoes swing silently above my head. Hummingbirds, tiny things, also silent, zip about the branches, buzzing by my ears. The little boy I was is crying on the ground as he twists branches and leaves to adorn the crown he's made. He hides it under a bush and sniffles, and I can remember how lonely he felt like it was yesterday. Another me, just as young, returns with flowers he snatched from the park before climbing down to the beach. He uncovers the crown and adds the small flowers before placing it on his head, talking to himself all the while. I kick off my soggy shoes and toss my balled-up shirt on top of them.

"Do you hear that?" A me sitting in this exact spot said to Albi, seated on the bench next to him. "Silence. Do you hear it? It's so lovely, isn't it?"

Albi grunted in acknowledgment, not wanting to disturb the stillness.

There are so many types of silence. An uneasy one. Its brother, the uncomfortable one. There are unrelated peaceful silences of endless varieties. Lonely silences and horribly suffocating silences, too, but this one is sweet. It has motion.

It has a flavor to it. It's moist and sweet and cool. Kissing someone after eating a Popsicle.

"Now, listen behind that . . . The trees . . ." I leaned back and exhaled, feeling the bark beneath my fingertips.

Albi intertwined his pinky with mine. I looked up into the unified canopy and slowly closed my eyes. I imagined I was still watching, using the glow behind my eyelids and the sound of the leaves to reconstruct the motion, foliage brushing against itself like a bow drawn across strings. Above, hummingbirds darted and hovered like miniature conductors, coaxing rhythm from the branches with every tremble of their wings.

"I can hear it," Albi said. "Kind of sounds like they're singing, don't you think?" He smiled and started to hum, and we sat next to each other, just breathing and listening to the silence.

After a while, Albi stood and walked down the small slope from the garden onto the beach. Kicking off his sandals, he swiveled his feet down and down again to avoid the scorch of the sun-cooked sand. He paused for a moment, relishing the isolation of our secret little kingdom before peeling off his shirt. "Let's lie down for a while," he said over his shoulder. He laid his shirt on the sand, then stepped out of his shorts, arranging them into a ghost-version of himself, soft limbs, empty and waiting. "Here. The sand's too hot. I don't want you to roast."

I stripped down to my briefs and smoothed my own clothes beside his, shaping a ghost-me for Albi to lie on. His scent billowed around me as I nestled into the fabric. He settled in next to me, his knee leaning gently against mine.

If I could've seen us from above, I would've seen his body on mine and mine on his. The two so closely twined, they'd be indistinguishable.

"We are one and the same, you and me. Isn't that a wonderful thing to think about?" I said. "Like if I were to break, you'd see yourself in all of my pieces."

"Well, aren't you the poet? And if I break?" Albi asked.

"Then I'll be even more alone than I was before I met you." I hadn't thought the words before I said them. I grabbed the fabric beneath me, rolling my fingertips over the woven fibers. "You are me. I was me once, but now I'm you."

There's something beautiful—but dangerous—about being that close to the water. Just lying there, feeling its presence. This huge, vast thing living beside you, moving and breathing. Lying next to Albi, I felt that same energy coming off him. He is something immense, beautiful.

Was. He was those things.

I stay in the warm sun a while longer, letting my clothes dry before putting them back on. The fabric stiffens and dulls. I think I know what I need to do, but these memories keep forcing themselves on me. I've converted my body into a walking memorial, a living eulogy, a pyre burning itself down. An offering of coins on the eyes.

Those eyes . . . long lashes blinking at me from across the dance floor. Eyes that once poured tears of joy, framed by speckles of sand. Eyes now deflated, eaten by worms. The warm amber gone. Honey with swirls of molasses. Sweet, sticky stares once stuck on me, now reserved only for the dirt piled above his head.

Sometimes, giving in to memory is the only way through. They rise like monuments on every path. I try not to think the thought, but that's only another thought about the thing

I'm avoiding. Obsession fuels compulsion fuels obsession. Spiraling, spiraling, spiraling until I give in, just to have one single moment of peace.

I've detached from life. I know it. I've abandoned everyone. And still I'm furious. No one came. No one pulled me out. It's absurd to blame them—my mother, this town—but I do. I'm angry. And tired. I feel everything so fucking intensely. It boils beneath my skin, cooks me alive, crisping my skin into *chicharrones*.

It's easy to say none of this would've happened if my mother had accepted me. Maybe she could've anchored Albi, too. If the church practiced what it preached, our love might've been a battle cry instead of a shameful whisper. Maybe the town wouldn't have lurked like a phantom, waiting to unearth us. And The Family . . . always watching, always reminding me I'm not the man they'd hoped for. They'd never have loved Albi. My mother, least of all. She needed me to become a man when my father left, not whatever this is to her.

But what do you do when the hands that made you belong to a woman, and then you're told to be a man? I became a scar to her. A reminder of what she lost and the person who left her behind.

When I was little, I believed there was something different inside me, something anatomically deviant. I imagined that if I ever had surgery or an x-ray, the doctors would find unique bone structures and organs never seen before. A secret magnetic field that warned others without me saying a word. And *that* was why they treated me differently.

I tried to release it however I could: stabbing needles into my fingertips, sitting perfectly still for hours imagining I was someone else, staring at objects to trigger a telekinetic blast. My mother would disrupt me with a *chancleta* to the side of the head, "*Baboso!* Don't do that. You're going to get stuck with that *cara de fuchi.* What did I do to deserve a feather brain for a son?"

Obviously, none of it worked. So, I invented a system. I scrutinized and evaluated every moment. The way someone said a word, the intonation. How they moved. How these movements differed between people. And if I blinked with intention, I could turn every moment into a snapshot. Each blink a frame I could study later, a still image waiting to be re-explored, zoomed in for overlooked details, dissected for meaning. While other children might cling only to happy moments, I considered every memory essential, especially the unsettling ones.

Kids remain wide-eyed to their surroundings, counting stairs, marveling at the day-to-day evolution of the foliage in spring. This alertness eventually fades in adulthood until what was once awe becomes merely background noise.

Not for me. The catalogs flip just behind my eyes. The dark ones sit on my chest. The warm ones cradle my head. They crackle in my skull. Leak out of my ears. Foam at the corners of my mouth. Bovine cud. Turning, tumbling. Experiencing and re-experiencing everything. Always.

I read once that cows are extremely intelligent. They seem like they are dumbly, blankly staring into space, but the mechanics of evolution cranked their dome-shaped eyes to the sides of their heads, letting them see nearly everything at once. Everything happening nearly three hundred and sixty degrees around them is perceived, yet they cannot see the bolt gun approaching in the thin blind spot directly in front of their forehead until it is too late. Never knowing it was the hand that fed them pulling the trigger.

A memory comes into focus. The hallway of the great blue

house on the hill. I watched from behind the bathroom door as my mother put on her makeup before bed. Her lips pursed. Her hand sliding the crimson stain: up and across, down and over. Reckless Rouge. A mist of perfume across her chest. One last check of her hair. She did this every night after my father left, as if he might return and find this impossible beauty in bed. As if he might regret ever leaving. Every morning and every night she turned herself into someone she thought he'd stick around for.

"Mamá, he isn't coming back," I said quietly.

"Excuse me?" Her head cocked. Fist clenched.

"I don't want you to waste your pretty makeup on him."

A flash of red-lacquered pain swiped across my mouth. When I looked up, her finger was in my face, and her face was very close behind that finger. She spoke low and sharp. "*Te voy a decir una cosa, hijo.* I will do what I want with my makeup. Do you understand me? Instead of worrying about what I'm doing in the privacy of my bathroom, why don't you go read your books or blink at a wall and leave me alone." She didn't move until my little legs had climbed the stairs and shut the door to my room.

The day my father left, the house echoed with my mother's screams. My tía's pleas. The twins clinging to her skirt. My father's back stiffening as he stormed down the steps. I remember his linen shirt, half-open and filled with air, swelling as he walked away from us for good. In that snapshot, I see everything around him: the framed print of the Virgin Mary slightly askew, a toppled chair, two bees buzzing about the flowering vines that snake their way around the window and doorway. And in the cloudy, gilded mirror, my small frame stood trembling, my frenzied eyes blinking.

A child can endure such intense feelings of otherness for

only so long before becoming inventive, building structures and mechanisms to cope with who they are.

I adapted. I adjusted the amount I spoke, the way I stood. Eventually, I realized blinking wasn't necessary. I could hold the shutter open in my head. Fifty frames a second. An evolution from analog to digital.

Though I do still suffer blinking fits when I lose control, like a lisp or stutter that emerges under stress, I discovered safety in restraint. That's what freaks do, right? You find your own way in the world until the people who fed and raised you shoot you in the forehead when you least expect it. No matter how smart you are, the bolt hits its mark in the end.

Stepping over the scissor-stone portal, I cross back into the land of the ordinary. My legs tremble as my mind orders me forward, but my body resists. Come on, Simón . . . we've done this before. One foot. Now the other.

Before I know it, I'm speed walking. Then running. I watch myself as if in a movie, curious which path this character will choose as the wind whips his hair and his grungy shoes slap against the pavement in time with some synth-pop soundtrack. Movie Simón flies past the jagged rock wall, soars up along the malecón, and reaches the plaza where the north and south meet.

Stalls litter the square. Farmers sell meager potatoes and tomatoes. Fishermen try to offload yesterday's catch before putting out the fresh stuff no one can afford. Mothers yell at their children. They yell at other people's children, too. A young man maneuvers a rattling bicycle with one hand and dribbles a basketball with the other. Laughter trills behind me. Children screaming, running. Music echoes off the plaster facades beyond the market. And an overwhelming urge to explode overtakes me.

I am a hummingbird in a gaggle of honking geese. A flutter of heavy pigeon wings. Hummingbirds feature often in my life. Maybe I feel a kinship because they're so unlike ordinary birds. A rare sight, set apart by natural selection. Their wings blur in figure-eights, hovering like something else entirely. Meanwhile, fat, clumsy pigeons waddle through every corner, forcing themselves on you with their dull eyes and duller motives.

My heart beats. Vision frays. Head rings.

The noise.

The people sliding around me. Banging into each other. Into me. I'm merely an obstacle. A massive field of flowers shaped like people moves around me. Boulders like buildings hold the sky up.

Before Albi, I was always thinking of ways to avoid human interaction. He had this power, this ability to enter a space before me, shifting the atmosphere into something I could slide myself into. But now the anxiety mounts. It eats away at the thin line separating me from everyone else. The only thing keeping my skin as mine, keeping it from bleeding into the air around me. I'm becoming a fine line around a silhouette. A clump of cells. Masses of atoms. Just here because they are. I feel myself spilling out onto the ground.

Head feels empty. Hollow ringing.

The chimes again. The water rising around my feet.

I don't want to drown.

The flower people morph back into birds—geese and gulls and pigeons—and I can't remember that they were never birds to begin with. They weave and swoop.

All the people. All the noise. The water rising.

"Whenever you get overwhelmed, mijo, you have to remember to breathe. If you focus on breathing, you won't be so focused on all of the people," my mother said once, holding my tiny hand in hers as my feet kept pace with the clicks of her heels against the hot pavement. "And if it's the place you're scared of, just imagine you are somewhere else. You control your mind, Simón. Remember that. Let it fly to safety if it needs to."

I find myself backed up against the boat dock. My breathing putters and falters along with my hummingbird heart.

I close my eyes and imagine myself soaring into the air, shooting upward, piercing the clouds, caressing the satin blue of the sky above them. The city tumbles up and down the hills below me. I map out every street, alleyway, and house. Breathing deeply, my lungs draw in every scent clinging to the muggy air. The salt blowing off the waves. Jose Maní's musk, soaked into his linen shirt as he sells peanuts along Milanés Street. *Torrejas* being flipped in oil by Señora Vargas for her good-for-nothing grandkids; the anise and cinnamon of the syrup swirls as she pours it on top. And Mamá's house perches on its peak just there. I smell her jasmine perfume. I long for her embrace. For her to hold my hand. To tell me to keep breathing.

A strong wind slams into me, pulling me sideways, dropping me out of the sky.

A pinch and a twist bloom on the back of my arm with a sting.

Tumbling out of my vision and back into reality, my head whips around to find Lenita standing in front of me, still gripping the skin of my arm between two fingers.

Her frantic eyes scan my face and body before she pulls me into a tight hug. I smell a hint of perfume I don't recognize.

"Finally! I've been hanging outside your place like some sort of professional stalker. I even asked the neighbors across the street if I could use their bathroom just to get a better look through your windows."

I gnaw on the inside of my cheek and pause, unsure if I can even form intelligible words, or if it'll come out as sobs.

"You look like shit, man." She exhales an awkward, forced chuckle and pushes my shoulder. "Figured you'd been sleeping this whole time. Guess not all sleep is beauty rest, huh?" Her voice is teasing, but her eyes don't match it. There's something unsettled behind them.

The last time we spoke was after Albi's funeral. I can't remember much about the funeral at all. Not really. My camera was in the shop, I guess. Flashes come back to me: the heat pressing in on me from every direction, a girl in the choir crying somewhere on the other side of the church, the casket closed in front of the altar.

I remember trying not to look at Father Cordero. I couldn't meet his eyes. We were never close. Maybe Albi wanted to keep that part of his life separate. Or maybe I did. Either way, his eulogy felt . . . off. Erratic. Vague. Maybe I was too numb to hear what he actually said.

For someone who remembers everything, it's cruel that I can't remember that. Not the sound of Albi's name being spoken, not the color of the flowers, not whether it rained or was sunny. Just the heavy, sticky air of the church, and how badly I wanted to leave my own skin behind.

Lenita came every day that first week. I told her she was suffocating me. Told her to get the hell out. I don't remember exactly what I said, only the way she left. Slowly, like someone stepping barefoot over broken glass, hoping I wouldn't notice how much it hurt. Now I know she didn't really go. She stayed close enough that I wouldn't notice.

"Hey, for real. How are you?" she asks, softer now. "I know I'm not usually sentimental or whatever, but this is the longest we've gone without talking. I want to be there for you. However that looks. We don't have to talk about it yet if you don't want to. We can walk, get some sun, catch you up on the *chisme*, whatever you want." Even if I remembered how to talk to someone who isn't made of thin air and misfiring neurons, she speaks so quickly I don't have time to respond. "Not much is open anyway. Whole town's either in church or pretending to be."

"What? Why?" I can only manage monosyllabic caveman speak. My voice sounds distant in my own ears, like it's coming from someone else's mouth.

"It's *Semana Santa*, Simón. Tomorrow's Easter."

My brain stalls a beat too long. Lenita slips her arm through mine, more gently this time, like a sailor's knot, tugging me forward. Her skin is warm against mine.

"Come on," she says. "Let's go sit somewhere and talk shit about people. We can see if anyone we went to school with has gotten fat or lost their hair." She winks at me, puts her other hand against my cheek, gently tipping my head to her shoulder.

Lenita has always been unassumingly gorgeous—sharp, irreverent, allergic to fragility. My opposite in almost every way. Growing up, she rejected every delicate thing I adored. But now I see her clearly: she's cultivated her own kind of feminine power, the kind that doesn't ask to be palatable. She's not trying to be admired. She just *is*.

I should've accepted her help back then. Should've

thanked her for showing up for me even if I couldn't accept the hand she was offering. I know I can rely on her now, but even that feels so impossible.

"Isn't your family expecting you?" I ask.

"Yeah, but I'm not missing anything." She shrugs. "They all yell at each other, play dominos, and get drunk. It's like a time loop of terror. I'd much rather be with my favorite person in the world." She pauses, her arm tightening around mine. "And I haven't exactly been having the best time either," she adds, quieter now. "I need this, too."

"I missed you, Leni," I say quietly.

"I missed you too, Simo," she replies with a rare kiss on my head. "More than your big dumb brain can ever know."

We leave the walk-up coffee stand and sit in silence for a few minutes, sipping from our cups shoulder-to-shoulder on the curb as people rush by and the sun climbs overhead. Wind whips behind a bicyclist who swerves around a woman with a wagon full of vegetables and blows the floral scent off Leni's skin again.

"Are you wearing perfume?" I ask her with more than a hint of judgment in my tone, shocked by the flowery revelation.

"Shut up!" she barks, sliding a few inches away in mock indignation. "I can change, you know. I'm embarking on a metamorphosis, *mamón*. Look it up in one of your books." She throws her head back and laughs, running her fingers through her hair in tight little clusters at the scalp, shaping them into tulip stems.

I turn to look at her. I hadn't noticed her hair was curled until now. She seems different. Her posture carries more poise, her steps have a bounce, her mood is lighter. This is about a man. I know it. She hasn't said anything because she knows it would be inappropriate, given everything that's happened. And I won't ask because I'm a self-centered prick. I should be able to set my grief aside and celebrate whatever has changed her. But instead, a pang of jealousy flares up, an urge to run home. It's not fair. She should be ashamed. She should be mourning with me.

A young man approaches, eyes fixed on Leni. She angles away before he can speak, shooting a curt, "No, thank you. I'm good." He lifts his hands, bewildered, then walks off mumbling.

"He was really handsome," I say, testing the waters. "You sure you don't want to talk to him for a second?" This is a test as much as an honest offer. I hope the venom I feel doesn't curl my words.

"Fuck no. Trying to pick me up while I'm sitting on the curb. I am a rose, not a dandelion. He wouldn't know how to handle all of this." She laughs, and I do, too.

"I'm sorry if I worried you. For being an asshole . . . I thought about coming to see you or calling," I say after the laughter tapers off. "But I . . . I don't know." My knees bounce with anxious energy, my ankles tangled together.

"Simón, don't be an idiot." She bumps my shoulder. "You never need to explain yourself to me. I'm always here. You're never getting rid of me." She rests her head against mine. "And don't you fucking apologize again. We don't do that, okay? We are never wrong."

"I do feel wrong." My voice catches. "I don't feel like me anymore, and I don't know how to make it right again." I shrink into myself as my arms fold around my torso, holding the pieces together. "I just want it to stop hurting." My eyes start to burn under their lids. I want to turn away from her, but I know if I move an inch, I'll lose control.

"I know, Simo." Her voice drops to a low hum, the kind meant to settle crying babies. "It's messed-up. All of it. And it's not gonna make sense for a while. Maybe not ever."

Her fingers find mine and grip tight. "But I'm here, okay? You don't have to hold yourself together for me. You don't have to be anything. It's just us. You and me. Like it's always been."

I nod and lean into her, heavier now. "Maybe we should get drunk," I say with an intentionally pitiful whimper.

She lets out a short laugh and jumps to her feet. "Hell yeah. I'll swipe us a bottle of something absolutely disgusting. Just like old times."

We meander through town, taking swigs from a glass bottle and tucking it back into Lenita's bag between pulls.

"You stole this way too easily," I say, still looking at the ground. "Not complaining, though. I love the seedy little skill." I wipe my mouth and hand her the bottle.

"I know, right? Especially with that old fool eye-fucking me the whole time. Guess he didn't notice my hands were busy 'cause his eyes were stuck on my ass. Men are sick." She takes a quick sip, then slips the bottle back into her bag. She looks distant for a second as tension pulses in her brow.

"I never asked," I say, recalling what she said earlier, "why you've been having such a tough time lately."

"Huh?" She blinks, then forces a shrug. "Oh, it's nothing. I was worried about you." She raises the rum to her mouth again before lowering it to ask, "So, what made you finally come out into the land of the living today?" She glances my way but doesn't linger, careful not to corner me. She hands me the bottle.

"My Tía Cachita came over." Another gulp of booze.

"Ew. Why?"

"She said Mamá needs me. And that I obviously need her. It embarrassed me, her seeing me like that. It felt like I either had to get up and try living again or give up completely. Kind of felt like I was in limbo—kept going to sleep and waking up, getting drunk, going to sleep and waking up."

I can't tell her the rest: that I'm losing my mind, seeing through the eyes of a fly smashing itself against my window. How I ended up at the beach without knowing how I got there. How Albi still talks to me. How I see him. How I imagine myself headless, handless, drowning. How my mind feels like an abridged version of itself. "I needed to get out before I missed my chance," I say instead.

"Simo," she says gently, "I know things are bad, but promise you'd tell me if they got worse? You can lean on me—I want you to lean on me. I'll help you carry it. Albi's gone, but—" Lenita stops and curls her lips into her mouth. It's the first time we've both heard his name spoken out loud in a long time. She looks like a fish gasping for water, eyes wide open and unfocused.

I wave it off before she has to fight for composure. "It's okay," I say quickly. "I'm okay. Well, I want to be okay anyway. I think I do need to lean on you. Coco too . . . maybe even my mom . . ."

"You actually want to see your mom? Wow. Now I know things are bad." Lenita repositions herself to face me and check my pupil dilation, but I edge away.

"Stop." I sigh. "It wasn't fair of me to vanish and leave everyone worrying. As for Ma . . . part of me misses her, part of me wants to blame her." I inhale and hold it in for a second before releasing it all at once. "I keep thinking she should apologize . . . to me, to Albi . . . I don't know." I pick up a pebble, but it feels sticky, so I drop it and wipe my fingers on my pants.

She looks at the pebble, which we both now see is gum, and we laugh. "Look, I'm just gonna say it. We both know your mom. You walked out on her. There aren't many women who would welcome a man back with open arms after that, let alone apologize to you . . ." She shakes her head and places the bottle in her purse before reclining back on her elbows. "She'll see your dad walking through that door before she realizes it's you, and you'll have a frying pan at the back of your head or a knife at your throat."

"I'm nothing like my father. My leaving was nothing like his leaving." I yank the bottle from her purse and take a burning gulp. My stomach clenches and heaves, but I swallow another mouthful. "Maybe I'll swing by and wish her a happy resurrection day or whatever. Whisper a Hail Mary and hope she doesn't throw a shoe at me."

Lenita wrestles the bottle from my hands and, with no warning, hands it off to an old man passing by. He flashes a grateful, toothless grin.

"I say we walk it off a bit," she says, standing. "Give you time to sober up. Then you can decide if you really want to risk your life for a holiday greeting."

She holds out her hand, and the skin feels moisturized and soft as I take it.

Chapter Four
Domesticated & Abandoned

The city exhales around us. We walk in silence, dodging people and waiting for cars to pass. Pastel buildings with crumbling corners loom overhead, held up by the memories of their former grandeur. Old ladies look out through windows, beyond the iron bars and out into space. Old men play dominoes in front of their houses, never saying a word, just pursing their lips and clutching the ivory tiles. A child climbs a street lamp while his older sister screams and flings a shoe at him from below.

As the booze seeps into my stomach lining, the gloom dissipates from my skull. My feet could be hovering over the pavement, my body floating along the preordained path. Such a dangerous feeling, this need for chemical intervention, but I welcome it all the same.

Lenita tells me some story about her cousin and a neighbor fighting in the front yard and how one of their shirts ripped, and her breasts swung two seconds after the punch and hit the other girl like a second wallop. I laugh, but the sound doesn't feel familiar.

The next story begins, and I see myself walking ahead of us. An even younger me than that first one stands in line against a wall. He is wearing a uniform and staring at his feet while the other children talk over and play around him. More memories piling up before me.

The old church comes into view—Albi's church, my mother's church. Albi runs ahead of us. I know he'll turn into the alley when he reaches it. And he does.

The current me is still walking, but I can't tell if I'm moving myself forward or being pulled. Albi circles back, half-skipping, half-running, and he looks like a child. I imagine him sitting at a table surrounded by other little kids as his mother presents him with a birthday cake. I can hear his voice asking too many questions, his big head encircled by a bigger dome of curls.

"C'mon, Simón! You're walking too slow." It was so out of character for Albi to be giddy, his cool facade chipped away by sudden, unbridled joy. I'd fold him up if I could, crisply crease him into a keepsake or a talisman to hold in my pocket and smooth between my fingers for good luck.

The main road isn't visible from where we now stand—Lenita and I alongside my other selves and Albi. Beyond the far side of the church lies an easement connecting the church and its small cemetery to a rectory and makeshift seminary behind it. From a child's eye level, the path would have been obscured by the cemetery gates and memorial stones, which explains why I never noticed it despite attending mass here twice a week.

A green wall of vines and their outstretched leaves flank one side of the path, towering higher and higher as we walk along. The slope crests, and at its peak a squat little door appears—a door for garden gnomes or faeries.

When Albi was still here, particular attention had been paid to the doorway, the flowers and vines trimmed back to frame the door like an illuminated manuscript. The foliage curled like expressive script around a gilded doorway, vines snaking arabesque trails, swooping and slinking. It was like a fragrant portal to another world. Now, the vines have overrun that door, tapping lightly against its surface as they unlearn all former restraint.

"I trim and prune everything here," Albi said, fumbling for the key as he noticed my gaze following the twists and turns of the greenery. He pushed the door open, waiting for me to step through first. Beyond the threshold lay a meticulously manicured paradise. "You have your beach, I have this," he beamed, arms outstretched in a Vitruvian way. An image of his naked body flashed behind my eyes, but I blinked it away. Not now, Simón.

A worn stone path lined with brilliant yellow blossoms threaded its way lazily through the walled garden. The plants nearest the path were low and neatly spaced, yet small variations kept the arrangement from feeling rigid, like one of nature's seemingly impossible mathematical equations. Behind these, Albi had placed taller species that rose and fell in waves of greens and purples, swaying in the breeze.

"I wanted it to feel like your eyes sort of follow the flowers along the path and then get sucked into the layers building up behind them," he said. "Like a story almost. Don't you think?" A hummingbird—always a hummingbird—zipped between us and around our heads before joining bees and whatever other pollinators were on the clock. It was like a story. A fairytale. "Most of these plants are older than us," he added, "but some are as new as this past spring. I took them from the little park outside the Grand Hotel. They were about to throw them out when the new stuff arrived to be planted for the season."

"Are we on a different planet?" I murmured, stunned by it

all, but especially by Albi's green thumb. Who knew a muscular, hairy man of God tending flowers would stir such hunger in certain corners of my anatomy? I slowly spun around, taking it in.

He'd cultivated this whole other world while all I'd offered him was a derelict beach. My struggling little handful of mango trees fend for themselves every day, listening to the prostitutes screaming in the park above them, condoms and trash washing up on the shore at their feet. These plants here had nothing falling on them but love and devotion. A choir sings to them several days a week, for heaven's sake.

The air seemed to glow, sweet and light, like a *pastelito*. The sounds of the city murmured miles away, and the dirt and grime of the alley on the other side of the vine-covered wall faded into fiction in this parallel universe. Even the pigeons looked happier, bathing in crystal-clear water and finding shade without a single care in the world.

"They don't wreck all your hard work?" I asked, nodding at them with a jerk of my chin.

"Nope! They just come here to zen out. Get clean water, rest a bit . . ." He bent down and plucked a fallen guava leaf from the path and tucked it into his pocket. "I actually really love the pigeons," he said a few seconds later. "Something about them still wanting to be around humans even though we're supposed to hate them . . . It really gets to me."

"I never thought about that. We really screwed them over, huh? Domesticated them and then abandoned them. That's really sad," I said, keeping with his slow pace. "I don't know. They still creep me out."

Albi walked me over to a little patch of flowers under a fig tree. There was a rock painted with little orange blossoms. "Simón, meet my mother." He knelt down and made invisible adjustments to the surrounding plants. "Mama, this is Simón, the guy I told you about." He stood up and smiled. He looked at me, and I crumbled.

"When my mother and I first moved in," Albi continued, "Father Cordero told me that fixing up the garden would be my chore. It was really run-down, basically a mating ground for cats back then. Pretty disgusting to hear. For the first few months, that is what I mostly did—threw things at the cats while they were screwing." He laughed and took his sandal off, holding it up like an annoyed mother, pinching his lips together in mock threat. "Once they stopped coming around, I had to figure out which plants were supposed to be here and then pull all the weeds out."

"How'd you know which was which?" I asked. "You were still a kid."

He brightened. "I developed my own method! Most of the mature plants were pretty obvious. But if I was unsure, I would place my fingers around the base of the plant, pinch it a little to see how fibrous it was, and then tug. If it came loose easily, it was probably a weed."

"So you didn't actually know," I teased. "You were just pulling things up and hoping for the best."

"Weeds have to grow fast to overtake the other plants, so they are usually flimsier and made of water for the most part. That's why they pop up out of nowhere after it rains. And their roots don't have time to get deep in the ground either. So yes, I do actually know."

"But you don't! That's an assumption," I blurted, the skeptic in me surfacing.

Albi lowered his invisible spectacles to peer at me over the nonexistent frames. "Or is it a hypothesis, Mr. Science?" he said, and I punched him lightly in the arm.

In the garden's dappled light, Albi looked like something from a religious painting. Haloed and sacred. Watching him tend to his flowers with such devotion, I thought about the tendons in his forearms. How those same arms had held me. Tended me. This garden had been his beginning. And like that other garden story, this one already held the seeds of its undoing too.

"I'm glad you had the key with you," Lenita says, standing next to me in the garden. My arm is wrapped around hers, and my other hand is holding a guava leaf.

I nodded. "I always have it with me." My voice slides out from my lips and drifts to the ground. I slip the leaf into my pocket.

She studies me for a moment, letting the quiet hold. "You've been deep in it, huh?" she says. "I mean, I get it. This place feels like . . . more than a garden." She rubs my back, then shifts her bag on her shoulder. She winces slightly for a second, like something tight pulled in her lower back. "I've been talking a lot," she adds, brushing it off with a laugh. "Sometimes I try to make things easier by making them louder. I don't know if that actually helps."

I glance at her. She shrugs, but there's something forced in her expression, something she hasn't shared with me. "You've got a lot to carry, Simón. I know I can't carry it all for you, but I'm gonna do my best."

"I think I want to sit here and spend a little more time with Albi," I say with as much volume as I can muster.

She pulls away but keeps her grip on my arms. "Take your time. Think. Maybe go see your ma, and I'll meet you at El Palomar later. I want to be there when you see Coco." She shifts her weight and lets her arms fall. "Are you still thinking about it? About seeing her?"

"I think I have to." I pull her into a hug. "Thank you, Leni. For being with me today. I love you."

"Of course, *baboso*. I'm always here for you." She kisses my cheek and pulls back, holding my gaze. "And I'll see you tonight, no matter what. Even if the visit goes to shit. Even if you don't go."

"I promise," I say.

She backs toward the garden door, one hand lingering on her lower back as she steps. The latch clicks. Silence settles in, and I sit down on a rock surrounded by flowers and grasses.

I try to force the apparition of Albi back into the garden to pick up where he left off. I hold my breath until I'm dizzy, thinking the strain might force another mental break.

After about twenty seconds, the grasses sway. And then the flowers sway.

A brown eye peeks out from under a leaf. And then a green eye blinks open. A furry brown head pops out of the brush.

"Sapo! Have you been following me around all day, *precioso*?" I say in the required mush-mouth pet-speak. Sapo springs out in a playful tumble and spits a cockroach at my feet. "Is this a treasure for me?"

He sits down in front of me and positions his paws as close together as they can be, waiting for me to look away; I do so, and he jumps into my lap. The cockroach springs back to life and scurries off down the walkway and into a bunch of flowers. It's a day of resurrections. Sapo purrs in the crux of my legs. "I've been spending time with your other dad." He pushes his head against the motion of my hands, and I kiss his closed eyes. "Yes, the more handsome one." He chirps and flops his back down into my lap, exposing his belly. "I miss him, too."

Sapo's ears perk up and flatten behind his head. His eyes go glassy as his pupils dilate, and he scrambles to his feet and off my lap before darting behind the rock I'm sitting on. Strange animal.

"And here's where I found a dead cat!" Albi called joyfully from across the garden, continuing his tour. "I pulled up a weed and there it was, maybe an inch under the dirt. So many black flies swarmed out. It was absolutely biblical." He walked over to the corner closest to the rectory. "Father Cordero helped me one time. I think he was unironically trying to be a father figure. But he threw his back out unearthing this St. Lázaro statue over here."

Time seemed to slip sideways in this place. What seemed like a day passed in merely an hour; it was like the sun decided to stop and rise again in the opposite direction.

Albi bent over to pull a dying leaf from a plant near the walkway. He lingered there for a moment, and I could sense a subtle tension in his shoulders. Suddenly, he sprang up from the ground, a new, more beautiful flower. "Let me show you my room," he said, turning quickly towards me.

Something in his walk felt off. It was still buoyant, but too measured, stunted almost. I watch my younger self and see his stomach lurch as he followed Albi's urgent stride into the rectory and down that narrow, windowless hall. I see him pausing and collecting his composure before stepping into Albi's room for the first time.

"Welcome to my chamber, good lady," he said, locking the door behind us. He bowed deeply and extended a hand out to me, his soft palm pointing upward like a velvet pillow for a ring to rest on, his fingers fanning out delicately. I could have licked each of them and taken the whole hand into my mouth. Instead, I set my hand on top of his, and he spun me into an embrace, steering me into a waltz around his room.

"Someone's feeling lively. That's usually my thing. Am I

gonna have to sue you for trademark infringement?" I asked with a shaky laugh. I'd never seen him so giddy. It unsettled me. I wanted him to be consistent, to ground me, to be the sturdy walls to contain my crazed, overanalytical overthinking.

"I don't know. I don't feel any pressure here, I guess." He shrugged and pulled me closer to him. My right arm wrapped around his shoulder, and his left hand settled on the small of my back. My mother's dance lessons sounded in my head. *This is the woman's posture, and this is the man's. His carriage is meant to support her like this.*

"We can finally just be us. No windows. The door's locked. The walls are made of stone. It's like a cocoon in here," he said, low in my ear.

"Or a tomb," I mumbled. A dull pressure had been churning at the base of my gut from the moment we stepped into the rectory, somewhere between a sudden dash to the bathroom or the reflexive lurch that comes from drinking too fast on an empty stomach. It had nothing to do with being alone with him in that way. I'd wanted that ever since I first saw his hands gripping the paschal candle during mass. The real dread gnarling up my insides was rooted in something far less sensual.

Intimacy typically begins by removing clothes, and removing clothes starts with the shoes—shoes I'd worn all day in the sweltering heat. Shoes that had absorbed summers upon summers of anxious foot sweat. "How do you get airflow in here?" I asked coolly.

He laughed. "We have a communal fan. I usually wedge it in the doorway a couple of times a week, just to move the air around. It's not a big deal. I don't work out in here or anything." He arched an eyebrow. "Unless you were hoping we might get a workout in together." He spun me around, too quickly, and then shoved me down onto his bed.

"Sir! This is a church!" I laughed, but my voice quivered as my mouth suddenly went dry. My tongue shucked itself from the roof. "Besides, I don't want you getting fired. Let's go to my place another day. No worries, really."

"This is the rectory. Totally separate building," he reminded me. "And they can't fire me; I'm here by choice," he said, sitting down next to me. "How many young guys do you think are banging on the door to get in here?" My hesitation clicked in his head, and he added gently, "But if you'd rather go, that's okay. I don't want you to feel stressed or pressured or anything. I'm just excited to be here with you." His shoulders sagged a fraction, his posture deflated, and I missed the giddy, carefree Albi that danced with me just seconds before.

"I was only thinking of you," I said, sliding my hand up his substantial thigh for a groping squeeze. "If you're okay doing it under His watchful eye, I don't mind seeing what's under the cloth . . ." I tried to sound mischievously casual and irreverent, as though I weren't freaking out about it being my first time touching a penis that wasn't my own or about having to remove these damned shoes in front of the unbelievably gorgeous man attached to that penis I wanted to touch with more than just my hands.

"In that case, let's get cozy." Albi kicked his shoes off and launched himself deeper onto the bed. "Come lie down." He tugged me backward by the hips as I sat stiffly at the edge.

My right foot inched the heel of my left shoe downward, my nose testing the air in microscopic increments. Every movement stretched in slow motion, feeling theatrically drawn out yet taking far less time than my brain reported.

"Hurry up, weirdo! What're you doing?" Albi said. He yanked me down, and I toppled over onto the bed, my shoe rocketing off in a comical arc. A warm, soft pungency hit my nostrils, freezing me like a dog caught raiding the pantry: frozen, eyes darting side to side.

"You okay? Did I hurt you?"

After a too-long pause, I opted for honesty. "I was worried about my feet smelling bad." I exhaled and took another breath in, reassessing the situation. "So I was trying to do a quick sniff test. I didn't wanna gross you out." I couldn't meet his eyes.

Sporting a devilish grin, Albi inhaled deeply and let out an exaggerated sigh of pleasure. His head tilted back, eyes closed in mock ecstasy as he sank to the floor, ferreting around blindly for my foot. His fingers met the skin of my ankle. His eyes snapped open, locking with mine. Slowly, he began peeling off my sock. One hand slipped under the elastic while the other tugged at my toes. The playfulness beaming from his eyes only seconds ago retreated, and a new bullish hunger flourished in its place.

My sock fell to the floor, and the cool air of his dungeon-like room chilled my skin as he lifted my foot to his face and softly kissed it, caressing my ankle with one hand. He picked up my right foot and repeated the ritual, never once breaking eye contact. My head was floating above my body. My ears rang with a hollow, tinny clang, and my arms hung lifeless at my sides. The only muscle that seemed functional was in my throat, swallowing nervously as he kissed the sole of my right foot and then returned to the bed.

He guided our bodies onto the mattress and pressed a kiss to my ear, trailing slow kisses along my jaw. He was on top of me. His body weight kept me from floating through the ceiling. His hands found my wrists and wrapped around them as he pinned me down, and the heat of his palms and fingers seared my skin like a serrated knife held over fire. His smile was immense, each tooth a continent.

I was smiling, too, but I felt like I could cry at any moment. I was so overwhelmed by this chill racing through me, even though my blood was boiling beneath the skin. My limbs went cold, and my teeth clacked as my body poured out sweat. My hands pulsed, now harboring hearts of their own, and twitched like mischievous raccoons itching to sever themselves and rummage through the dark.

Albi began a quick transformation, too. His face faltered, melted into something both urgent and uncertain, like eating ice cream sliding down a cone—still delicious, but rushed. His smile faded, his eyes scorched the space between us. I looked at his mouth, his soft lips barely parted, and I could almost see his jaw tremble. He made a dry gulping sound, and I knew he felt that same freezing-feverish sensation.

His face moved closer to mine. My raccoon hands wanted to rip him to shreds. I wanted to touch every inch of his body at the same time. Every microscopic moment was happening, and I wanted to witness all of it, all of him, all at once. I wanted to dislocate my jaw and swallow him whole. My brain flicked through devious variations of lovemaking I'd never thought of before. Positions to place my mouth against his. Parts of his body to grab. Ways to grind into him in ecstasy. All of this without any actual comprehension of the mechanics of desire, nor how to navigate them with a real pulsing body on top of mine, pinning me down.

My lips tingled as he pressed into them. My mouth watered. His tongue slid between my lips, and the hunger was unbearable. *Devour him. Swallow him whole*, my brain told me. I had never expected someone's mouth to have a flavor. You think of how it would feel, how to maneuver your tongue, but

I never anticipated the flavor I'd encounter, the sweetness, the warmth. I desperately hoped that mine tasted half as good to him. His mouth opened with a gentleness, but his tongue was desperate to wrestle mine into submission. The necessity of it all, the yearning beading off of him told me it might be his first time, too.

He released my wrists, and the raccoon hands grew minds of their own to match their hearts. They immediately sprang into action, going in separate directions, pulling my arms around his waist in their mad dash. I pressed his body against mine. Grinding my hips into his, feeling his stiffness that rivaled my own.

He twisted his body around and let out the smallest gasp. I felt his smile against my lips as I continued kissing him. He nuzzled into me, still twisting and wiggling like he was trying to burrow into my body. I wanted to tell him it wasn't any warmer in there, that I was freezing, too. Instead, I held him tighter, crushing him against me, hoping we would coalesce into one. Reverse mitosis.

He sucked in air through his teeth, and my mind clawed its way back to humanity. "I'm so sorry." I released him. "I couldn't tell what to do, or not do . . ."

He began feverishly kissing my chest, his curls lightly brushing and bouncing against my jaw and mouth as he made his way back up to my lips. "No. Don't stop," he said with his teeth against mine. "I'm just so happy."

I felt monstrous. He was giddy, giggling, while I ached to tear him open and plunge inside him. I wanted my arms to fuse around his torso, never releasing him, intertwined forever in a Giambologna abduction scene.

"I want to keep you," I breathed into his hair.

"You've got me now, haven't you?" he replied. I pulled him

tight against my chest. Then, with a swift pivot, flipped us both so he landed beneath me. Surprise flashed in his eyes. "I didn't know you were that strong," he gasped.

Now on top, I snarled and dove into his neck, biting lightly at first, then harder, then gentle again. His arms coiled around my head, nails digging into my scalp. I had no idea what I was doing, just following the frantic impulses of my body, afraid I would go too far and hurt him or scare him away. His teeth were on my neck now. My right arm held him close to my chest, keeping him suspended, levitating a few inches above the bed. An exquisite exorcism. A blind foot hooked into his half-unbuttoned shorts and wrenched them down in a series of graceless tugs, like a hyena tearing flesh from a carcass. I barely recognized my own body. Adrenaline pumping through my veins. Passion obscuring any moments that might be awkward or clumsy. Hyenas don't feel shame, and neither did I.

A guttural noise escaped his lips as he kicked his shorts the rest of the way off. Albi's spit cooled my neck, his hands still rooted in my hair. "I want to taste you," I whispered breathlessly against the side of his face, the words worming their way up his cheek and into his ear, moistening his hair and sticking to his skin. I pulled back, trying to capture every detail of the moment. His delicate lashes, the satin skin, the warm brown of his eyes, the veins in his forearms. I wanted to worship every inch of him. I wanted to destroy every inch of him just the same.

He didn't blink, only shifted his hands from my head, trailing down my back to rest on my ass, each palm searing like charcoal. "I want to taste you first," he said, slithering out from under me in one fluid motion, reappearing behind me while I remained hovering over the crumpled sheets.

An arm pressed against the small of my back, another hoisted my hips upward, sending my face into the mattress. A warmth hit me and spread into my stomach, infecting my heart. My chest seized, my mouth gaped, but no sound escaped. I wanted to bite the mattress, or my hand, his hand. I searched desperately behind me for something of him to grab onto as his grip tightened and his face buried itself deeper and deeper. His stubble rubbed against me like sand. His tongue danced around, pirouettes and pliés.

Cold air hit my wet skin as he suddenly released my hips. His body fell on top of mine, and he kissed me from behind as I twisted to meet his mouth. I could smell myself on him. I felt changed. He felt different to me then, too. Older, somehow. Aged. Fermented.

"You wanna try?" Albi asked, biting his lip. He grabbed my dick and stroked it.

"I don't know. There's no way I'll be as good as you. I've never done this before," I said, still panting, trying to crush his body into mine—partially to break his gaze, to hide away for a second, but also to be as close to him as possible.

"You think I have?" Albi laughed, taken aback. "I must be a natural then," he said, smug, his hand still wrapped around me. My skin tingled all over my body. "Pretend that you're eating a mango. That's what I was doing. Like you're getting the meat off the pit."

"Sounds sloppy," I said, distracted by the wet pleasure below my waist as he took me into his mouth. I held his head gently and felt the rocking of his skull.

"Exactly," he said with a sinister glint in his eye, his mouth watering, teeth reflective as mirrors. A beast had taken his place. All the better to eat me with.

I lowered my mouth to his chest, inhaling deeply as my

face slid across his body hair. Scents of pepper, vanilla, incense from that morning's mass, the saltiness of our intermingled sweat. I kissed his belly button; he chuckled breathily. I kissed his hip bone; he gasped slightly. I kissed the other side, and he turned his pelvis so that his cock was staring at me, eye to eye. A newfound boldness took hold, and I grabbed him by the base and then guided the entirety of him into my mouth. The heat emanating from him made me salivate. He cupped the back of my head, guiding my rhythm against his rolling hips. My hands slid up his torso and back down again. The air thickened. I couldn't breathe.

I grabbed his hips and pulled myself away from his pelvis, letting his cock slap against his stomach while I moved down and began licking the tender space where thigh meets groin. A heavenly patch of the smoothest skin, dusted with fine black hair. He curled his hips upward, begging for me to keep moving down, so I went even slower, watching him squirm and writhe. The power thrummed through me, a dizzying sense of control over his every shiver, every gasp.

Eating mango can be a very messy process. The juice. The slippery meat. The hairs caught between teeth. I refused to waste a drop, miss an inch, hairs be damned. He glistened with my spit, and I thought of how digestion starts with saliva. I wanted to break him down, to devour and digest him.

His body shuddered as I held his hips like handles. Seeing him relinquish all control, seeing his body collapsing in my hands sent waves through my body, and I let myself go with the current. Out to sea. Tumbling under the waves. Naked on his bed. Damp, panting.

His head fit perfectly in the curve of my neck, my arms wrapped around him, our legs intertwined. We had been changed. I was sure of it.

At first, he twitched and spasmed as he fought off sleep, but soon he found the right position, and I did too. With Albi's arms around my waist, his chest pressed against my back, I felt his breathing gradually slow. The motion of his rib cage, heaving rhythmically, steady against my back, ticked the seconds away. Then minutes and hours. I tried not to breathe out of sync with him, as though mismatched breaths might remind him this was all wrong, that we were not one and the same. Like our competing breaths might knock him out of slumber, and he'd know this was a mistake, and he'd push me off him and beat my face in, suddenly aware of my absurdity—the absurdity of what we had done.

Things think themselves differently when you're alone. Having another person around forces even your inner monologue to reshape itself into something more acceptable, more "correct." It seasons your reactions to match the palate of the company. Anything to avoid conflict, to avoid causing discomfort. I remember hearing a song once, and my mouth could hardly contain how much I adored it. The magic of it. The feeling in my stomach. I remember sharing it with Lenita and realizing within two seconds, as she started talking about something else, that it wasn't anything special to her at all. And I questioned its worth. Did I even like the song? I remember feeling silly and sad. It was shameful. How can someone be so passionate yet so fickle?

When he woke up, he kissed the back of my head, the sound muffled, consumed almost entirely by my hair, moist from his breath, wrapping in and around itself like the roots of some overgrown forgotten potted plant. Then he kissed my neck. His breathing remained controlled and consistent, and I consciously matched it again, even though my heart felt like it couldn't find the beat of the same music. And I realized I'd have to fake waking up so he wouldn't know I hadn't slept, pretend I hadn't been obsessing over our shared breath all this time.

I felt unbearably neurotic. More so than normal. We train ourselves so deliberately and diligently to be the person we need to be for whoever is around us—to protect us, to protect them—that it truly is a bit sociopathic. And the guilt that stains the situation, any situation, knowing that we are lying every word of every conversation. Even then, with a man I had just slept with. The man whose ass I had just lapped up like a mango. I felt like I had to pretend. I felt compelled to perform.

"Relax, Simón." His lips lightly caressed the back of my ear as he whispered, somehow even gentler than the breaths his words replaced. "Your heart's about to explode." He kissed the back of my head again, and a warmth spread from that point, igniting each follicle like granules of gunpowder, each hair a fuse. I imagined my head exploding briefly before tamping down the spiral.

"I keep thinking about . . . everyone," I managed.

"Who?" Albi interrupted. "No one matters right now but us." His shoulder nudged mine from behind. Another kiss planted.

"No, not what people think. Not in that way." My voice stumbled over itself. "I mean all the people I've pretended to be. The people I feel forced to be. I thought I had to be perfect even for you. I imagined that once this happened, I'd finally feel free—that my old life would get left behind and this new better one could start." I stared into the dark. "I pretended to be asleep. I never slept. I concentrated so hard on matching your breath so you'd feel like we were the same. So, you'd know that this meant something real. That it's good and okay, and . . ."

"Oh my God, Simón." He exhaled gently. "Just stop it, please. You're thinking way too much about this." His grip on me loosened as he tried to get a better look at me.

"Sorry, I . . . I just thought—" I moved away from him, and cold air rushed between us.

"No, not about us." He reached again, tugging me back. "We are real. This does mean something. But we're not the same. That's not the goal." He paused. "I don't want to dissolve into you, Simón. I think love should make us more ourselves. Not less."

His hand traced a circle on my stomach. "You keep trying to become one with me. But what if the miracle is that I already love you as you are? All your pieces, all your fears. You don't have to be perfect. You don't have to disappear."

I didn't respond. I couldn't.

"I know it'll be good and okay because it already is more than that. It's not perfect, but nothing is. Perfect things never change. They don't need to. I want to grow, and I want to see you grow. If you're perfect or pretending to be, there is no way for us to grow together. I'll be like vines growing up around a statue. You'll crumble." He curved his arms tightly around my waist.

"That's not how I want to live." He spoke softly in my ear. The words wrapped around me like his vine arms. "Not now that we have finally found each other."

My whole life was spent documenting every second of every moment, every gesture, every unsaid word, every subtle shift in posture. Obsessively dissecting it all. Replaying it over and over, convinced the meaning lived in the details. That I could parse out the how and why behind it all. And then Albi came along. My brief blip of absolute silence in the middle of a crowded dance floor. I no longer needed to search for anything. His world built itself up around me, protected me. Without his breath against my ear, without his skin next to my skin, I'm stranded. I'm floundering.

The dull haze of the booze wears off, and I'm left feeling vacant. Used up. Waiting, frozen, hoping my lover returns with a warm, damp towel to clean me up. He'll never come. I know he won't. The garden grows before my eyes. Pigeons surround me. The guava leaf is still in my pocket, under my hand.

Just say what happened to him and what you must now do, and your world will begin to spin again.

A voice. Urgent and caustic.

Just say his name, and the spell will be recast, and you will know what to do.

It's in my head.

Just say it all out loud, and you will be able to feel something, anything again. Just say his name and what he did. The mornings will sound however you'd like them to.

It's only in my head.

Just say it, and he will come back, and he will love you, and you won't be angry that he gave it all up because he knew that you could be happier elsewhere.

Like you could be happier.

You could be happier.

You could be.

You could.

You. You. You. You. You. You. You.

"You ever seen horses playing?" I asked Albi. "One time, I went to this ranch outside of town. We didn't have to drive far.

We went a few times, actually. Two times, we had to take the bus, and those trips weren't very fun because we were packed in there like corn kernels, and since it was going out into the country, it had a lot of country people in it if you know what I mean. Anyway, it was owned by some guy my aunt was dating. The ranch, not the bus. The horses were beautiful, and they were all standing around most of the time. They look strong even just standing there, you know? They don't posture about and act tough like humans do. They just are. They'd all be standing around eating grass, shitting, pissing . . . a lot too . . . but then one of them would start to jump and kick. Bucking and prancing. Front legs, back legs, front legs, back legs. Sometimes the other horses joined in, and they all stomped the dust together and ran and ran so fast it was almost like they forgot they were just horses on a ranch. They became a river." I became aware of my rambling and trailed off. "But a lot of the time a little baby horse was jumping around on his own."

I tossed my head around and flung my arms like the foal, laughing as I stumbled and kicked at the sand, ending in a half-hearted cartwheel. Albi watched me with his head tilted, black curls brushing his temples, a smile sprouting under his stubble. I wondered how often he shaved but didn't ask.

"Your eyes are so beautiful when you talk about things you love. You usually have a restlessness in there. Inside your head. Like you can't decide what not to think about. But just now you looked like those horses you described. Dancing, prancing until you forget who you are." He paused. "If you could be any animal, do you think you'd be a horse? I think I'd be some kind of bird."

"Maybe a horse," I said. "But they're always in a group. No autonomy. I need space. Actually, I'd rather be something in the water. There's more planet to explore that way. Maybe a giant squid . . . No, that's weird . . . Ugh, I don't know now. Actually, yeah, I'd be a horse. Or a dog . . ." Normally, I'd clamp down on these back-and-forth rambling fits, shut down out of embarrassment. But not with Albi. Part of the fun was rolling along with it until he snapped.

And right on schedule, Albi dramatically yanked at his hair and rolled his eyes back into his skull. "Simón! You can only choose one. I wouldn't have asked if I knew it would devolve into this. Why do you always do this?" He groaned and laughed as he pulled me down onto his lap and pressed a kiss into my back. He loved that I always had something to say, even if it was nonsense. Like he always had someone to talk to, even if there was nothing to talk about.

"You have to pick one. Right now. No more cocoloco rambling. The witch is coming in three seconds to cast some spell on you. First thing that pops into your head in three . . . two . . . one . . ."

"A pigeon. I'd be a pigeon."

"No way! You're not a pigeon kind of person," he huffed.

"You made the rules," I reminded him. "That's what popped into my head."

"But why? They're so boring and dirty. I've seen you kick them away millions of times. You hate pigeons."

"I do hate pigeons." I shrugged. "But think of the ones in your garden. You made them a little bird bath and a cove to rest in."

"Just because they're gross doesn't mean they shouldn't have someone looking out for them. And they were there first, so I made it look nicer. Purely for aesthetics." He was lying. He liked having them to care for. He filled the basin with fresh water every morning, swept the walkway, and arranged leaves in a bed for them to sleep on, but he never fed them because he was worried about more coming around and shitting on everything.

"Now that I think about it, seems like a pretty sweet deal to be a pigeon," I continued. "There is food everywhere. They get to hang out at the beach or on the boardwalk all day. They are alone sometimes, but also hang out together, walking up and down the town, around the shops . . ."

"Nope," Albi cut me off. "You can't make pigeons sound glamorous enough that I believe you want to be one for the rest of your life. Go again."

"Rules are rules. Tell the *bruja* I'm ready for my wings." I lifted my chin and spread my arms out, unfurling my feathers for the first time, clucking my neck and cooing.

"Yeah, and a club foot and bird flu." Albi dove, fingers first, into my armpits. My arms clamped down around his fingers, and he immediately began wiggling them around. I thrashed about, laughing and yanking him around by his trapped hands.

"You'd still love me if I were a pigeon." I cooed and tilted my head to one side and the other, kicking up dirt behind me as I pecked toward his face.

"Gross! Stop!" He freed his hands from underneath my arms, stumbling back a step. "So disturbing." He sniffed his fingers and winked at me.

"And that's not disturbing at all," I muttered.

"No. I love the way you smell. Also, you never asked me what animal I would be. Selfish."

"Okay, what animal would you be? A sensitive little bitch, I'm guessing?" Too far. Why do I always go too far?

"You gotta count down from three, Simón. Jesus. What is wrong with you?"

"Fine. Three . . . two . . . one."

"Shit. I'd be a pigeon too." He tilted his head in my

direction and paused for a second before descending upon me, wings spread, cawing over my laughter.

Chapter Five
Cuarenta, The Impossible

"Listen here, *mijo* . . ." My mother stroked my right cheek and rubbed my left earlobe between the fingers of her other hand. A tiny Simón covered his neck with raised shoulders, chin glued to his clavicle, as tears landed on the tops of his bare feet. "I know life seems too much to handle sometimes. The world can be tough and mean. It eats shit up, shits it out, and if it wipes right, it will never think about that shit again. You are not shit. Do you hear me?" Her voice scratched with the temporary raspiness that follows a bout of screaming. "You can be the whole world if you let yourself."

It's strange to picture her yelling now. The poised, elegant woman she pretends to be these days would never risk her image with an outburst. She wouldn't curse or indulge the pathetic behavior I see in this memory. She always had a regal air, but after she changed, a layer of concrete hardened just beneath her jasmine-scented façade, shielding her heart even from her only child. She didn't hug anymore, rarely laughed out loud. I never saw her cry, though once or twice I heard muffled sobs from another room. She never failed to provide for me, but after my father left, it felt like she left too. The softer version of her walked out with him.

My mother's name is Cuarenta. Abuelita gave birth to her on her fortieth birthday, and she always told the story in a way that made Mamá seem like her personal little miracle. The doctors had insisted she was barren, that she would have had children long before her twenty-first wedding anniversary if it were possible. The contractions trumpeted the news of this impossible pregnancy, and that same day my mother arrived on the tiled floor of the foyer. To my grandmother, the name Cuarenta stood for patience and perseverance, a reminder that things happen when they are meant to happen. But I don't believe Mamá ever fully embraced that notion—patience was never her greatest virtue, before or after the change.

When my Tía Cachita was born nine months later, they named her Milagro, shelving my mother's title as the family phenomenon and making way for the true miracle of the family. Tía Cachita would have everyone believe that, anyway.

Mamá still lives in the big blue house at the top of the hill—the house she was born in a little over fifty years ago, sold to my grandfather by a doctor who fled the country at the first rumblings of revolution. From our rooftop, we would watch the sun set diagonally across the city as it sloped down, finally plunging beneath the water of the bay. She would settle into her soft white bed of sand for the night, and I would imagine her just below the surface, fishing boats dotting her hair, as the sky glowed with colors refracted through the water like a prism. The waveless hour reflected the city lights as they slowly blinked on, one by one, accompanied by a star or two. The city stretched for miles along the coast in either direction, expanding the longer you looked at it, and there we sat, right in the center of it all.

It's only two floors, but the ceilings soar twenty feet into the sky, every plastered inch radiating a brutal confidence. This house could, at one moment, make you feel welcome into its grand halls and, the next, more insignificant than a passing fart.

When they first built it, a breathtaking blue supposedly coated the Caribbean colonial exterior, but after a century of sun and salt, the color fizzled into the bleached yellow tinge of time. A somber dullness occupies every atom of the building. At first glance, it still whispers of that majestic blue, but upon closer inspection, the color vanishes from memory like a skunk backlit by passing headlights, gone before you register its shape, leaving only the acrid stench of its fear behind.

And yet, several moments throughout the day, when the house's color perfectly matches the sky, the structure flings itself into another realm. It transforms into a palace of clouds. The windows, doors, and gutters float in midair, and you can't define the exact point where the walls blend into the heavens. In those fleeting moments, I felt at home. Not only in the house, but in the world.

I long for my mother. For her stories. For her hands guiding mine, her feet guiding my feet. I even long for her reconfigured love, barbed and misshapen though it may be. After holding such lazy hostility toward her, I never expected to crave anything tender from her again. But looking up at that blue dot sitting atop the city like the point of a crown, nothing seems more comforting than her stern stare.

Everything I left behind in that earlier life still waits at the peak of this hill, pinned in place like insects on velvet. The thought burns in my throat. I feel my old insecurities itching to twist back into place, synapses primed for doubt and shame, yet I square my shoulders. The elevation rises under my feet. My toes grip the insides of my shoes. I am breathing. I am in control.

I hear them before I see them. My cousins, the twins. Camilo pinches two cigars between his lips and a bottle of rum under his arm, and Caridad is carrying a small pot of food. I wonder if they forced my mother to make whatever's slopping around inside and imagine grabbing it and dumping it over Cari's head. They're yelling at each other about something, anything, like always.

Tía Cachita follows shortly after in an impossibly short blue dress, frills framing her clavicle and more frills bordering the nearly visible crotch of her panties. She looks a bit foolish wearing high heels on this hill. Her toes clench the open fronts of her shoes, her body teetering forward dramatically, as if she's about to take flight. I love her. She always makes me laugh with how unapologetically she acts, how irreverently she dresses. She lives against the currents of normalcy; in a way, I suppose we have that in common.

Mamá hates her sister, though she'd never admit it. Elder daughters are never truly appreciated. They're inevitably appointed proxies to the mother, with no opportunity for contest or contempt. And although my mother was only several months older than Cachita, she was forced to be a second mother to her, becoming the third and fourth hands, the third and fourth eyes of my grandmother. Over the years, Tía Cachita left and returned to this house many times, always relying on my mother to rebuild her life. After every failed marriage, every bad fling that sent her trailing after some man or another, she came back, shameless as ever, head held no less high than before, knowing that my mother would be right where she always was, in that big blue house.

She was living with us when she got pregnant with the twins. They're less than two years younger than me, and we look almost identical. Everyone in town always said I was the spitting image of my father, *El Puñal.* The Dagger. Do with that information what you will.

My aunt spots me and throws her hands into the air. "Simón! You bring your handsome face over here." She bounces toward me, exaggerating every step to animate her breasts for the nonexistent suitors lining the street. She lives as though trapped in a telenovela, the camera always panning to catch her reaction. Someone is always watching. Never a genuine word slips from her lips, nor a subtle expression graces her face. She said once that she tries not to smile to prevent wrinkles, but it's such a struggle because she's just so, so happy. My mother was seated beside her, face made of still air. Motionless. Emotionless. My mother, who never smiled anymore. My mother, whose life was ruined by her choice of man and some karmic retribution that saddled her with a younger sister with a vacuum cleaner for a pussy.

"Hi, Tía. I like your dress." I kiss her cheek. "Very festive."

"I'm so proud of you for listening to your tía, the genius! I knew my powers of persuasion could snare any man. Even you, *Puñalito.*" She thinks she's being clever, referencing my father while tossing in a tactless, benign jab about me being gay. The only thing less clever than her is her dim daughter, stuffing her bra with napkins picked off the street just a few feet away from us. "Now go see your mother. I can't deal with that sour face of hers for another second. She can yell at you for once and leave me alone."

An urge to slap her across the face—to send her teeth flying and her frilly dress spinning like a windmill in a hurricane— slides into my head. I'd never actually hit a woman, but I'm still ashamed of the anger swelling inside of me. I know she's harmless. Like someone singing off-key. Mildly annoying, yet somehow endearing.

I nod my chin up at my two cousins. Cari ignores me, but Camilo surprises me with a soft smile. We exchange greetings, and my aunt walks away without saying goodbye, yelling at Caridad to hold the pot upright.

"Hey, Simo," Camilo says as he sets the bottle of rum on the pavement. "I got a new car. Figured it might be nice to take a drive sometime. I actually made you a tape of songs I thought would be good for a road trip." He fishes the cassette from his backpack. "It's mostly your kind of music . . . you know, old lady songs, stuff to iron to . . . but I still think it'd be chill. Let me know when you're free or if you'd even wanna do something like that." He hands me the tape and gently grabs my arms. I think he's going to hug me, but then he just slaps my shoulder before jogging to catch up with his mother and sister.

For a moment I don't move. The air around me thins. My hand closes instinctively around the cassette, like it might fall. He's supposed to tell an inappropriate joke, say something ignorant I can laugh at for the wrong reasons, and go back to listening to the sound of waves crashing between his ears. I wish I would've hugged him. I wish I would've told him I loved him for the first time in our lives.

My eyes burn with that familiar moist heat, and I close them tightly before opening them again and looking directly at the sun.

I don't remember pressing the button, but I hear the muffled chimes of the doorbell bouncing off the wooden furniture inside as the water begins pooling around my ankles. My hands dangle in front of me, thumbs fidgeting with their respective fingers, while my eyes blink wildly, trying to preserve a few snapshots before whatever happens next, documenting the calm before the storm. The door swings open in the middle of my blinking fit. It was too fast; there was too much silence. I imagine her standing at the threshold for two years, waiting for this moment, for me to come home.

As it creaks to a halt, there, framed in the impossibly large doorway, stands Cuarenta, in her fifties. Her hair folds in on itself in an elegant, tight bun like a black hole, and her face, painted subtly yet meticulously, sits faultless and stern. She stands there for a moment, and as her eyes scan my face, her eyebrows give the faintest shudder. She lifts her chin and tilts her head to the right, but behind long, mascara-coated lashes, her eyes remain stationary within their moving sockets.

"I wondered if you'd make me spend yet another holiday alone," she says. "I had to sleep through *Noche Buena* just to survive the embarrassment of having an absent son, and don't get me started on Mother's Day." Swaying aside to let me in, she moves like a length of chiffon hanging in an open window on a still summer night. Her feet still don't make a sound.

Suspended in the foyer, just inches away, stands yet another me, waiting in anticipation before the scene resumes. I make eye contact with him and nod for him to proceed. I know what this is. I know who it involves and what parts they all play.

"Mamá, this is my friend Albi. The one I've been telling you about. You probably recognize him from church; he studies under Father Cordero." I stepped in farther, grinning and motioning Albi into the house as my mother's shrewd eyes darted between us.

No impostor escapes unmasked under her jurisdiction, and this woman knows how to judge. My mother delivered a dry "Alberto," taking his hand with limp fingers, one eyebrow slightly cocked.

"I'm sorry, *señora*, but my name is Albi. Just Albi." His voice squeaked, throat tightened by the tense introduction.

Daggers pale in comparison. My mother's eyes were launching machetes, so I quickly pivoted. "Did you know there is a garden out in front of the rectory? I had no idea! Albi is the one who takes care of it. He tends the old plants and has added a ton of new things, too. It's really impressive."

Albi shuffled his feet and waved the compliment off.

"Yes, yes. Father told me about it years ago, but I've never seen it. That's a private building. It would be indecent, and you know I'd never put the good Father in that position." Quickly dashing the sign of the cross twice across her face and chest like holy water, she cleansed herself of the suggestion of immorality, pressing her right thumb and forefinger to her lips, and spun on her heel, kitchen-bound. My mother cared about appearances almost as much as she enjoyed dismissals.

"I can bring you and Simón there together one day, *señora*. You'd be my guest," Albi offered, raising his voice to keep up with her retreating figure. His hands twisted together, desperation curling his fingers into tight leather braids.

"*Si Dios quiere*, Alberto," she said over her shoulder.

I see my old self grabbing Albi's hand and squeezing it. His gaze fell to the floor, and his head turned away from me. I squeezed his hand again. The current me wants to reach out to squeeze the other hand.

Standing up to her wasn't an option back then. The Family sticks together. The Family knows what's right and what's wrong. They do anything to protect the integrity of The

Family. The son does not move out. The son grows up and gets married to a nice woman who moves in, and they take care of The Mother together until she dies. That is the way things are. That is how things are done, but I could never have gone through with it all. Not after knowing what it feels like to be happy, to be in love. To laugh sincerely and smile with my whole face.

I have failed The Family. I have failed my mother. I see that me from two years ago, holding Albi's hand. I look at their chests, and their breathing is in sync, the way I always dreamed.

We dashed upstairs, giddy as schoolboys. I never had a friend like him growing up, and I don't believe he did either. I did have Lenita, but she was a girl, so our interactions were limited. We never had sleepovers or hung out alone at each other's houses.

Safely in my room, I closed the door behind us, and we threw ourselves onto the bed. "I know my mom can be intense," I said after a minute. "She doesn't mean to be so rude. At least, I don't think she does. She's just a bit . . ."

"Callous? Hateful?" Albi offered.

"Harsh." I shrugged and leaned back on the bed. "But fair."

"I'm sorry. I was so excited to meet her and to be around a mom . . ." He sighed. "I think about mine all the time." His voice cracked. "You know, Albi isn't even my real name. That's what my mother always called me. Father assumed that was my name since she didn't call me anything else. And when she died, and I went to live with him, my real name sort of faded away. No one says it right anyway, so it doesn't feel overly sentimental or anything. Just another name. I even say it in the Latin way when I introduce myself now."

"Tell me the right way. The sentimental way," I said, propping myself up to look at him.

"It's pronounced more like 'El-bee.' Everyone says it like 'All-bee' or 'I'll be,' but the vowel sound needs to be deeper."

I give it a try.

"No, it's not as round as an 'A' or flat like an 'E.' It's sort of in between. In your throat."

I try again.

"That's perfect! My mother would be proud . . . though . . . maybe not of . . ." He gestured between us, and a small laugh, unsure in every way, slipped past his lips.

"But the pronunciation was good!" I added swiftly, steering the conversation back into safer territory. "Do you want me to keep calling you Albi? Or would your real name be better? We can repackage you and start selling the real deal again."

"No. I like Albi better. It reminds me of my mom. Especially when you say it the way she used to." He blinked hard and kept his eyes closed. "It means 'my heart' in Arabic." His voice cracked, hot and strained. A single tear dropped from his eye, landing on the fabric of his shorts, and his hand darted to cover the darkening spot.

I inched my body close to his. "If you're Albi, then I'm Albi for you too. You're my heart, and I can be yours if you let me. If you want me to be."

"*Enta albi. Enta hayati.*" He turned to me and grabbed my face. "I love you, Simón. I loved you the moment we first spoke."

"I think I loved you longer than that," I said.

"Always have to one-up me, huh?" He kissed me, and his tears slid against my cheek.

We lay back and looked up at the ceiling together. Cracks stretched from opposing corners, spreading across the ceiling.

I imagined them meeting and the whole roof falling in on us. End this while it's beautiful, God.

"My mom snuck us over here from Syria when I was really young," he said, voice low to preserve the stillness. "She'd never have been allowed to leave my father, let alone take me. His only child. His only son. She never talked about it. Don't know anything about anything, really. It must have been a bad situation, though, to travel half the world. She'd heard about the casinos they were starting to build over here, how much the town would be growing, how many jobs there would be. She tried really hard, but she could never fully get the hang of English or Spanish, so she didn't find work as easily as she'd hoped. Eventually, we met Father Cordero. I don't remember how. He gave her work cleaning the church and the rectory. She cooked and sewed. I kept him company. He taught me how to read and write using the Bible. My mother didn't believe in the religion, but she did believe in Father. In his kindness. It's so strange looking back at it now, this fake family, but it was stable and full of love. Even if it sort of felt like living between two worlds."

"Did you believe? Do you believe?" I asked.

"I guess I do. I don't know any other way. You have all of your books, but I only ever had one," he said, and it felt like such a poignant thing to say in such a throw-away manner. "I think I have to believe in something to feel like I have a place. Did the stories actually happen? Who knows. But I do know they have a lot of meaning to a lot of people."

"Even if they say we're wrong?"

"They don't say that *we* are wrong. It's the action. And anyway, I don't want to talk about that right now, Simón."

I turned toward him. "Your mom believed in *you*. She left everything—her home, her language, her family. She broke all the rules they wrote for her, even the sacred ones. All because she thought your life could be better somewhere else.”

He blinked slowly. I couldn't tell if he was crying again, or if he was tired.

“So maybe it's okay if you break a few of those rules too,” I said, barely louder than a whisper. “If it means being happy. If it means being loved.”

He didn't say anything. He pulled the sheet higher up around us and tucked his leg beneath mine.

“Let's take turns then. You teach me things from your book, and I'll teach you stuff from mine.”

“Actually, some of the best stories aren't even in the Bible. They all happened later. Part of seminary is learning about the saints, and every morning we start the day learning about the saint being recognized on that feast day. Sometimes multiple. They all have these crazy miracles that happened to them and super-gruesome stories about being murdered.”

“Miracles and Murders it is!” I said, failing to mask my excitement at the prospect of avoiding theology and going straight to the good stuff. “Tell me the goriest one you can think of.”

“I knew you'd go for the deaths and not the miracles. You're a monster.” Albi laughed and shoved me. “Hmmm, let me think. This is tough.” His feet kicked and swung over the side of the bed, and I counted the times his thigh hit mine as we lay there. “There was St. Bartholomew. He was skinned alive. They cut strips of his flesh off while he was awake, and they eventually had to chop his head off 'cause he wouldn't die. Father has a painting of him looking like a skeleton and holding his skin across his shoulders like a cape. You can see the fingers and hair flapping in the wind.”

“Fucking disgusting! That's a good one. The beheading

was definitely for theatrics. I think he would've died of blood loss before they finished skinning him. And he definitely would've passed out from the pain before that. Especially if they were taking the time to do it in strips. How tedious! They could have just flayed him like a cow. Much more efficient. No reassembly of skin cloak required. Tell me another."

Hours and hours passed us by, him telling me stories, me dissecting them to check for validity or argument. Cringing dramatically at the more gruesome details, laughing about how demented we must be to find entertainment in these horrific tales. Our feet kicking, legs brushing against each other, we continued staring at the ceiling, talking and laughing into the night with a cloud of macabre circling us like beautiful vultures.

The aroma of coffee woke us the following morning, sneaking under and around the door, slightly ajar. I stretched my legs. My arms repeated the motion. My knees cracked. My eyes fluttered closed before spreading wide with terror.

The door was open.

My stomach slammed against my pelvis. I had closed it. I know I did. Maybe one of us forgot to close it again after using the bathroom. Nothing happened. We were both still wearing the clothes we had on the day before. We kissed and cuddled and slept fully clothed. In the same bed. My mother had seen us side by side. In the same bed. Maybe the door unlatched itself. Maybe it was Camilo or Cari being nosy. No, that's no better. They would surely tell her some dramatized version if so.

Shit, shit, shit.

Descending the stairs, I heard the clinking of dishes. The floorboards creaked under my weight as I approached the kitchen, and the clinking stopped. Be ready for anything, Simón.

One coffee cup, a mark of red lipstick along the rim, sat on the table where two would be on any other morning. A part needed to be played, and I had a script to follow. Simón, the son, fallen from grace. "Good morning, Mamá. How did you sleep?"

Silence. The *cafetera* sat cleaned, upside-down, and drying on the lip of the sink. My mother's hands perched on the edge of the countertop as she faced the window above the sink that overlooked our small garden. The light from outside shone on her slicked hair.

"Albi and I were thinking of going to the beach for a morning swim, and afterward we'll pass by the bakery. Do you want *pastelitos* or anything?"

"No."

A bike flew by the open front door; its bell clanged flatly from left to right and away. Birds sang on balconies, on rooftops. Neighbors chatted indistinctly.

"I can go to the bakery now if you are hungry," I said after a few dead seconds swayed between us.

She threw the dishrag into the sink, sending suds and water airborne. There it is. "Do you think a pastry is going to heal my heart from the disrespect I have suffered?"

All I could do was stare at the back of her head. Her shoulders were squared, her skirt tight around her small waist.

"Do you think I want bread carried to me in those filthy hands?" She whipped around. "What you choose to do in the streets is none of my business. I never meddle. But you will not sit here in front of me, acting as if you did not bring evil into my home." She didn't shout, and her voice didn't falter as she slowly walked toward me.

"Mamá, I don't know what you're talking about."

Her open hand connected with my face, but I refused to break eye contact. She taught me to never show weakness, so I stared back at her and squared my own shoulders to match hers. She slapped me again with the back of that same hand. A ring snagged the skin of my cheek. My jaw clenched, and my chin lifted.

"Don't you dare lie to me." Her words were almost hisses. Every second I stood there, I could feel her coiling up tighter, poised for another strike.

"We did nothing. I am not lying. We stayed up having a good time, just talking. Then we fell asleep."

"Having a good time or having sex, there is no difference to me. A sin is a sin whether you are doing it or thinking about it. I have eyes, hijo. I know what you two are to each other. I thought you loved me enough to put that behind you. But I see how you repay me for everything I do."

"Mamá, please. Don't act like that. I didn't do anything to you. We didn't do anything wrong. What can I say to prove that to you?"

She flattened out her skirt and repositioned her blouse, tucking it back in tightly. The dismissal was imminent. She looked back at me with pure indifference and said, "All we can do is pray. I will pray for you like I always do, and you can pray for God to show me that this way you are choosing is right. If it's his will, he'll change my mind."

"Ma, you can't be serious. I'm not going to sit around and hope that some idea will magically pop into your head to understand me."

"Then leave. I cook. I clean. What do you do for me

besides test my patience?"

"If that's what you want, I'll go pack my things."

"Your things?" Her dismissive cadence was gone, replaced by grit, a corrosive disgust. "What have you bought for this house? Everything in this house is mine." She didn't slam her palm into the counter to drive the point home. She didn't need to; her voice, her words were final enough.

"I'll pack some clothes. You can check my bag before I leave if you'd like." Even at that lowest of lows, I could not bring myself to disrespect her. Truthfully, I didn't even want to.

She didn't say anything as she calmly wiped the counter and shuffled around the kitchen, cleaning the already spotless surfaces.

I went upstairs, grabbed a bag, and shoved clothes into it. Shoes, books, whatever would fit. Eventually, tears fell in as well. Albi waited silently on my bed, watching me pack, waiting for a sign as to what I needed from him. He was love personified, patience, perfection. I knew then that I could walk out of this house, and I would be all right.

Above his head, on the wall behind my headboard, a crucifix had hung for decades. Standing on the bed, I snatched the thing off the wall, revealing a sun-bleached outline of the cross, and threw it across the room, out the second-story window and onto the street.

My eyes were swollen, but I feigned a big smile and slung the bag over my shoulder. "Let's go for a walk. I have an errand to run before we hit the beach." He kissed my shoulder. I placed my hand on the small of his back.

Albi and I left the house without another word, and the sound of my mother rustling around the kitchen trailed behind us. The bright light of the new day slowly climbed up our bodies as we walked out onto the street and stepped over the crucifix, face-down on the pavement.

My mother snaps her fingers in front of my face. "Do you want coffee or are you going to stand there with your mouth open?" She shuffles past me and into the kitchen. Her standard kitten heels prop her up two extra inches, like always. "There is no excuse for a woman to be flat-footed. Do I look like a duck to you?" she used to say.

"I guess I wasn't sure what to expect. The last time I was here, you refused me coffee," I say, stepping into the kitchen. Every detail aligned perfectly. Every spatula, spoon, and serving tray neatly placed in its assigned space.

"That was because I was angry. I'm not angry today."

"Okay," I reply, my voice devoid of emotion. Like the kitchen, she hasn't changed a bit.

"Simón, please don't start already. You just walked in."

"I said, 'Okay.' I didn't mean anything else by it, Ma." I did. I meant two years' worth of things by it. Two years that she did nothing with. Nothing except stew in my absence.

She clicks her tongue, purses her lips, and shoots me a sideways glance as she packs the coffee into the basket of the percolator. I look at her hair, slicked back in a bun, her eyebrows drawn on in precise arches, her housecoat perfectly tailored by her own hand. "Did you get a telephone yet? Your aunt told me I could call the corner store, and they would let you call me back when you're in next, but that is too bothersome. What if I'm not even home when you call? Do the planets need to align for me to talk to my son? No, no."

She flips up the top of the *cafetera* to check on the coffee and prepares the sugar to be whipped. "Your cousins are driving me up the wall. I want to gnaw my leg off. They tiki-tiki-tiki all day long. Fighting and yelling, laughing and yelling. So much yelling. You and I have more self-respect; we don't carry on loud like that. I'm living with animals. And you should see them eat . . . *Muchacho* . . . Cari has gained so much weight. They left right before you arrived. Did you see her on the street? She looked like she was wearing a napkin when she should have used the whole tablecloth." Cuarenta, The Queen of *Chisme*.

Stifling a laugh, I pull out a chair and face the stove. This visit is about business, not gossip and idle chitchat. "Mamá, don't you want to talk about that? About not speaking to each other for this long?"

"What is there to discuss? We are speaking now, aren't we? I'm glad you came back home. Okay? I was disappointed in you for not coming to your senses, for not coming to see me. So, of course I didn't call. But I've forgiven you, and you being here tells me I'm forgiven, too." She shrugs her shoulders and claps her hands. "*Ay, y ven aca*. I've got to tell you what happened with that drunk *viejo cagalitroso* José Maní and one of the mannequins that Maria puts outside of her shop."

"Mamá, please. I love you. And I've missed you. But I haven't forgiven you."

"You think you're the only one with problems. Is that it?" Cuarenta, The Impossible. Yet again, she refuses to meet me halfway. As if the fact that she's also struggled locks us in a stalemate. As if I played the same role in her pain that she did in mine.

"You kicked me out. For no reason. I offered to get you pastries and you offered me the door," I reply. My heart is beating. I am breathing.

"I still pray for you." Ugh. "Every day, I pray that you are happy and healthy and that Jesus lights the path for you." She continues on with her prepackaged justifications, convincing herself more than me. She hears nothing I say. "Life is not easy, *mijo*. It holds you down all on its own without you adding more weight to it. I wanted more for you. Is that so bad?" These words would be delivered tenderly by any other mother, but mine shoots them out like bullets. "If I was ever hard on you, it is because I love you. I did everything in my power to give you a better life. An easier life. And you've gone and thrown that all away. I never wanted you to struggle and now look. Just look at you." As she motions up and down at me, I know she is not wrong. I do look like shit. My clothes are salt-crusted, and so is my hair. My eyes are red and swollen. I haven't eaten in days, and I'm one gust from becoming a human kite. But I won't give her the win.

"*If* you were ever hard on me? You were always hard on me. You really don't see that you made things worse? You weren't protecting me, you were protecting yourself. I was finally not alone. I was finally happy. Happy! Do you even remember what that means?" My heart beats faster. Breathing shortens.

She stands, wipes her hands as she inspects the coffee burbling up into the carafe, and pours this first spurt of coffee into the sugar waiting to be spun. "Did you come here to criticize me? Is that it? Call me a bad mother, ruin my day?" She begins whipping the coffee and sugar. *Clank clan clank clan clank clan.* The gritty mixture becomes smooth as it fills with air, lightens, and turns into a thick foam; the sound of the stirring follows suit. *Cluh cluh clank cluh cluh clank.*

I walk over to the shelf with the fancy china set, the one we used on holidays and special occasions, wondering if they ate on them last night or if my being gone halted any frivolity in this house. My aunt had threatened to sell them on several occasions— "They are mine just as much as they are yours. Papi only gave them to you because you got married first. Look how that turned out."

Glancing past the standing plates to the photographs behind them, I see my grandfather on a boulder in some park, wearing slacks and a knit collared short-sleeved shirt. He looks like a Latino Paul Newman, with shellacked black hair and gold jewelry competing to be the most reflective. The photo, shot slightly from below, captures his head cocked to the side, grinning with only half of his mouth, the opposite eyebrow arched. He would give me this same expression when I explained things to him as a young boy, looking down at me and grinning, that one eyebrow flexed. He would pick me up and dance with me. We'd all eat together and laugh. But all of the happiness and joy in this house is gone. Just like the picture now resting in my hands, it's all a memory. I feel the dissonance in my fingers, and it itches in my toes.

Mamá notices me looking at Abuelo's photo and turns the gas off. "Your grandfather would have hated all of this if he were still alive, you know. He would have hated to find out about you." She pours the sputtering coffee into the sugar mixture and motions for me to sit, but the blunt force of these words leaves me reeling.

"Why would you say that?" The words tumble out limply. The brutality living in this tiny woman.

"Your father, too. He was a narcissist, *machista*. You may look exactly like him, but you two couldn't be more different. He would have burned this house down to hear these conversations." Her hand flies up and down, motioning at me, side to side, then back to her face and chest in another haphazard sign of the cross.

"Well, he's gone," I say as my mother brings her fingers to

her lips for the final movement of her theater production. "He is not here, Ma. He left. And it doesn't fucking matter to me what he would think. Or Abuelo. They aren't here to tell me how disgusting I am." Her teeth are gritted at my profanity. "You are doing well enough with that on your own." I take my coffee like a shot of liquor. The liquid scalds my throat and leaves my tongue raw. The caffeine hits my stomach like lead, and I feel unbearably hot.

"Stop using profanity in the house," she almost whispers. "I hear enough of it from your good-for-nothing aunt and her brood of *comemierdas*." Her chin lifts, indignant. She looks toward the kitchen door, picks up her coffee, takes a prudent sip, and places the cup back in its exact spot. She swallows, and I worry the caffeine and sugar will only fuel her fury, causing her talons to unfurl from under her frock. Cuarenta, The Harpy.

Instead, she takes a deep breath and says, "Let's eat. You look like you haven't been eating. I'll heat up some *pernil* from last night. Black beans and rice, too. I know I was supposed to make fish, but I couldn't let the pork go to waste. I'll confess tomorrow."

Mamá spins on her heel and retreats to the stove where her powers are strongest. She moves quickly now, as if momentum might spare us both the trouble of saying anything more. This is how she makes peace, by pretending it was never war.

"I have some *maduros* I need to fry up before they go bad, too. How's that sound?" she asks as she stirs the beans with one hand and checks the pot of rice with the other. Her rice was always fluffier than anyone else's. "Lemon juice and salt, but shhh, don't repeat that."

When she was happy, I'd ask her to teach me her recipes, and she'd always respond: "Go play, Simón. The cooking will be for your wife to do. This isn't anything you need to concern yourself with. Anyways, I always start by chopping the garlic super fine and then . . ." She taught me about balance. Every flavor has an opposite, and you need a dash of that contrast to create harmony in the dish. Every savory dish got a spoonful of honey. Every sweet thing got a pinch of salt.

"What a nice coincidence. Pork, black beans, *maduros*. All of your favorites," she says, her back still turned. The kitchen floods with concentrated aromatic pockets of citrus, garlic, cumin, and oregano as the beans simmer beside slow-cooked pork shoulder, bubbling gently.

"Yes, but my all-time favorite thing you would make was plantain soup," I say, still a bit stunned by the ongoing rollercoaster of emotions.

"Would make? Was?" She pauses as if building suspense before beating me over the head with the scalding spoon of beans.

My heart beats faster. Contain yourself, Simón. Play her game, eat, and leave.

"You're the one that deserted me. I could have made you a hundred pots of that soup in the time you've been out in the street doing God knows what." She says critical words, but her playful tone makes my skin itch. Blood surges to my face. Fists clench. The constant tip-toeing, the constant need to censor myself to circumvent her temper pushes me over the edge.

"I didn't desert you, Mamá. You told me to leave." I want to calm down, but my mouth starts spewing. "You told me to leave, and when I did, you acted like I disappeared on purpose. Like I walked out the way he did. I stood right there, and you looked through me." My finger shakes as it points at the kitchen floor between us. "You made the choice for me to walk out and then called it mine. You saw I was in love, and you couldn't stand that for the first time I wasn't sitting around being angry with you anymore." My mouth runs ahead of my mind. "And me being a faggot made it worse. Albi being a man added a turd cherry on the shit sundae."

"*Qué te calles ya!*" The wooden spoon slams into the counter, sending black beans flying. Dark streaks cut across the wall, skins sticking to the ceiling. "I was a good mother to you. I took care of you all on my own. I did everything for you." Her words bounce off the walls and fly out the window. She picks up the spoon again and points it at me. "This way you want to live is not natural. That is what I was taught, and that is what they still teach. Do you think I should be happy about that? About you parading around town, skipping down the street with your *amiguito*? For everyone to see?" Wisps of hair have escaped the tight bun and surround her forehead like an untrimmed hedge. "I was a good mother. But to you, I'm a monster." My mother's shoulders hammer into her ears, holding her head up, preventing it from rolling off into the simmering pork. Her cheeks are flushed, sweat beading on her brow as her chest heaves unevenly. I imagine her heart seizing, her body collapsing, and think to myself, *I just killed my mother.*

"Mamá—"

"*Basta ya, Simón.*" She holds on to the counter, looking down, breathing heavily. "I've had enough."

The shouting's over, but its weight stays in the room, thick and insurmountable. Her posture rebuilds itself. Vertebra by vertebra, the stone woman reconstructs herself. I sigh and turn to go to the bathroom. She clicks her tongue and begins fiddling with things on the counter, busy-bodying herself about the kitchen.

Everything in this house remains exactly as it was when I left. Beyond the kitchen, old French rococo chairs still flank the long table, its waxed surface lined with porcelain statues mid-dance: one girl converses with a bird, another lies peering into a porcelain puddle, her hair forever swooped and draped in a Mucha swirl, cascading into ground and water.

The same paintings hang on the same walls—my grandmother's paintings. She re-created scenes of her small village from memory. None of them have people, yet you can hear the grasses rubbing together, birds chirping, cicadas buzzing. She used to say the only thing she didn't miss about living there was being itchy all the time, but she would move back in a heartbeat to escape the city's clamor and just breathe. One painting shows a fence in the foreground with a field rolling for miles behind it. Brown smudges dot the landscape, and when I asked what they were, she said they could be anything I wanted. "That's the magic of it all," she told me, motioning around, not only to the paintings, but to the house, and maybe to the whole world beyond it.

I pass the hall bathroom beyond the table and decorative chairs. Tía Cachita and Cari share it, and it is inhospitable to human life. My mother stopped cleaning it years ago after finding a condom and half-eaten flan, covered in flies, behind the sink. Now, stalactites form inside the toilet bowl, and hair strands lace every surface. Toothpaste cakes around the sink. The wastebasket overflows with soiled napkins, and mildew funk seeps from all fabrics.

Leaving that squalor behind, I make my way into Mamá's pristine bedroom. My mother's powder room opens with a faint fragrance of jasmine, rose, and talcum. The vanity displays three fragrance bottles and a scalloped powder box that could've been presented by some wealthy dignitary's attaché, with its gold accents and silk lining. This box has been sitting in this spot my whole life. The vanity mirror seems smaller than I remember. I slump forward, curling my spine to fit the top of my head inside the frame. Patina sprites swarm around the edge of the glass like a reverse halo. A previous me, twenty years ago, rested his small hands on the marble plateau, eyes barely peering over the bottom edge, trying to see himself.

I look at my body, barely fitting in the same mirror I wanted so badly to see myself in all those years ago. Rummaging through the drawer past the blush and eyeshadow, the makeup brushes and the hair brushes all set in assigned places like some diagram in a catalog, my fingers blindly find what they seek. I take it out, remove the cap, twist the body, and smell the wax. Reckless Rouge. Five-year-old Simón below me did the same. He applied the lipstick exactly how he saw Mamá do it. Bottom lip first, half of the top lip, and then the other half. He practiced smiling. He pretended to be at a dinner party. Earrings hung, dangling from inside of his ears, and he felt beautiful. Like Mamá. He put a necklace on, and he was suddenly powerful like her, too. The lipstick stained his skin, so he wiped it off as best he could and darted to the kitchen for a red paleta. Sloppily devouring the frozen thing, his fingers were red, his chin was red and his lips a touch redder. He developed tactics like this. He invented new ways of lying to be able to feel beautiful. Powerful.

Memories flicker behind my eyes, and I see him again, maybe a hair smaller this time. His toes flexed against the tiles, pushing his small head up and up. The party jewelry hung from his neck and ears. He tried to gaze at himself in the vanity mirror, but could barely see his eyes. As his hand reached up blindly searching above for rings to plunder from the jewelry box, the necklace became tighter; it dug into his neck, and pressure built behind his eyes. The damned thing was cursed. It lifted little Simón off the ground, suspended for a small boy's lifetime. Begging for slack, he clawed at his neck to unhook the fastener, but his body continued to ascend. He couldn't unhook it. He thrashed until his eyes landed on the mirror, and for the first time in his little life he could see himself fully. The earrings sparkled, still lodged in his ear canals. His lips were bright red, but his face was blue. And to the right of his watering eyes, another set seethed with revulsion.

Everyone in town would say, "*Qué guapo eres!* So handsome! You look just like your father!" But seeing our faces reflected together, I knew I could never be like this man. Puñal's eyebrows crushed downward, half-obscuring eyes that curved maniacally. His lips snarled over his teeth like a rabid dog, blood pounding visibly in his neck. He didn't speak at first. I hung there, asphyxiating, limbs slack, hands clenched around the beads. I was game, ready to be drained and gutted. My eyes bulged from their sockets, and he waited, almost patiently, for them to plop out so he could snip them off and string them to his belt as a warning to the others that he'd skin them alive, too.

My father launched a large glob of spit onto my reflected face. The mist of his violent spray moistened my cheek. "Dressed like a whore. You're no son of mine. Disgusting rat." He spat again, hitting the same spot. "Maricón." The first glob absorbed the second as they slid down the glass.

My body sailed backward as he flung me by the necklace. The chain snapped. A cascade of opalescent beads and plastic stones suspended around me, hitting the wall a fraction of a second after my body. The force knocked one of my grandmother's paintings to the floor with us—a young foal nursing while its mother gazed back with sad, jet-black eyes. The beads dug into my skin, pressing against bone. He squatted in front of me, denim stretching and knees popping. He leaned close to my ear and slit my throat with a final "No son of mine," then cracked his palm against the light switch. His broad shoulders turned away, silhouetted in daylight, before he slammed the door and left me crumpled in darkness. It was the first time I remember hating myself, the first time I remember him walking away. It seemed I would only remember him walking away.

I heard my mother enter the foyer, high heels announcing her return with a light click clack click as she hummed some song or another. I scrambled to my knees and scooped up the beads and fake gemstones by the light slinking in from under the door. My neck was on fire, my eyes still adjusting to the darkness and the cloudiness of tears, but I couldn't let Mamá know I had broken her necklace. That my father had disowned me. That he spit on her belongings because of what I'd done. I propped the painting on her vanity and climbed up to wipe the spit with my shirt. It left a streak on the glass, but it was only noticeable from below. She told him she was making arroz con pollo that night. He left without a word. He came back for dinner later that night but wouldn't look at me. My lips were still red, but my neck was redder. They yelled at each other, and he punched a wall. I hated myself. My mother stroked my cheek and rubbed my ear when we were alone. She told me something I have saved in a snapshot somewhere. Something about the world eating you up and shitting you out.

I blink hard, trying to conjure that memory. My clammy grip around the lipstick loosens, and I leave it on the vanity. All these years have passed, yet nothing has happened. Even after going through so much, I remain that same little boy. No, merely a husk of him, like some decorative gourd. When he hit that wall, his soft insides seeped out, and his skin hardened into a fibrous shell. I became conditioned to the emptiness. Glad to be sad.

I'm not a son. I'm a disgusting faggot.

Why did I come here? I've set myself up over and over again to relive my grief. I allow my mother's grief to compound with my own. This legacy of sadness, passed down like my grandparents' china. I didn't want to fight. When I arrived, I felt so resolved to reconcile. And now, all I want is to make her cry. To force her to shoulder blame that isn't hers alone. It's just . . . simpler sometimes when there's a villain to vanquish. When fury has direction, the obstacles along the path become mere mile markers. But I know what the final obstacle is. And it isn't my mother.

The powder room door opens, and Mamá is standing in front of me with an expression I've never seen draped across her stone face. Her gaze falls to the lipstick on the vanity, then darts directly into my eyes. Her lips part, but no sound escapes. It's a subtle softness, like the prelude to a cry.

And suddenly I understand her. We understand each other.

Her frame shrinks. Cuarenta the Beast becomes a field mouse, squeezing her malleable skeleton through a crack in my wall. She scurries inside, surveying everything at once. And for a moment I see all of her too—not the all-powerful mother, but a girl. A daughter. Cuarenta Linda, whose hair was once wild. Whose gold hoops swung when she danced with me. Who rubbed her feet against mine to get warm at night.

I feel her heart breaking when I walked out with Albi. When she saw me with him just hours before that. It breaks every morning since as she sits in the kitchen drinking her *cafecito* alone. She's understood all along. Through all these years she knew exactly who I am. And she's deathly afraid, not of who I'll become, but of what will become of me.

"Simón, I . . ." Her voice falters. The wrinkles around her

eyes deepen. Her elbow twitches, almost reaching for me. What has she seen inside me? She knows something now. The ruins of my insides told her everything. That sly little mouse.

I step forward, maybe to rub her shoulder, maybe to pull her close. Maybe to let myself be held. But before I can touch her, she straightens.

Then—a knock.

Two seconds later, another.

"Señora?"

My mother's eyes double in size. Her hands shoot up to her hair, frantically smoothing the strays, smearing grease and bits of food onto the left side of her head as she darts past me, slinking toward the mirror to salvage whatever dignity she can.

"Señora Cuarenta, it's Father Cordero. Just stopping by to wish you a happy Easter." His voice is light, almost breathless. It's hard to imagine that voice commanding a pulpit.

Of course. Of fucking course, the priest shows up during the one hour I visit my mother in two years. I feel my whole body shift into that familiar tension—practiced, instinctual— the posture I reserve for people I need to perform for. And this isn't just any priest. This man raised Albi. Loved him. He probably knew about *us*.

For a moment, I can't move. My hands tremble faintly, but the rest of me stays frozen. I picture Albi's voice echoing in this man's ear. What did he say? Did he speak of me with pride? Did he tell him how we laughed? How we touched? Or did he protect me with silence?

Before I can think better of it, my body carries itself to the foyer. I swallow the rise of something in my throat. Shame, maybe. Or anger. Or that pathetic need to be recognized as someone broken.

He stands humbly in the doorway. Black shirt, black pants, black shoes. His collar's undone, his slacks slightly wrinkled. A snake oil salesman like all priests, sure, but maybe a gentler one than I'd let live in my memory. A priest who was once a young man I knew. Who knelt beside my grandfather's coffin. Who once handed me a paper dove at Mass and told me I was born to fly.

"Oh, Simón! I—uh—I didn't know you'd be here. I thought—um—I guess I assumed your mother would be alone and wanted to stop by since I was alone this afternoon as well." His voice crackles. He shoves his hands into his pockets, rocks back and forth on his black trainers, and takes his hands out of his pockets again.

Alone. "It would be indecent, and you know I'd never put the good Father in that position," she'd said not so long ago. My mother, once so scandalized by the idea of being caught alone with Father Cordero, doesn't seem to mind now. Interesting. I make a note to use this revelation to my advantage later.

The silence stretches between us, and I let it. We both know who we're not talking about. What we're not talking about. Finally, I nod and gesture him in with a languid hand. "My mother's freshening up. She got beans in her hair," I say, and sit down at the table without offering him a chair.

He hesitates, then takes the seat beside me. Presumptuous little bastard. Still, there's a part of me that notices how small he looks in this house. How his hands tremble when he folds them.

"You know, Simón, I'm really glad you're here." He pats my shoulder gently. The contact catches me off-guard. I flinch, not a full jerk, but a subtle recoil. Some muscle memory for the recently traumatized.

He jumps and withdraws, startled by the reaction. "I think

it would be nice for you and me to sit down. To check in with each other," he continues. "I know you're not active in the parish, but I'm available if you'd like to talk through things. We all need someone to share the darkest parts of our souls with."

I exhale slowly, jaw tight. "I have nothing to confess, but thanks, Mr. Cordero." Not Father. That title belongs to someone who raised you. Who stayed. Hell, I wouldn't call my own biological father that.

"That's not what I meant. I thought it might help us both to talk through things. To vent. Priests need friends, too." He shakes his head. "That sounded strange. I just meant grief is a struggle better faced with company. And I'm here. For you . . . If you need someone. Albi told me—"

My mother enters the kitchen, and I breathe deeply for the first time since the black-clad windbag started rambling. "Father, what a surprise!" she says without a hint of surprise. "My son came to visit, and we were about to eat. Please join us. I made plenty."

"Oh no, I couldn't. Not that hungry. Too many treats after Mass this morning," the priest says as he pats his belly. "And I'd hate to impose on family time. I'm sure you have a lot to catch up on." My eyes narrow into slits. His gaze snaps from my mother to me and back to my mother.

"Just eat a little, and I'll pack you a plate or two to take home. It reheats wonderfully." She flits over to set his place. Wonderfully. Huh.

There's no such thing as not-that-hungry in this house. She heaps food onto our plates as if we haven't eaten in days, and in my case it's true. She sets the mountainous servings before us and returns to the stove to serve herself what looks like three grains of rice compared to our helpings. The streaks of black bean splatters on the off-white walls frame her and

Father Cordero like an expressionist cage, the tableau suddenly turned otherworldly. He doesn't mention the gruesome crime scene, and neither do we.

The priest prays over the food, thanking the hands that prepared it, causing my mother to bow her head even lower across from him. The rest of the prayer eloquently drags on. They both say "amen" with the same voice. Their hands move as one, making the sign of the cross. They kiss their thumb and forefinger with closed eyes, and I imagine if I weren't here, they'd be kissing each other's fingers, and their eyes would be open.

My appetite vanishes at this thought, and I idly twiddle the utensils in my hands as the priest raves about my mother's cooking. My mother haphazardly dodges the compliments with a slight smile, an it's-really-nothing wave of the hand.

They begin chatting about this morning's service, and I imagine myself climbing into the garbage can to be compacted and shipped away. I hear the conversation as if prerecorded. I could have heard it dozens of times. Like a computer, my brain can anticipate and populate every next word in succession. Every predictable turn of phrase arrives on cue. Like a computer, I feel nothing and blankly vibrate as the words are produced.

"Yes, he's a new member. He's only been to mass maybe two, three times."

"And he left with that young woman just like that?"

Every syllable drives me deeper and deeper into a toneless madness.

"No, you see, she's lactose intolerant . . ."

"Mmmm . . . so she can't eat cheese or anything?"

Every syllable becomes a new object with which to stab my eyes out.

"Nope. Nothing with milk at all."

"Uff, I could never live without cheese, I'm telling you . . ."

Every syllable scooping deeper like a spoon.

"Me neither."

"How does she do it?!"

I take the spoon, and the cold metal shines dully in my hand. I twirl it in my fingers, thumb the ridge that divides concave from convex.

"She doesn't. She eats it anyway!"

I plunge the metal tip of the spoon's bowl slowly, deliberately, into my eye socket.

"*Ay no. Qué locura*! What happens?"

The gelatinous tissue gives, and blood squirts out; fluid drips down my cheek.

"She gets gassy most days. But sometimes it gets worse . . ."

"*Pobrecita*. Rice pudding either, huh?"

I scoop out the eye and hold it level in front of my face, pinching the spoon between two fingers. I do that trick that everyone learns in primary school to make a pencil turn to rubber.

"Nope. Especially not that. Or flan."

"That would be me too, you know, eating it anyway. But it's all in moderation. She doesn't know when to stop is all. She eats too much. I would have a little cheese here, drink a lot of water, *y ya*."

She snaps her fingers as I launch the eyeball, sending it sailing through the air in front of her face. It slaps into the priest's tissue paper skin and slides down his cheek as he continues talking about dairy products.

They sound like an old married couple. The casual drop-in as if they are the best of friends. The gossip. The laughs. The black bean on his tooth. My mother, who hasn't eaten a bite. It all expands inside my head until I snap.

"Albi is dead." The words scrape my throat, first time spoken aloud. "He's dead. Buried in the fucking ground." My stomach lurches into my lungs. Heat bubbles beneath my skin, eyes burning dry. "And all you can talk about is dairy?!" I'm standing now, fists tightened at my sides.

"Simón, please! Not right now. We can talk more about this after Father Cordero leaves." She turns to the priest. "My apologies. He hasn't been well since his friend left us. But I know you understand that."

The priest looks uneasy. He shuffles in his seat, the exact dining chair my mother swears was once sat on by Hemingway himself. An awkward gulp slides down his throat as he sits on his hands and stares at the tabletop. The sweat stains, old and new, around his collar and under his arms seem to ebb and rush like waves, flowing and receding abruptly with his labored breathing. The salt deposited on the fabric creates a white stiffness in those areas, while other areas of his black garments wear thin to the point of near translucency, his olive skin visible where the thin fabric clings to his moist body.

Since he arrived, I'd avoided looking directly at him, but like a dog smelling cancer in its human companion, I'm suddenly aware of something awry in his ordained aura. His eyes have sunken a bit since I last saw him. His lips crack with dryness, and his hair has not been cut in some time.

"He wasn't my friend." I pause to clear my throat before speaking again. "He was the love of my life. And he didn't leave. He died." I can't contain the swell of my words. The angry tide rushes back like a tsunami. "He's rotting underground, and it doesn't even matter. Because you wouldn't accept him," I say to my mother. "Because you would've kicked him out if he stayed with me," I hiss at the priest. "Because of all this bullshit you've built to feel superior. Because you'd rather see people stomped down than admit you're wrong. Because your cult teaches shame and fear and calls it love. Because you want us just as miserable as you are. It's all about control, isn't it?"

My voice breaks.

"And now here you are, seducing my mother? Spitting on your own Lord's teachings?" I look at them both. My mother, silent in her apron. The priest, eyes wide and unblinking. "You're hypocrites. All of you." My lungs run out of air, but I don't breathe in. I turn for the door. I know it's not solely their fault. I know the part I played.

Then, a meek voice behind me. "I lost him too, Simón. I loved him like a son." The words sound wet, like they refuse to leave the back of his throat.

The birds are still singing outside. A car passes, then another car. Someone laughs down the street, and I cringe at the grating noise of it.

"You didn't even know him. Not the real Albi."

"I understand. You're hurting. You want to find someone to blame," Cordero says.

I blame myself. I blame him. I blame my mother and the city this house sits at the center of. And as I had done hand-in-hand with Albi not so long ago, I walk through the front door, open and illuminated.

"You're such a St. Simeon," Albi's voice teases. "Always up there praying for a world you won't let yourself belong to."

"I don't pray," I mumble back.

"Prayers aren't always to God, Simón."

And without another word, I step down from my childhood home. From this towering pillar. A stylite, forced to end his isolated prayers and meditations. My feet hit the pavement, and behind me, all I hear is silence.

Interlude: Lenita

The piss stick sat on the bathroom counter like a loaded gun. Two pink lines. No room for misinterpretation.

Lenita squatted on the toilet, knees knocking against the cramped walls of the closet they called a bathroom at Dr. González's office. She'd been in there too long. The nurse had already knocked twice. The antiseptic smell burned her nostrils.

Two goddamn pink lines.

"Leonora? The doctor needs the sample for confirmation." The nurse's voice sounded bored, as if women discovered their entire futures derailed every fifteen minutes in this cardboard outhouse.

Lenita tore off a square of toilet paper, swiped it between her legs, and chucked it in the bowl. No blood. Six weeks with no blood. She'd blamed it on stress, on that fight with her mother, on anything that wasn't this.

"Coming," she called, her voice steady despite the earthquake liquefying her insides.

Twenty minutes later, the doctor's cold hands pressed against her stomach. The way he touched her, like she was some biological inevitability rather than a person, made her want to knee him in the teeth. He talked about weeks and trimesters and prenatal vitamins. Words slid off around her ears and down her shoulders. Comprehension lagged five seconds behind.

"Congratulations," he said without looking up from his clipboard.

"That's a matter of opinion," Lenita muttered, tugging her shirt down over her still-flat stomach. His eyes flicked up briefly, mouth tight with judgment. Fuck him too. "How far along am I?"

"About eight weeks. The nausea should peak soon, then taper off by the second trimester."

"Great," she said, sliding off the exam table. "Looking forward to it."

Outside, the afternoon heat slammed against her, so she walked faster to create her own breeze. With no particular destination, her feet plodded on autopilot while her mind spun free. Eight weeks. Two months of carrying something inside her without knowing. The thought made her skin crawl. Her body had changed allegiances without consulting her first.

At the corner of Plaza Vieja, she stopped to catch her breath. A group of children chased each other around the fountain, screaming and laughing like feral cats. A girl with two messy braids tackled a boy into the dirt. The boy's mother rushed over, brushing him off and scolding the girl, who stood defiant, chin lifted.

"Atta girl," Lenita muttered, a smile threatening her lips.

The girl reminded her of herself, all knees and elbows and ferocious energy. But then came the thought: would her kid be like that? Would it have her sharp edges or Ramón's gentle ease? She tried to picture Ramón's face and felt a chill. Two months of dating. She barely knew his mother's name, or whether he liked his eggs runny or firm. How would he react to this news? Men were all the same when backed into a corner. For all she knew, he'd question whether it was even his. The prick. Maybe he would be happy. The idiot. She huffed and sped up her gait.

Passing a fruit stand, the smell of produce made her stomach clench. Without warning, she doubled over and vomited behind a parked car. A woman passing by crossed the street to avoid her. Smart move, lady.

When she straightened, wiping her mouth with the back of her hand, her eyes caught on a mother adjusting a tiny hat on an infant held against her chest. The baby's head lolled against the woman's collarbone, trusting and vulnerable. The mother's hand cupped the back of the infant's neck with practiced precision, a gesture so full of care it made Lenita's throat tighten.

She'd never been gentle with anything in her life.

Her house announced itself before she even turned the corner. Her youngest sister's attempt at trumpet practice bleated through the open windows. Lenita could picture the neighbors' faces pinched with irritation, counting down the days until someone "accidentally" dropped a brick on that goddamn horn.

The front gate creaked as she pushed through. Her father was on his knees in the small patch of dirt they called a garden, carefully tending to the stubborn oregano that refused to die despite the shade and poor soil.

"*Mija*," he said, looking up. His face was damp with sweat, but his smile was easy. "You're late for dinner."

"Sorry, Papi. I'm not hungry," she said, helping him up. His hands were rough from working all day, then coming home to wash dishes and scrub floors. He liked feeling useful. And staying out of the way.

Inside, chaos reigned. Abuela and Tía Constanza argued about a telenovela character's morality while her mother shouted into the phone about a missing delivery. Her sisters whirled through like miniature cyclones: Luz still wielding that wretched trumpet, Dulce fiddling with some jewel-covered knickknack that was definitely not hers, and Mariposa stretched across the couch painting her toenails a violent shade of orange that would absolutely stain the upholstery.

"Where have you been?" her mother demanded, covering the phone's receiver for a moment. "Your father saved you dinner."

"Had work," Lenita lied, moving toward the stairs.

"Work on a Saturday afternoon? Since when do they need you at the salon on Saturdays?"

"Since today," she snapped. "New boss, new hours."

Her father materialized at her side, a plate covered in aluminum foil in his hands. "Take it upstairs, *mija*. I made your favorite. *Ropa vieja* with extra olives."

The smell, usually irresistible, made her stomach roll again, but she took the plate. "*Gracias*, Papi."

"And take a shower," her mother called after her. "You look like you've been dragged behind a bus."

Lenita slammed her bedroom door, muffling the cacophony below. Her room was the only space just for her in the madhouse. She set the food on her desk and collapsed onto her bed, staring at the ceiling. Inside her, cells were dividing. Building something. Someone.

She pressed her palms against her stomach. Nothing felt different, and yet everything was. She tried to summon hatred for the cluster of cells, this parasite hijacking her future, but found only a hollow numbness instead.

A heavy thud against her door made her jolt upright.

"Lenita!" Dulce stage-whispered through the crack. "Let me in! Mami's looking for her earrings, and I need a place to hide!"

"Not now," Lenita hissed back.

"Please! She's gonna kill me this time for real!"

With a sigh, Lenita opened the door a crack. Dulce slipped in, fourteen years old and already wearing enough makeup for three women. In her hand glinted one of their mother's gold hoops.

"What the hell is wrong with you?" Lenita snapped, snatching the earring. "You want to get shipped off to Abuela's sister in the country? Because that's what's going to happen when Mami catches you."

Dulce threw herself dramatically across the bed. "Worth it. Joaquín thinks I look hot in big earrings."

"Joaquín is seventeen and has the brain of a lizard."

"You're just jealous because Ramón's screwed you over."

The comment hit like a slap. "What are you talking about?"

Dulce examined her nails, suddenly fascinated by her chipped polish. "Mariposa said she saw someone that looked like him at El Tambor with a girl from the resort. All over each other, she said."

The world tilted slightly. Lenita sat down hard on her desk chair, the plate of food rattling. "When?"

"Last night supposedly." Dulce looked up, her face softening at whatever she saw in Lenita's expression. "Hey, are you okay? You look weird. Like, green weird."

Lenita swallowed hard. Eight weeks. Two months. She counted backward, landing squarely on that first night with Ramón, when the condom had slipped and he'd laughed it off. "Don't worry, I'll pull out." Fucking idiot. Fucking men.

"You know Mari, she's kinda blind. And dumb. It prolly

wasn't even him." Dulce moved closer. "Leni?"

"Get out," Lenita said quietly.

"But Mami—"

"GET OUT!" The scream tore through her throat, shocking even herself.

"You're a psycho." Dulce scrambled off the bed, eyes wide, and slipped out without another word. As soon as she was gone, Lenita lurched forward and dry heaved into her trash can. Nothing came up. Nothing left to purge.

She'd been so stupid. Thinking Ramón was different because he'd brought her flowers and cooked her dinner. Because he made her laugh and didn't rush her. All that shit about staying together, starting a business, having a future. Lies to get into her pants. And she'd fallen for it like some pathetic, love-starved teenager. Even if Mariposa was lying, the doubt existed now.

How was she going to do this on her own if he really did turn out to be like every other guy? She couldn't rely on her sisters. Abuela was too old. Her mother? No, she knew the children her mother raised. That left only one person.

Simón. She thought of how great a father figure he could be. How solid he always was, how constant. Though he hadn't been around since Albi died. She couldn't even think about it. It hurt too much. She knew Simón would never be the same. Her smart, funny, fragile friend.

When she was eleven, three boys had cornered Simón behind the school. He'd been smaller then, softer if anyone would believe it. His voice hadn't dropped, and his mannerisms flopped and popped. Lenita had heard his yelp from across the yard and ran without thinking, her backpack abandoned in the dirt.

The tallest boy had Simón pinned against the wall, his

forearm pressed to his throat. The others circled like vultures, taunting. "*Marica*," they hissed. "You're like a little girl."

Lenita had stomped up to the biggest one and, with one swift motion, punched him in the gut and spat on him as he crumpled to the ground. The boy howled, releasing Simón, who slid down the wall, gasping.

"Touch him again," she'd said, "and I'll aim lower next time."

The boys scattered, hurling insults over their shoulders. Cowards, all of them. She helped Simón up, brushing dust from his uniform with brisk, efficient swipes that hid how badly her hands were shaking. Not from fear but from rage.

"You gotta learn to fight back, Simo," she told him, her voice gentler than she'd intended.

Simón looked at her with those big green eyes, wet with tears. "Why do I need to when I have you?" He laughed as he wiped his cheeks, leaving streaks of dirt behind.

She punched his arm lightly. "I won't always be around, dummy."

But she had been. Through every heartbreak, every disappointment, every moment he'd needed someone strong enough to absorb the worst the world could dish out. And he'd been there for her, too, in his quiet way. He was the only person who saw past her armor to the soft, bruised parts underneath.

Hours later, when the house finally settled into the relative quiet of night—Abuela snoring, her parents' murmured conversation behind their bedroom door, her sisters each tucked into their own corners of the house—Lenita sat cross-legged on her bed, the pregnancy test balanced on her knee.

Two pink lines.

Growing up, she'd never wanted kids. The thought of being trapped like her mother, drowning in other people's needs, made her throat close with panic. She'd planned to get out, see what existed beyond this suffocating city, build something that belonged only to her. But plans change. People change.

She placed her palm flat against her abdomen, trying to feel something, anything, that might tell her what to do. The skin felt warm. Ordinary. Inside, this thing was growing with single-minded purpose, indifferent to her crisis.

Maybe she didn't have to be like her mother. Maybe she could be like her father instead, finding quiet purpose in nurturing, in creating order from chaos. Or maybe she could create some maternal identity entirely new and never seen before.

Her finger traced the two pink lines. She thought about that girl at the fountain today, fearless and unapologetic. She thought about punching that shitty kid in the gut all those years ago.

Maybe this was another kind of fighting. Another kind of protection.

For the first time since seeing those pink lines, Lenita felt something crack open inside her. Not fear or anger, but something tender and ferocious, primitive and new. She didn't know if Ramón would step up, or if she'd be any good at this motherhood thing. But she knew how to be brave. How to protect what was vulnerable. That seemed like enough for the moment.

"All right, you little shit," she whispered to her abdomen, to the mitosis occurring inside it, to herself. "But you have to be well-behaved, okay? I'm not gonna have some *mocoso malcriado* running around."

Part III
We Are Animals, After All

Chapter Six
Postage

Early evening malaise settles in as the streets empty. The sun slips down the sky, colors leaking from it like toxic fumes. Heat radiates from the pavement into the thin soles of my worn shoes. It creeps under and between my toes, around my ankles, winding up my legs. People abandon their laughing, their yelling. My pulse punches me in the throat. I count the beats: one, two, three, four. The children have stopped jumping from high places. Even the dogs are napping now. A cart's wheel creaks and wobbles around a corner. A radio crackles and thrums a faint song. An apocalypse occurred while I was in that kitchen. The rapture sucked up all the god-fearing people and left me alone.

The memories of Albi and myself still run around me, but I am alone. Finally alone.

I imagine I could revert to one of these earlier versions of myself. I could fictionalize my body and fit the parts back into a shape that made sense, that felt right. But at what cost?

A bell chimes. The twinkling circles my head as the door to the corner store opens and closes.

Albi's head passed between cans and bottles. He grabbed two packs of multicolored paper and turned to me. "I have this idea to make your new apartment a little homier," he said.

"Are you going to make me some paper chains? Maybe a few hand-bird pictures for the refrigerator?" I said, fingers absentmindedly poking objects on the shelves. A week had passed since my mother kicked me out. I'd found a small apartment closer to the bay, down the hill from my old home. It had its own stores, its own parks, its own people.

"No." Albi moved towards me but didn't touch me. "My idea will also help block that window behind your bed that looks directly into the old guy's place. The one that is full of newspapers and old containers. He's always standing at the window because I think he has nowhere else to stand in there. So, I had an idea to give us more . . . privacy." He nudged me and lifted his brows twice.

The windows in my apartment extend from about two inches above the floor to about two inches from the ceiling. They tower over the room, leaning inward as if the sky would fall on top of you if they went those two inches higher. The building must have been converted into residences from something else. The height of the ceilings isn't traditional, and the wood planks in the floor are different sizes, different grains. I noticed these things but didn't care enough to investigate. Man-made things don't interest me. Buildings, cars, sports, politics. Blech. Ask me why the sky is blue, and I'll tell you about the scattering of light by gases and particles, the way color moves in waves, how it refracts and bounces all around us until it slips through the tiniest opening in the eye, to be shaped into color by the brain. The phenomenon of sight. It's extraordinary. But people prefer facts about ceiling heights. I don't know why.

"Now, let's separate all of these colors into groups." Back at the apartment, Albi began arranging the paper on the bed under the window. "Put all of the greens there, the blues there. We'll need orange, and some white, some purple and yellow. Have you guessed what scene it'll be by the colors? Ask me questions, and I'll give you hints," he said. This sort of game was one of the many reasons we fell in love. So I played along, even though my mood hadn't rebounded since the fight with my mother.

"Is this scene real or fictional?" I asked.

"I think both?"

"Come on."

"Technically, it's fictional, but inspired by true events."

He could probably hear my eyes rolling dramatically backward into my head. "Okay . . . Is it in nature or in some kind of civilization?"

"It is in nature just outside of civilization."

"Made-up place based on someplace real . . . in nature but close to people . . . I think I got it," I said, picking up some of the green and orange papers. "Is this place yours or mine?"

"Ugh. You little shit." He threw the colors we wouldn't be using over his shoulder. "It's both of ours! I want to do a little bit of my garden and a little bit of your beach. Watch." He ripped a corner off a piece of green paper and licked it like a stamp before sticking it to the window.

"Postage to another world," I said and grabbed another piece of green paper, this one darker, and ripped a piece off for him to lick and place. "Do you think it'll stay?"

"Hmmm, maybe we can coat it with a ton of hairspray," he said while placing a purple shard in the mosaic growing on the window, vines and flowers blooming. He captured the levels of his garden, undulating and flowing, which then morphed into the canopy of my mango trees.

"If you squint, you can already tell what it's gonna be," I

said optimistically. "You gotta put a pigeon-shaped piece of paper somewhere."

"This is the pigeon, dummy," Albi said, pointing at a purple and gray lump near the bottom of the window. "Should I also add a used condom in one of the mango trees? Make it more true-to-life?"

The paper mosaic blossomed as the sun set, our spit infused into every fiber of every scrap of color. His kingdom flowed into mine. His garden framed my beach, and the sky over both dissolved into the real sky on the other side of the window as we reached the limits of our arms.

"We've gotta sign it," Albi said, grabbing a pen and writing his name on the pigeon. I signed just below him, and we took a step back to admire our work.

With the bed blocked from view, Albi pulled me close and wrapped his arms around me. The setting sun cut between two buildings and lit up the entire scene we created. "If you squint, you can tell exactly what it's supposed to be," Albi said, echoing my reassurance from earlier. "And now we're safe and sound in our little home. What do you wanna do first?"

"You have any spit left?" I asked, grabbing his crotch.

A rustling behind the counter brings me back to the present. I'm still standing in the doorway of the store. The teenage girl at the register looks scared, like I might flip a shelf or take a shit in one of the aisles. Her arms wrap around her bare belly as if her halter top suddenly feels too short.

"Hi. I'm sorry—" I flatten the front of my shirt with two quick swipes before turning back toward the cans I saw Albi pass behind. "It's been a rough day."

"Yeah . . ." She eyes me, incredulous. "Looks like it." Her gaze narrows as she inches toward the door, ready to make a mad dash and leave me here to ransack the understocked shelves and empty till.

"I really am sorry. I didn't mean to make you uncomfortable. I was trying to remember something." The words slide out of my mouth like a bucket of eels. "I'm really missing someone. I feel like I'm going kinda crazy. Maybe I leaned on them too much, and now I'm kind of falling all over the place."

"Uh, do you need water or something?" The distrust in her face shifts to uneasy concern as I slump too close to the fruit paste display. "I can call someone if you need help getting home."

"Yes, please. Water would be nice. And the phone, too. That's actually why I came in the first place," I say as she steps out from behind the counter.

"Sure. The phone is right there. Please don't touch anything else, okay? I'll be right back." She speaks as if my toddler brain can only comprehend slow and deliberate enunciation. She shuffles past me, and I move back, not wanting her to feel any more threatened than she already is.

I pick up the receiver and turn the dial.

"*Dígame*," Lenita's voice pounds into my ear, loud and blunt to be heard over the laughter and clanging going on in the background. Her house is pure chaos. She lives with her parents, three younger sisters, her grandmother, and a great-aunt who never married. Her dad does all of the cooking and cleaning in the house. He says he likes to take care of everyone, but I think it's to distract himself from all of the noise.

"Hey, it's me." I realize I'm screaming into the phone, so I pause and relax my shoulders. "Just left my mom's place," I say, quieter now.

"Simón! Oh my God! Finally! I've been sitting around all day like some old lady waiting for her stories to start. How'd it go? Tell me everything," she yells.

"You sound like you expected me to be dead. I'll tell you about it later. Let's meet at El Palomar. I need to get absolutely pissed." I see a tin of cat food and drop it on the counter, along with some crumpled money from my pocket, still damp with salt water.

The girl returns with a glass of water. She grimaces as she grabs the money and wipes her hand on the back of her shorts. I mouth an apology.

"Uh, duh. Coco's hosting a show tonight, so she'll already be setting up. We can go whenever. I just need to freshen up. See you there!" She sends a kiss through the phone and slams the receiver down before I can respond. I hang up and turn to thank the attendant.

"El Palomar, huh?" She chews a piece of gum and pops it inward against her teeth.

"Yeah, it's a little place way out on the other side of town," I say and grab the glass of water.

"I know what it is." Her lips curl in on themselves into a toothless, smug little smile. I want to drag her out of the shop by her hair, push her to the ground, tell her not to think about me like that.

She was meant to be a shop attendant with shop attendant thoughts. But her knowingness transforms her into something else. An omniscient being. No longer a background character, but someone who truly sees me—my posture, my shifting expression, the way my hair looks from behind. She hears my voice as it actually sounds, not warped through the bones of my skull. And because of that, she knows me better than I know myself.

"Okay, well . . . thanks for the water." I take a gulp and wipe my mouth with the back of my hand, anxious to leave before she alerts the townspeople of my true monstrous identity.

"Have fun," she says, then adds with sudden sincerity, "and I hope you get to see that person you're missing."

"Thanks. Me too." I grab the cat food and pull the door open. The bell chimes again as I leave the shop.

A small old woman stands at a flower cart across the street. She smiles and waves me over. I ask for a small bouquet. She moves like a mother in a movie. Deliberate and delicate. She selects a collection of flowers, wraps them in brown paper and snips twine, looping it around the bundle. Her white hair rests in a bun, and the wrinkles around her eyes spread like wings. Everything about her calms me: the small arch of her lips, the sunspots speckling her skin, the knots of her finger joints.

I hand her some money, and she pins a gardenia above my heart. She steps back, appraises the flower on my chest, and pins another one beside it. My arms wrap around her before I know what I'm doing. She smells of roses, though she has none for sale. Her arms close around me, both hands rubbing my back. My chest aches, and the pain reminds me to breathe. I inhale deeply, imagining she's my mother, or that my mother was her. I imagine lying belly-down, drifting to sleep as she strokes my back.

"Everything will be better tomorrow, *hijo*," she whispers, again and again.

A man once sent a letter to the radio station, a confession of love for some unnamed person, and the host read it aloud as if he were the man himself. "I never knew a love like my love for you. My brain is empty without thinking of us. My heart will stop beating if it can't beat alongside yours."

My mother was crying while listening to the letter being read. I touched a tear on her cheek, but she only stared forward. This was when she first began to break. She looked like someone else. I followed the tear's path with my finger while she sat motionless, like a mannequin. I wondered if she knew this man, if she imagined the words were for her, and whether she'd ever move again. All I could think to do was curl up beside her like Snowball, the Pomeranian that lived next door. I curved into a ball, nestled against her, and cried too. She stroked my hair, and I jumped because I thought she was still Mannequin Mamá. "Don't worry, Simón," she said. "It'll all be fine in the morning."

"Everything will be better tomorrow, *hijo. Tú verás.*" The old woman says it like a fortune being told.

I realize I'm still holding on to her, arched over her tiny frame. I begin to unfurl my spine to regular height, a signal that I'm all right, that this moment can end. She lets go but catches my hands before they fall away. With a firm squeeze and a single wink, she kisses my left hand and then the right. I want to ask her name. Ask if she has children or grandchildren. But I don't. She seems like the kind of mother who beams at the mention of her children, and I can't bear that.

"Thank you, *señora.* I needed that." I kiss her cheek.

"I know." She places her hand over the two gardenias and hums an old bolero. The vibrations travel from her throat, through her fingertips and into my chest. Her warm smile spreads, and her wrinkle-wings soar again.

A small band plays on a corner a few blocks down. The music bounces off buildings, tumbles over a woman's phone call, and under a honking horn. There's music everywhere if I take the time to listen.

The city seems more beautiful the more I look at it.

The old woman's voice repeats in my head. *Everything will be better tomorrow.*

Then my mother's. *Don't worry, Simón. It'll all be fine in the morning.*

Chapter Seven
Every Day Is a Struggle,
Every Day Is a Blessing

"Teresa of Avila was buried and disinterred several times after her death. Each time they dug her up, they chopped off a piece of her body. Once an entire hand, then a finger from the remaining hand, a leg, an arm. They sawed the extremities from the corpse and scattered the relics around the globe," Albi read from his notes at the desk while I folded laundry.

"Jesus Christ." I grabbed a pair of his underwear from the basket, doubled them over into a small square, and placed them in the organized arrangement of clothing on the bed. Sapo stood from a pile of shirts he'd been laying on and shrank himself to fit perfectly over this new addition.

"Teresa described seven mansions in her interior castle before she died and was dismembered. Each mansion you occupy takes you closer and closer to God. She also described four stages the soul takes to become fully integrated in union with the Lord," Albi recited.

"Sounds like a video game. I wonder if she had to reach all four stages in each mansion or if certain mansions correspond to certain stages," I said. Albi grunted and added more notes to the sheet. "She's also the nun that would levitate and orgasm, right?" I asked with the crack of a towel before rolling it and putting it in the closet with the rest of the laundry, apart from that one pair of underwear.

"While being penetrated by an angel, no less," Albi added with a bland drawl.

She seemed mythological, removed from Catholicism entirely. The church and its followers revered this woman so violently, they kept digging her up and slicing away to own a piece of her. That epileptic body became an idol to be worshipped. The same flesh that convulsed in ecstasy at angelic visions would be repeatedly pierced by crazed fanatics after death. I imagined her spirit watching from above as they scattered her parts across the globe, feeling each chunk's pleasure like phantom limbs.

Albi described her in a way that made it all seem implausible, but I pointed out that, unlike Jesus, there were actual historical records that proved these things happened to her. She kept diaries and records of her own.

"Yeah, but they probably inflated the story to draw attention to her convent. Start a new pilgrimage or something . . . I don't know," Albi said.

"Like a publicity stunt?" I laughed, slamming the Saint Feast Days book shut before flopping onto the bed. "She was a post-medieval rockstar."

Albi chuckled. "I don't believe she was constantly cumming midair. It seems outlandish."

"And some random homeless guy saying he is the son of God doesn't? We can go out to the boardwalk right now and find three other guys with that exact idea rattling around their heads." I rolled over and used the book to prop my head up.

"What are you trying to do, Simón?" He'd been leaning back in his chair but returned the legs to the floor. "I don't like it when you make fun of me like that." His gaze dropped to the floor.

"I'm not making fun of you. I just think it's funny, is all."

"Well, it's not funny to me. I've dedicated my life to this homeless crazy man."

"I'm not homeless anymore. Look at this place!" I yelled and dove in to tickle him. He shrugged me off but quickly grabbed my hand and pulled me to his chest.

"I know you don't believe in it, and I appreciate you listening and helping me study. But you always try to demean everything. It makes me feel like you think my work is silly. That I'm silly."

"I'm sorry." I kissed his head. "Tell me more about the church people chopping up the poor old lady."

"That's enough." He rolled his eyes and tossed me off his lap. "Why don't you go to Coco's house and have her little game of solitaire tell you what to do with your life."

I laughed, punched his shoulder, and then kissed it, but he just looked at the wall for a moment, face slack and unreadable.

"You know I don't think your work is silly, right?" I asked.

"You act like it's all a joke," he said quietly. "But I don't think you realize how much I need to believe it's real."

I opened my mouth, then closed it.

"Anyway," he muttered. "That's enough saints for today."

I nudged his foot with mine. "Fine. I'll go ask Coco if the cards will tell me how to stop being such a jerk."

"Not likely," he said, finally glancing at me with a small shake of his head. "Unless they can point you in the direction of a brain surgeon."

Tarot is not traditional to Santería, but Coco would consult the cards after reading my shells for additional clarity. The orishas screamed through my readings, she said, their spirit energy palpable as they pushed her to tell me everything. My path split endlessly, too many choices to make sense of any single direction. She'd ask me to set an intention, something concrete, distinctly night or day, no space for dusk or dawn, then pulled the cards. The Hanged Man. The Fool. The Lovers. Yet she was still puzzled, her brows furrowed. Coco's skin held an otherworldly luminosity, as if a glowing mist hovered above its surface, making the permanent line between her brows more striking. She wore that furrow proudly, calling it her third eye, a mark of honor, proof she knew how to think.

When I first met her, I wanted to hide myself, fold into smaller spaces or fade into walls. She'd pinched my right ass cheek and said, "*Suelta las nalgas*, or you're going to start a fire, *papito*." She told me I was so uptight that if I were to fart, a diamond would fall out. I longed to break free of that rigidity, to let my hips swish, to let my hands dance with my words the way hers did. To draw attention and welcome the stares that followed. As a kid, I'd sit in church, eyes clenched shut, fingers laced so tightly the skin stretched translucent over my knuckles, praying to be normal, to be like everyone else, to be anything but me. Each night I'd pray the same way, then cry myself to sleep, waking up disappointed in myself for remaining unchanged. Still a sissy. Coco taught me to be different. To love that difference.

"People aren't going to trust you. They're not going to trust that you're not dirty or sick in the head just because you say so," Coco said, tucking sheets around her couch cushions after Mamá kicked me out. "People never believe someone different from them. And I am as different as they come, so I know." She smoothed a pillowcase and then another. "Live your life, Simón. Things won't get easier, but they'll grow predictable. Once you can anticipate stupidity, you can outsmart it."

Under a forceful hand, a sewing machine will swallow fine silk. There are very specific steps you must take before sewing this delicate fabric, things you learn only by working with it, not forcing it. Like my mother, Coco carried a self-assuredness that was learned as much as it was earned. Life had tried to force both women into submission, but they adapted.

My mother taught me to sew young, though perhaps unintentionally. I'd watch her in the kitchen, memorizing her movements, absorbing her conversations as she'd reach for her cookie tin atop the refrigerator. That secret box held her treasures: bobbins and thread, needles, tiny scissors, and her worn thimble. Whether cooking or sewing, she choreographed the motions with the same graceful precision. She knew exactly what to do and when to do it.

Where Mamá's grace came from precision and control, Coco's flowed like water finding its path. As she finished making up the couch, tucking in the last corner with that same careful attention my mother gave to her hems, I felt a familiar ache. I lunged forward to hug her. Her monumental body seemed much smaller wrapped up in my arms. I made us some tea, and we sat together on the couch, our feet intertwined. We cried and laughed until I fell asleep.

Lenita leans against a street light in front of the old house that hides El Palomar, Coco's house. Her loose hair tumbles around her face in caramel waves. She sees me and launches her newly fragranced body in my direction. "These chicken feet give me the creeps. This one looks like your toenails before I started doing your pedicures." She kisses both of my cheeks and slaps my ass.

"Well, it's been a while, so I hope you sharpened your tools."

"It's a medical mystery how someone so cute can have such heinous hooves," she says, tossing her hair behind her shoulders.

"Everyone's stress manifests in different ways. Maybe mine comes out through my feet." I grab her arm, and we turn away from the street.

"True. When I get stressed, I get super gassy, but you already knew that." She lifts a leg and yells, "Fire!" launching a fart at me, before landing and running ahead towards the back of the house.

"You're a beast." I catch up with her, and she laughingly turns, sending her curls in motion. "A beast that's suddenly curling her hair. What's that about?" I grab a lock of hair and twist it around a finger before throwing it at her face.

"That's the problem with keeping friends from childhood. They never want you to change. I'm a mature and beautiful woman now, Simo."

"That farts on command."

"My metamorphosis is ongoing," she says before sticking her finger up her nose and wiping it on my face. "Did you buy me flowers?"

"They're for Coco. I wanted to thank her for letting me take the time off. I picked them up after I left my mother's house."

"Yes. Let's get down to business." She claps her hands and looks at me expectantly. "Tell me everything. How is the ever-so-pleasant Cuarenta doing?"

"She's fine. Still refuses to face anything. She acted like she forgave me—basically wanted to move on like nothing happened. Didn't want to talk about it at all. You know, typical if-we-don't-acknowledge-it-doesn't-exist kind of thing." We move into the shadow of the building, and I rest my back against the side of the house. "We had a big fight. Expected. But then I also blew up on her and Cordero before storming out of the house. That part wasn't planned."

"You yelled at the priest?" she asks, wide-eyed, with a slight grin forming at the corners of her mouth. "What was he even doing there?"

"Well, I sort of think they're fucking."

"Wait, what?! Why didn't you lead with that? This story just got so much better." Leni positioned herself an inch away from my face, holding her breath in anticipation.

"Yeah, he came over while I was there to 'check on her' because he thought she'd 'be alone' this afternoon," my fingers dramatically mime the quotation marks around the words.

"Is that it? I thought you found nudy pictures of him, or you like walked in on a handy j. Maybe he actually was just checking on her." She huffs and settles against the wall next to me.

"I mean, there was an energy in the air too. It's hard to explain. She is always talking about decency and not being alone with a man, but it seems like they do this often. They were gossiping like two old ladies after mass."

"What if he's gay?"

"Stop."

"Maybe he is! It would explain why he took Albi under his wing like that."

"If that's what you wanna call it. He obviously didn't do enough. Or he'd still be here."

"He took care of Albi after his mom died when he could have just sent him to an orphanage or something," she reasons while thumbing the bulge in my pocket. "What the hell is that?"

"It's food for Sapo." I slap her hand away. "Maybe he was in love with Albi's mother. Maybe he's a serial philanderer."

"You've met the man, Simón. He has no game. I think he's a repressed homo."

"I hope not. I don't want to claim him."

"Imagine if they actually are doing it. Everyone's gotta get laid. Your mom especially needs it. She's so uptight. I hope Father Cordero is giving it to her really good right now." She humps and spanks the air until I push her into the wall.

"Speaking of getting some … Who is it?" I ask while she's caught off guard.

"Who is what?"

"Who is the guy giving it to you?"

"Honey, I'm an independent woman. I don't need a man to give me anything."

"Okay … who are you giving it to, then?"

"I don't want to talk about this," she throws her hand up, blocking my face from her vision.

"Since when?"

She hesitates. And for a second her voice softens. "Since you started looking more breakable than usual." She clears her throat and pushes forward. "Let's go back to making fun of your uptight mom. Does she still pull her hair into the tightest bun of all time? I bet when she releases it, her face falls three inches. That kind of tension has to do some permanent damage."

"Lenita. I am fine. You acting weird is worse than letting me self-destruct on my own. I'm fine. I feel better than I have in a long time. Now tell me about him. How good is he in bed? How long?"

"It's only been like two months. I didn't tell you because …"

"No, how long?" My hands start together and then slowly

begin to separate. "Tell me when to stop." My hands continue to separate—much longer than expected—and she finally blurts out an abrupt "Stop."

"That big?!" I stare at my hands in disbelief, mouth agape. "That's too much. Talk about permanent damage."

"Yeah, and girthy, too." She cups her hand into a large C and shakes it in front of my face. "You know what, maybe that's the distraction you need. Want me to be your wingman tonight?"

"I'm good. This body is closed for business. I'm not ready for anything like that with anyone. Don't know if I'll ever be. And especially not something that big."

"Girl's night?"

"Girl's night." I grab her hand and kiss the back of it.

"No men. Just us." She quiets, wraps an arm around my waist, and pulls me toward the stairs that head down into El Palomar.

It's late in the evening now, but we are the only ones there besides Coco. She's stocking beers and shuffling clean glassware from the storage area to the serving station. The deep lines dark between her furrowed brows release like a startled school of fish as she looks up and sees Lenita and me enter. "The prodigal son has returned!" she exclaims as she dramatically lifts her arms to receive us, her bracelets clanging together at the ends of her crucifix figure. "We've missed you around here, *mijito*." She releases Leni but wraps her arm tighter around me. "I'm wasting away to nothing over here doing your job. This is physical labor I'm not used to anymore."

"These are for you, Coco." I pull away from her grip slightly and hand her the flowers. I began working here after leaving Mamá's house. Albi and I walked here after the fight, and Coco left no air between my question and her answer. She offered me a job that very night and a place to stay while I looked for an apartment of my own.

"Look at how well he treats me. And they say all men are dogs." She hugs me again and sets the flowers on a crate full of bottles that were just delivered. "If you're a dog, you're well-trained, Simo." She grabs my face and kisses my forehead.

"Let me help you," I say as I grab the crate and move it behind the bar. "I'm really sorry I haven't been back to work. Sort of lost my mind a bit." I unwrap the flowers and separate them into a few empty bottles. "Not sure that I have found it yet, but being out of the apartment makes me feel a bit more normal. I need to be back to normal."

"Simón, don't worry. I'll always be here. The work will always be here. You take care of you. The only good you'll do crying in these faggots' drinks is if they're margaritas. Saves on the salt. But while you're here, yes, grab those cases and help me out." She waves a bejeweled hand at the bar area, and I get to work.

"Coco, it's a mess back here!" I grumble and huff as I remove things from the shelves and place them where they belong. "What happened to all of my systems? I had everything organized and efficient."

"What good is a system without an operator? I'm not a factory worker, cariño." Coco begins pouring three drinks as Lenita grabs one chair to sit in and another to put her feet on. "And you," Coco says to her with a sly look in her eyes. "I've heard you have a little boyfriend."

She shoots Coco a look that says to leave it alone. "Ay, no, I don't want to talk about that."

"Tell us! What's his name? What does he look like? How

did you meet? Why haven't you brought him here to meet me?" Coco prods.

"Wow. How refreshing. Simón only cared about how big his dick is."

"And apparently he's not that little," I shout from below the bar.

"Men . . ." Coco rolls her eyes and crosses her arms. "Wait, how big is he?"

"Huge, Coco. Like too big to be useful," I quickly add.

"Anyways!" Lenita yells. "His name is Ramón, and he works with one of my cousins. He's tall and sweet and has a huge dick, okay?"

"Does he make you happy, or is this purely physical?" Coco asks.

"He is lovely. He buys me flowers before dates, which is actually kind of annoying because then I have to carry them around. Guys do that for the spectacle of it so people walking by will think, 'Oh my god, he's so thoughtful. What a man!' But I honestly think he does it to make me feel good. He even cooked me dinner one night, and it was delicious."

Ice hits my teeth, and I realize I've downed the cocktail in one gulp. The cold liquid coats my stomach, and I close my eyes and wait for the numbing to take effect.

"Are you two looking for a third? I could use a home-cooked meal," Coco jokes as a sly hand refills my glass.

"So that's the thing. I am not sure how he would react to coming here," Leni says, looking at her hands. "That's why I haven't brought him yet . . ." She's shrinking, cowering almost. It's odd to see her like this.

"Better to rip the Band-Aid off. You're not the type of woman that can be with a bigot. Period." The blunt response from Coco snaps Leni out of her embarrassment.

"I guess I'm scared for the dream to be over. There aren't many men that . . . I don't know . . ."

"That would be okay with us?" I say and motion between Coco and myself. A sharp pain strikes my heart, and I down my second drink to push it away.

"You know what I mean, Simón." Leni regrets saying anything. It is written all over her face. "I just meant I wanted to stay in our bubble before real-world bullshit pops it."

"She's right, Simón. We are on the outside. This is a different world than what those men are used to." Coco wipes down the tops of tables and repositions them around the room. It seems so tiny in here without the bodies adding to the atmosphere.

"No, you both are my world. And I would never give you up for any man. It's just been a strange time with you being . . . away, Simón. And I have leaned on Ramón as a distraction I guess."

I pour myself another drink and step from behind the bar. "It's okay. We get what you mean. And whenever you do want us to meet him, we promise to be extra gay and sassy."

We clink our glasses together, and the sound rings in my ears as my empty stomach digests the booze. My cheeks feel hot, and my ears buzz. I kiss the top of her head, pick her feet up, and place them on my lap as I sit across from her.

Through the tiny windows near the ceiling, the last dregs of daylight slip their rosy fingers into the room. I feel a little prick of hope. I made it through the day. That sun saw me from my room to this room. The rays that tumbled through my window a few hours ago rolled across the floor and down the steps, through the city, into the water and back out again. They lit the path here, and it seems like it might be possible— to keep going. Some people leave, and some people stay. I'm gonna be someone who leaves. My wings are buzzing, tense with anticipation of flight over fight. Why fight? Why do anything when nothing matters?

I lean my head back and close my eyes. The booze swirls through my body, mingling with blood, brain fluid, and the water that lives inside me. My body rocks with phantom waves, like after a day of swimming. The swaying of a memory.

I see the room outside my closed eyes. Albi dances by himself in that way he dances. He moves his hands more than his feet. He creates shapes in fluid motions with his arms, leaving his hands trailing behind like a waving flag. He'll cock a hip up, drop it back down. I'm dancing with him now, too. The floor fills with bodies. We're happy. We're pieces of a whole. A herd of bipedal animals stampeding in a musical circle. Albi twists and spins at the center. An animal like the rest of us, though, I realize now, he's a different species entirely. The world around us had been reconstructed by vastly different brains in vastly different skulls.

"I guess my skull's too thick," I huffed, throwing a soiled rag to the floor. It made a funny, damp squelching sound as it hit the concrete. Normally, Albi and I would have giggled at that, so I kicked it to have the final word.

"Simón, you're not listening." Albi's voice carried across the empty bar, too loud in the afternoon quiet. "It's not about your thick skull. You're ignoring what I'm saying."

"I have a lot to do." Glass clinked as I hoisted bottles onto the bar, arranging them with mechanical precision, each label facing forward, each space between them exactly the same.

"Either give me your keys, or I'll just see you later this week." He extended his hand. His muscles rippled, tensed from forearm to clenched jaw.

"You're the one who doesn't want to be seen with me. So go." I stacked glasses with more force than necessary. "I'll

come to the rectory after work if I 'get over it' like you said."
My attempt at a scowl collapsed into something wounded and
pitiful, like a cartoon of a sad animal.

"We have your apartment now. We don't need to go there."
He put his hand down and breathed in deeply. "I have to start
keeping things separate."

So, Albi could see me, but I couldn't stay. I couldn't exist in
his life in any way that might force the church to look directly
at us.

His words stung, but it wasn't only the tone. It was the
echo of someone else's voice behind them. Father Cordero's
gentle way of supporting terrible ideals. Maybe he told Albi
it was okay to care for me, just not to live with me. Not to be
seen. Not if he still wanted to be a priest.

Albi said he needed to keep things separate. But everything
in his body—the tension in his shoulders, the way he barely
looked at me—said it wasn't just a separation of church and the
state of our relationship. It felt like the first quiet dismantling
of a future we had barely begun to build.

"I don't know what you want from me. Sweet at home,
stranger in the streets? Just fucking say that, then." I stopped
my frantic organizing and stood in front of him. "But you
can't fuck me one night and pretend not to see me the next
morning."

"Please don't curse at me." He crossed his arms in
front of his chest and looked down at the floor. "I'm really
overwhelmed."

"Well, I am too." I stepped out from behind the bar, closing
the distance between us. "But you need to talk to me. You can't
start treating me like trash out of nowhere and expect me to
fall in line." I ducked my head to catch his downcast gaze.
Sunset light caught his eyes as his eyelashes parted, turning

the brown to amber. "I need you to tell me what you want, Albi. Even if it's just this once. Even if it changes tomorrow." I took the keys from my pocket and slipped them into his. "I promise I'll learn. I'll do anything for you."

"Be patient with me. I'll figure out how to navigate this." He stepped closer to me, touching the toes of his shoes with the toes of mine.

"*We* will figure it out. You've got backup now, remember?"

Is that all it takes to be okay? Belonging somewhere, to someone?

Turn the handle, open the door. Flip the switch; there's light. I am You; You are Me, and because of that transmogrification, *We* are still alive?

A chorus of cackles descends the stairs, scattering my vision of Albi. I open my eyes to see him running up the steps, a different version of myself in scrambled pursuit. I can hear my voice. I can hear his. I'm laughing, but he's singing, and it drowns everything out, so I sing along.

"Is he drunk already?" A shrill voice pierces the still air of the empty room, followed by the clucking of four other din-producing bodies. "Stick to being cute, Simón. Singing isn't gonna pay your bills. In fact, I might have to send you a bill for my audiologist."

They call themselves Las Locas. Five grown men who perform schoolgirl dramatics with the tenacity of gossiping old women. We don't know any of their real names, but their hyperspecific nicknames—Pata de Palo, La Cachifloja, Pelona, Tucán, and Sin Bemba—fit them so perfectly that learning them would only disappoint. They bend the world to accommodate them, never shrinking to fit in. Their screams ricochet off walls. But dare look their way, and they'll tell you to mind your business. Do I like them? Not always. Do I love them? Inevitably. Today especially feels like a day to embrace them.

"No, not drunk yet, but I should get there quickly if I want to drown out the oinks and grunts from you pigs." I raise my glass into the air as they squeal in delight.

"You wish you could get a bite of this rump roast," Pata says, slapping his thigh and jiggling his ass from side to side.

"Maybe you ordered wrong. All I see are pork rinds," I reply. Las Locas erupt in a fit, and they demand to buy me a shot. No greater feeling exists than the triumph after a proper, good old-fashioned gay showdown. I feel witty, electric, unstoppable.

"Shots, Coco!" the group sings in unison. At the end of the bar, Lenita watches with her untouched drink, chin resting in her palm. She's looking at me and smiling. I want to cup her face, kiss her, bury myself in her curled hair and weep. My vision lags by two frames, so I stand still to do a reality check. The room isn't spinning, and my hands still seem relatively familiar. Nodding to myself, I join the others for the shots as Sin Bemba recites some poem about a man wearing leather and his friend wearing lace, and something else happens, and then he sits on his face. It sounds like a blessing. Laughter starts and stops in undulating spurts as we swallow the consecrated liquor. Behind my eyes, I see my mother at mass; she's standing, kneeling, standing again. The chanted prayers. The Blood of Christ. Peace be with you. And also with you.

Stumbling back to Lenita, I feel the drunkenness wobbling in my knees. My body begs to keep moving or it will collapse. "Let's dance. I wanna dance," I say, pulling her toward the center of the room.

"Your drunk ass probably needs to dance," she says as she spins herself away from me and then back into my body like a wave. "Now, dip me!" Our bodies flow toward the floor, and

I instinctively drop her into the crux of my left arm, spinning her twice as we stand upright. We both gasp in wide-eyed shock that I didn't collapse on top of her, and our synchronized surprise sends us into fits of laughter.

"I missed you, Simo," she says in my ear.

"I missed you too."

We move around the dance floor, and a pang of longing grips me. Like I miss her already, like I'm scared to miss her again. I wonder what she would feel if this were our last dance. I want to laugh, but I want to cry. It sloshes around. A valve has broken inside me. Everything keeps building up, and it leaks out slowly or quickly, depending on the position and motion of my body.

Las Locas blur at the edges of my vision. Leni's smile flashes as we twirl. Coco greets someone. Ice clinks against glass. Leni speaks, but her words stop vibrating before reaching my brain. I see her face, but she isn't there. My skin hangs loose over meat and bone as I sway to the music. A rhythm crawls up my legs as I melt into the floor. I could expand into air, evaporate, cease to exist. No more mornings not wanting to wake up, no more nights spent wishing I was asleep already.

My eyelids snap closed like malfunctioning shutters. A second rhythm trips over the one my hips and feet obey. My head echoes, empty like a camera obscura, everything upside down and reversed. The lights absorb my dissolving body, colors flashing against my eyelids. I'm dancing with my eyes closed, and a familiar thought, yet foreign in many ways, creeps along my skull's inner walls, fingers trailing over brain matter.

"Simón?" That voice. I pretend it's his, knowing it isn't. I grab hands that aren't his, and we spin. He's on the ceiling, smiling at the other me. They mirror each other's hip swivels, arms slicing the air, until they collide and bounce apart like slow-motion physics. I leap to catch them both, soaring upward. The other me kisses his hand. I kiss my own, then bite it. I remember when my hands abandoned me. When I sank into bed and died.

My body creaks and swells like horror movie strings. My insides rattle like loose change and old receipts—a junk drawer sliding across the floor. Ceiling Albi is telling Ceiling Simón something, and they both look upset.

I spin until the room surrounds me in a blur of itself. It becomes an orb with me at its center. Levitating like Teresa awaiting rapture. "Let us breathe for you, Simón," the nuns will say. Her four devotions burn into my flesh, and I wonder which mansion I'm in. They want my body. They want my devotion.

"Get him on the floor!" a nun with Lenita's voice sings. Arms slice through space and air to grasp me from all directions. Chop me up, ladies.

"Don't hold him too tightly. He'll break his neck." They're all singing. They're a choir. They lift me skyward and hold me against the sun to blot it out. Soon they'll boil me in oil like a true disciple. My skin will crackle and harden around muscle and bone. The disciple whom Albi loved. My body convulses in the heat, dancing atop the popping grease, slapping against the surface tension like a leather strap.

And now a canon:

Voice 1: "He's not having a seizure, is he?"

Voice 2: "He's just spasming or something, right?"

Voice 3: "That's what a seizure is, dumbass."

Voice 4: "Should we make him throw up now?"

What a funny song.

I try to open my eyes, and I see Albi's shoes. The floor holds me up by my back. Strange how this floor has known only my feet until now, except for that one failed breakdancing attempt when my left hand touched it for a moment. His shoes walk away. They're ascending the stairs. They'll step out onto the street. Las Locas keep singing. Their voices are like birds. Not songbirds but carrion eaters. They shriek and squawk to make a scene, to claim the roadkill.

"I am fine. I am fine." I sing back to them, staccato from the ground. "Get off of me. I'm fine." Vomit spills horizontally from my mouth and left nostril onto the floor.

I try to push myself up, but my hand slides through vomit and my face slams into the ground.

Lenita hoists up my right side with a guttural grunt while Coco crouches at my left. Las Locas part as Leni booms, "Fucking fuck off if you're not going to help, idiots." They scatter to different corners, giggling and chittering before scrambling back together like flies swatted from a picnic blanket.

Coco directs Leni to carry me to the back room. They lay my body on the old couch. Coco kneels beside me with a wet rag, cleaning bile from my face in soft smooth caresses. She looks to Leni while wiping my neck and then my hands. "Could you go wipe up the mess on the dance floor before one of those silly cows takes a tumble? They would fall on purpose just for the drama of it."

"Don't worry. I got it." Leni grabs the T-shaped mop from behind the door and drapes Coco's rag over it before heading back into the bar. "Get out of here," she shouts at the bodies crowding outside the door. "Don't any of you have anything else going on in your lives? It's Easter, for fuck's sake."

"We're worried about him," one of them replies. "Is he okay? Is this about Albi? It's been forever."

"Mind your own business. You wouldn't know what

mourning looked like if it fucked you in the ass."

"Well, of course not; it would be behind me." A fit of giggles explodes while one voice screeches out a fake orgasm. Their voices begin to fade as the horde moves away from the door.

Coco gives me water. "Ignore them. There are people who watch *novelas*, and people who star in them. You think Verónica Castro worries what my Tío Chucho thinks? She doesn't even know the goat fucker exists. Lucky bitch." Her fingers brush my cheek with a tenderness reserved for puppies or a crippled child that wins a rigged race.

I feel tiny. I'm no longer me, just a picture of me in a locket.

"I'm really sorry. I'm not that drunk. I'm not sure what happened." The air stagnates with the smell of vomit on my shirt and in my nostrils. It's embarrassing, yet all I feel is an emptiness so profound my ribs want to crush inward against the vacuum.

She shushes me and brushes my hair away from my forehead. "You don't have to explain anything to me. You're grieving, *lindo*. You don't owe anything to anyone."

"That's the problem, though. I don't have anyone to owe anything to. I made Albi my world. I made myself into love for him. I don't know who I am if I'm not his anymore."

"Just because he isn't here to receive your love doesn't mean it doesn't exist, that you don't exist. Letting that love die now would dishonor you and the memory of the man you love." She rests her hand on my heart, tapping lightly. "You hear that? *Love*, in the present tense."

I nod slowly. Something in the air shifts.

"Coco, he doesn't listen," Albi said once, storming into the room. Coco followed and pulled the door partially closed.

"It's not so simple for me," he continued. "I can't just start over like he did. And Cordero isn't making things easy either. I'm screwed no matter what. I feel like I'm breaking in two."

"*Te voy a decir una cosa, guapo.*" Coco took a seat at one of the vanities and motioned for Albi to sit on the stool next to her. "Sometimes, when something breaks, the pieces are large enough to glue back together. Other times, it shatters so completely it can't be fixed. My whole life, I hated who I saw in the mirror, in pictures. I hated the person people talked about when referring to me. I was so cruel to myself that it hurt. It was painful to live inside my own skin. Every shirt I wore suffocated me. The pressure of fabric on my legs made me sick to my stomach. And I knew exactly why. I knew how to fix it, but I thought the love I had for my family was enough."

I had been eavesdropping right outside the door, watching through the crack. Coco paused, her eyes flitting to me and back to Albi, his hands folded gently in his lap.

"When I finally decided to show the world who I truly was inside, I had to choose. To either shatter myself or shatter my family's version of me. When I shattered the need for my family's approval, they never spoke to me again.

When I shattered that false image of myself, the real me was already there. She was waiting with open arms and so many beautiful things to show me. There was nothing to fix, Albi. My skin was the same skin as before, but it didn't hurt anymore. I grew my hair out, and it tickled my shoulders. I wore dresses, and they felt like clouds. My given family may have decided to take back their love, but I found a new family. One I chose for myself." She grabbed his hands. "This is your journey. You're deciding which road to take. Not Cordero. Not Simón."

"I'm scared, Coco," Albi whispered. I had never heard him say those words before. I'd never seen his face like that, raw with fear. Suddenly aware of my intrusion, I stepped away quietly, returning to work with my heart thudding strangely.

I look up now, meeting Coco's patient eyes. "I heard what you said to Albi . . . about how you started over."

She nudges my chin, winking. "And you have a choice now, too, Simón. You can take what life's given you, or you can respectfully decline and find your own way."

"I'm tired, Coco. I've already shattered everything once. We built a new life. We made a world together that we cooked in, that we slept in, and that we loved each other in. We were so happy. I don't understand how it ends like this. We had everything planned out. We were happy."

"I know he was happy with you. The world you made together was beautiful, but you are still Simón. And Simón is still alive and has a lot of life to live. You have to let him."

"There is no Simón anymore." I sit up, and my head spins. "My skin doesn't hurt like yours did. I don't have skin. There's nothing left for me to fix, no pieces left to glue back together."

"Then you might have to create something new. It's now or never," Coco says sharply. She stands up and offers me a hand. "I shouldn't have to tell you how precious life is. Get up and get used to being you again."

I grab her hand and stand, unable to lift my eyes from the floor. "Coco, there's something else. Before Albi died—"

Just then, a flying cockroach lands on her arm, sending us both screeching and jumping onto the couch, clutching each other amid the screams. She swats it away with a dozen frantic swipes, and it takes flight, landing on the wall.

The shock dies down, and we collapse onto the couch, laughing so hard my diaphragm cramps. We laugh and laugh until I realize I'm weeping. My breath comes ragged and wet. Coco cries, too. She holds my head against her chest, her bracelets clanging in my ear, and they sound like a Sunday morning. Her tears fall into my hair as I fold deeper into her.

"It hurts, Coco. When will it stop hurting?" I gasp, clutching my stomach as overwhelming reality rains down on me like baseball bats.

Coco kisses my head, and the sound is muffled in my hair. "Every day is a struggle. Every day is a blessing." She swallows hard and kisses my head again. Her lips meet my scalp at the same time as her tears. "There's no easy fix to how you feel. This pain will never get better. You adapt to it. You come to terms with it, and you figure out what comes next after what has passed. It will never stop hurting, but I'll always be here to rub your chest when you feel like it's too much. *Sana, sana, colita de rana . . .*" She runs her hands over my heart like a miracle worker.

We sit in silence as our tears stop falling and my breathing steadies. Clinking glasses and laughter spill into the room from the bar. "We should get back out there before these heathens rob me blind." She loops her arm through mine and looks me up and down. "But first, let's find you a clean shirt. You smell like rotting fruit."

"I'll meet you out there," I say. "Love you, Coco. And thank you."

"I love you too, *mi gran varon*," she says, pausing at the door. As she turns the corner, people applaud and scream about how thirsty they are.

I find a short-sleeved nylon button-down in the lost-and-found and swap it for my soiled shirt. Layers might shield me from whatever comes next, so I grab a jacket from the box and slip my arms into that as well.

I practice smiling in the little mirror the queens use to touch up their makeup. I read that the act of smiling, even forced, releases endorphins, serotonin, and dopamine. A series of glands and brain chunks are triggered by those specific muscles functioning at the same time, and they assume you are experiencing pleasure. Like a pulley system releasing the happy floodgates. I blink a few times and stretch my lips into various configurations. It'll be okay. I'll adapt.

Everything will be better in the morning, I think, through a fake smile. It will all be better in the morning. My lips part and separate from my teeth, and the moist sound makes me want to vomit again.

The floor vibrates with music and the shuffle of a dozen newcomers who must have arrived while I was falling apart in the back room. I wonder how many are here because they have no family to be with on Christmas, and how many are faking their smiles. A drink thrusts itself into my hand, and after a hesitant sip I gulp it down. Las Locas applaud, teasing me for being macho as they squeeze my arms and pinch my chest. I laugh and brush them off, saying they're not my type.

"Oh, we know what your type is. You like tall, dark, and handsome like every other faggot in this town," Tucán says, rolling his eyes and clicking his tongue. His voice is high-pitched and lilting, in stark contrast to his weedy frame and slumped shoulders.

"No one is his type now. Not after having Albi. Uuf. What a man," Pata de Palo says, fingers still digging into my arm. Ice cracks and crunches between my teeth like a glacier calving. "That man walked in and we'd have licked the ground beneath him. Couldn't believe it when we heard. Another round? No lime for me, Coco."

Another drink is placed in my hand, and another word about Albi's beauty gets tossed into the air. They know nothing about him, about his true beauty. His soft humming while we drifted to sleep. The way his long lashes overlapped his eyebrows when he was concentrating. The cleft in his chin. The soft contour of his cheekbone sloping down to his jaw. His knee between my knees. His knuckles knocking against mine as we walked around town. They know nothing.

"You were so cute together. So unexpected. What a tragedy. When we heard what happened, we couldn't stop crying," one of them says. My hand aches to cover his mouth and nose and watch his eyes bulge out of his head. Cry now, I want to say. I'll give you a real reason to cry. My mouth seals shut, fists clenched. There are dozens of things I want to say, but my brain speeds over them like potholes. I rumble inside, unable to speak.

"How are you dealing with all this? Tell us everything." Sinister interest glints in his eyes. He's a stage villain with a poisoned dagger, a mantis poised to strike. "Must be hard not to blame yourself. We're here for you. Let it all out." Another drink appears.

Isabel Panocha pushes in between us on her way to the back room. Her face is painted and glitter-encrusted, but she's wearing floppy basketball shorts and a tank top stretching over her barrel-chested torso. She lifts her baseball cap an inch and playfully sneers at us over her free arm like Nosferatu at Ellen's window.

"You don't know how to welcome royalty, or what?" she says as she struts past, suddenly overcome by a ghost of glamor.

"I don't think the court jester is considered part of the royal family, Panocha," Pelona says, dodging the bar rag Isabel launches lazily at him.

Leni grabs my hand and pulls me close, like a flying buttress stabilizing my stony weight. She nods at me, and we turn to leave. Skulking away from the dance floor, I keep my gaze down but my posture up, Mamá's phantom hand still tapping my lower back to stand up straight.

Bodies fill the room now. They kiss each other, they laugh. Their feet touch the ground while I float by—a ghost whistling a forgotten tune.

Coco weaves through the crowd, a sparkling gown now haloing her body. She kisses Lenita first. "Get him home. And next time I see you, I expect Ramón to be the one attached to your hip." She embraces me, kisses both cheeks and then my lips before hugging me tightly again. "Adapt, Simón. You have to adapt." One last kiss is planted on my forehead, like last rites before an execution.

We climb the stairs hand in hand as Coco quiets the crowd. "Welcome home, my children. Lent is over, so let's indulge a little," she says, lifting her hand. Everyone claps and whistles while she begins singing *La Gloria Eres Tú*. I look at our hands and remind myself that one is mine.

The street lights glow piss yellow, casting shadows of poles and wires across the crumbling pavement like some jaundiced Mondrian. The world could seem so beautiful if only I allowed it to, if only I saw it as sunshine yellow rather than piss. If only I saw Leni's hand in mine and not Albi's. The lucky number thirteen.

I look at my shoes again, and they are still the same shoes I've been wearing all day. The same shoes I have worn for two years. I rewind them in my mind, and they get brighter. The sweat and saltwater stains ripple and recede, and the frayed edges mend. I see them standing on so many different surfaces. Soil of the garden. Sand of the beach. This exact pavement and others, too. Crossing over from grass to pavement to rocks.

I was looking at my feet, and Albi laughed. "Are you ever going to look me in the eyes?"

"I'm still nervous. I feel awkward," I replied with an embarrassed chuckle. Slowly lifting my head, my eyes found his, pinched at the corners. His lips were wet and red, parting as he breathed out a small "ah . . . there he is."

He looked at me as if he knew who I was and all the reasons why. I felt cozy, like I was at home, like I finally knew who I was, too. He looked at me like my skin was transparent, every cell and atom visible at once. He looked at me, and I was home, but all my cabinets and drawers stood open. A poltergeist revealing all my disorganized truths, my painfully visible faults.

"Don't worry. I'm nervous, too. But I don't want that to get in the way. It's just you and me right now." His smile brightened, and the drawers closed. The cabinets cleaned themselves like in an old show about a good-humored witch.

We turned and walked close together down the alley, our uneven strides causing us to collide continuously. Each small bump was an arrow shooting into my heart.

"You okay?" Leni is here. Albi is not.

"Yeah. Just drunk. I'm sorry." My arm is still intertwined with hers.

"I will sew your mouth shut if you apologize one more time." The air moves slightly and I smell her perfume, the product in her hair. She's majestic.

"I wanted to have fun with you tonight. I wanted to start over." My legs turn gelatinous, and I prop my body against the wall. "I think I can be fine, but then I'm not. And I think Pata de Palo is funny, and then the bitch is not even funny." I shift and shake my head. "And I am to blame. I am. It's all my fault."

The words spill out, and I try to control them, pronouncing each one carefully, slowly forming the sentences in my mouth so I don't sound so drunk.

"Don't listen to those hens. They're just pecking around the dirt for drama. You are not to blame. Ignore them and let them eat shit."

I close my eyes and feel the stone wall against my head. My cheek lays itself against the cold, rough surface. I start to whistle the tune Albi would always hum. Lenita hums along, leaning her head against the wall, facing me like a mirror.

My body slumps heavier, the weight of it multiplying with every second. I could knock the building down, and the city would follow like dominoes—white faces and black dots sliding across each other in a fluid motion of destruction.

A hand comes up to my neck. It's warm and soft.

Leni continues in a hushed voice, "Simo, I have to tell you something. I . . ." She pauses and takes her hand away. A wave of cold air takes its place. "I'm pregnant. I'd love to say I don't know what to do, and how could this happen and all that bullshit, but . . ." A quick sniffle cuts the revelation in half. "But I'm happy," she croaks. "I haven't told anyone yet, not even Ramón. Shit, I barely know the guy. I didn't want to tell you today, but I just . . . I need you, Simón. I can't do this alone."

The night swirls around us. I try to form words, knowing exactly what she needs to hear, but my mouth feels stuffed with cotton. Pain becomes a wall between us.

"I know the timing is shit," she continues, wiping her eyes. "With everything that's happened. But I don't know what to do. I don't know how to be a mom. You have to remind me to shave my own armpits most days." She forces a laugh through her nostrils and wipes her nose with the back of her hand.

"How long have you known?" I manage.

"Almost two months. I wanted to tell you when I found out, but . . . you know," she trails off.

I look at her—really look at her for the first time in weeks. The slight fullness in her cheeks. The exhaustion beneath her new perfume and curled hair. While I'd been drowning, she'd been silently carrying this new life, alone. I know exactly what I'm supposed to say: "Oh my god! That's amazing, Lenita! Don't worry. I'll raise this baby with you. It'll be a heteronormative fairytale." I know what she needs to hear. But my heart can't conjure the excitement she deserves. Guilt hits me square in the back of the head like a hammer. The thought of accompanying her through motherhood, of a life forming inside her, jolts me like a jump scare. I want to say I'll be there for her. I want to say I'll be there for her child. But I can't. I can't even be there for myself.

I stagger away from the wall, rubbing my temples, waiting for the feeling to pass. Then the world goes white. An instant later, my face collides with the wall and then the pavement at Lenita's feet. Streaks of what should be pain but feel more like cold wetness streak across my skin before everything falls away. I'm ready to shatter. Ready to become something new.

Chapter Eight
Home

"Let's go swimming!" I grabbed Albi's hand as we left El Palomar—his palm hot and moist against the cool night air.

"It's 2 a.m. We're going home," he said, leaning away from my tugging.

"Time doesn't exist. You've been brainwashed." I tripped and, laughing, hopped to regain my footing.

"Yeah, at least I have a brain, Pigeon Boy." He gave in to my jerking and yanking, his arm rolling loose in its socket as I skipped and leaped, pulling him like a rhythmic gymnast's ribbon. "Let's go home. I want to relax with you."

When I looked back, he was smiling. He glanced away, laughed, then met my eyes again. His hair bounced a beat behind each heavy step. I imagined what a younger me would have thought to see this. A man holding my hand. A man, smiling and full of love, holding my hand in the street.

"We don't have to swim. I don't want our anniversary to end yet. Let's just be you and me out here till it's over," I pleaded, spinning around to curl myself against him like croissant dough. "Two years!" My shout echoed until Albi covered my mouth and then pressed a kiss to the back of his hand.

"Fine, just be quiet. I am going to need to sleep at some point. I meet with Father at eight tomorrow," Albi conceded.

"I work at eight, too. Suck it up, buttercup."

"You work at a bar. You don't start till eight at night, asshole." He shoved me and took off running toward the beach. His shirt filled with air and sent him skyward, hair streaming like clouds. He was a kite dancing through the night sky, swooping from side to side, diving then rising. My grip would always keep him tethered, safe from being swept away.

I grabbed his shirt to reel him back as I took the lead. He thrust his left foot in my path, and I leaped over this assassination attempt—our laughter carrying through the shock of my sudden athletic prowess. We ran and ran, and I thought of the horses on the ranch.

Albi reached the seawall first, vaulting over it onto the rock and rubble below. He stripped his shirt off, tossing it at my face in one last attempt at sabotage. The smell of his skin and hair enveloped me. Vanilla and oud, smoke and sweat. I stopped running and held the cloth against my face. No other scent would ever be so sweet.

Folding his shirt, I stepped down from the large slabs of rock onto the beach. The mango trees swayed. The waves rumbled softly. My clothes piled up on the sand, and I placed his shirt on top. His pants sprawled halfway to the water like a warrior, slain in battle. I jumped over the casualty and began sprinting once the cold night breeze hit my naked body and tightened my skin. I dove in and swam underwater toward Albi.

A swinging scythe of water cracked against my face as I breached the surface. Water drained from my nose as I wiped my eyes and forced out a hoarse, pitiful cough. His devious smirk vanished, and he labored quickly through the water to embrace me.

"I'm sorry, Simo," he said with a laugh, trying and failing to sound remorseful as he stroked my red face. "I thought you'd dodge it. You were so sporty earlier." He laughed again, leaning in with closed eyes to kiss me.

Before our lips met, I hooked my foot around his ankle and shoved his chest backward, sending him plunging underwater before he had time to gulp down any air. Hooting and yipping up at the sky, I dove on top of him, pressing his shoulders down as he flailed. He wriggled free, spinning us around, and wrestled me into submission. His arms locked tightly around mine, pinning them to my chest as waves splashed up around us.

"You're dark-sided," he said, spitting water over his shoulder and clearing his nostrils. "An eye for an eye, huh?" He dunked me underwater, but this time, the motion was gentle, like a baptism.

He held me draped over his arms, floating on the water's surface. He was the Virgin Mary, and I was her son. Albi della Pietà. His monolithic arms, beaded with moisture, dwarfed me like some ancient tree roots surrounding a temple as he slowly spun us around. His chest was a hair-covered wall of stone, and I was chained to him, a willing Prometheus offering not only my liver but my entire body for all of eternity. As he squeezed my body closer to his, a lip caressed his nipple. Then a tongue. The roughness of hair against my face, the skin below the hair tightening. He released my legs, and I drifted downward, the salt water flowing over and under me like infinite, delicate laminations. Our bodies collided, and he pushed my head down to his nipple again while he groped around underwater. Catch and release, catch and release. I dove under and took him into my mouth, blowing air out through my nose. The bubbles slid up my forehead, catching in his body hair like glimmering pearls.

His hands gripped beneath my arms, pulling me up for air I hadn't even missed yet. He pulled me into a hungry kiss. "I love you, Simón," he said solemnly.

"I love you more."

He led me out of the water and up the beach, his thumb tracing slow circles over my hand as we walked. Passing his discarded pants, he picked them up and used them to dry me off, starting at my shoulders and working his way down. When he reached my waistline, he dropped to his knees, kissing each hip bone and then the swell of my crotch. The water on his skin had evaporated, leaving constellations of salt scattered across the broad expanse of his shoulders. My fingers found the back of his neck, tangling in his damp hair. I could feel the blood pulsing in his veins, see the air swirling around him, alive and electric.

There was no world beyond us. No beach apart from the sand beneath our feet. Our shared heat created a simmering energy, thick and undeniable, as if we hadn't done this twice a day, every day, for the last two years. As if this were our wedding night, and the act itself hung above us, ripe and waiting. A mango to savor and suck.

I placed my hand on his lower back, guiding him down to the sand before laying my body over his. In that moment, his body was the only thing in the world I was touching. He wrapped his arms around me, crushing me against him. His legs tangled with mine. A low growl escaped from one of us. He spat into his hand. His fingers danced around. I arched my back. He spat into his hand again, and I pressed myself harder against him. Hours could have passed. Generations come and gone. Lifetimes lived by everyone except for us.

The sand scattered from our bodies as we plunged into the water. After the warmth we'd shared, the cold was shocking and sharp, tightening everything inside me. We left the water and walked back up the beach, the night still heavy around us. The air hung suspended in place as we pulled our clothes on over our wet skin.

We moved in silence. It felt like the night could stretch on forever.

Everything was still and dark. And then it hit me.

The stone soared through the air, weightless. The silence wrapped its fingers around it all. Everything suspended in time, like a mouse's neck clamped in a trap. A fly on glue. Then it hit me.

The stone struck my face. And suddenly I was home.

Not the kind of home you feel after a week away or a long day at work. Not the kind where you walk through the door and pause, marveling at how everything remains just as you left it. Not one thing out of place.

This was something else. A different kind of home.

A home like instinct. Like flinching. Like crouching low when you hear footsteps overhead. A home made not of memory but of muscle, coiled tight. A home you always feared was all you deserved.

What I'd thought was home—at our beach, in our bodies—was the eye of the storm. A quiet dream surrounded by violence.

This was the real place. The one that had been waiting for us all along.

Heat streamed down my skull in a slow flow. It pooled in my ear. There was no pain, only a stunned emptiness, and I don't remember sounds, only the sight of Albi standing over my horizontal body, panic carved into his face. He dropped to his knees, clutching the side of my head, his eyes darting frantically. I tried to push myself up, but the sand clung to me, pulling me back. My head buzzed. A high-pitched whine crackled and faded as I staggered to my feet.

Then it hit me. Clarity slapped me awake, and I heard three voices. Three men.

"Get out of here, Albi," I hissed, scanning the pathway over the rocks. "Go. Hide in the trees." Albi froze. "Go!" I shoved him, and he stumbled back, falling hard onto the sand. Scrambling to his feet, he darted into the shadows of the mango trees as three men clumsily descended the boulders leading to our beach.

The men were laughing, stumbling down the boulders I'd climbed since I was a child. "I nailed that faggot right in the head. You both owe me drinks for a month."

Blood dripped from my jaw onto the dry sand, leaving tiny beads of crimson in a circle. They reminded me of my mother's necklace digging into my neck as my father choked me. My hand went up to my throat, and the thudding of my body made me realize I was running toward the voices.

My body surged forward, air slicing past my face as I ran. The stone that had hit me moments ago bit into my palm, its jagged edges digging into my skin. "Hey, asshole!" I screamed, hurling the stone at one of the men.

He turned to look just as it struck his throat. The stone fell to his feet with a hollow clatter, and he gurgled—a sound like a clogged bathtub draining—before dropping to his knees, hands clutching at his neck.

Adrenaline surged around my heart, and I rushed forward, slamming my fists into his face. His nose shattered under my knuckles, and his head bounced against the rocks beneath us.

My bones beneath muscle beneath skin collided with his bones beneath muscle beneath skin. My head rang with an empty, metallic echo as punch after punch sent shockwaves up my arms. Soon, my hands slid off his face, slick with blood, until a blunt force cracked against the back of my head.

Then another hit. And another.

I collapsed onto the bloody, broken man beneath me. Kicks swung down on my gut, each one snapping like a whip. Pain bloomed in my side as a rib cracked. But I didn't want it to stop. I wanted to absorb it all for Albi.

I told myself this was where I belonged. They hit me, and I knew I was home. They seemed to understand my place; they knew exactly where I was supposed to be. My body begged my brain to shut down, to go on standby until it was over. But I kept thinking about Albi.

I sat up, hands wrapped around my head. I turned my body into an obstacle. Another boulder in the pile.

Stay hidden. Stay hidden. Stay hidden. The mantra looped in my mind, matching the rhythm of each punch. This wasn't his home. He shouldn't feel at home here.

The fists kept coming, relentless and disembodied. A creature with four fists it launched and retracted in mechanical spurts.

"Faggot's not giving up," one of them panted.

Then Albi burst from the shadows and tackled one of them. I heard grunts, and could only picture his skin bruising, tearing. Every blow to him was a blow to me.

I got to my feet quickly and grabbed a rock, hoisting it over my head. I kicked the man grappling with Albi, knocking him off balance, then hurled the rock downward. He raised his hands to block it, but the stone broke through, crashing into his face. He crumpled, and I drove my foot into his gut. Again. Again.

Albi scrambled away. So did the third man. His wide eyes kept expanding as I kept kicking. He shuffled farther back, away from me. In fear.

Fear of me.

Am I the monster?

The sudden pause in violence snapped me back into place. My hands trembled, not knowing what to do now that they weren't hitting anything. My skin tingled as pain set in, burrowing deep, catching in every nerve.

If I could see the future in that moment, I'd see a note. Flowers on the dashboard. The note slamming into my face again and again. He wrote me a note and picked me flowers from his garden. I didn't feel at home then. I felt like I was in a house. Any house. A place I'd been left for dead.

The third man sobbed, crawling toward the others. Hands in the air. Begging for me to stop. The crashing of the waves became audible once more, and we slowly climbed the rocks, dripping blood and unable to speak, as the men groaned and writhed among the rubble.

We walked shoulder to shoulder through the voided night. No wind. No twinkling stars. Only us, moving through a world on pause.

His knuckles glowed dull red. His lip bled. But the wounds were superficial.

Each breath sent a sharp pain through my gut, so I kept them shallow. My eye was swollen shut, and blood still dripped from the side of my head. My whole body ached, but I was so relieved for it. I was grateful it was me and not him. He'd be fine.

My hand brushed his. He jerked away, too quickly to be

intentional. The brutality had infected him, seeped into every muscle. I could feel it tightening everything between us. And I worried what would happen when morning came.

I needed him to touch me. Wrap his pinky around mine. Tap his elbow against mine as we walked. Just to know he was okay.

That we were okay.

"I gotta sit for a second," I said, lowering myself to the pavement. I looked up at Albi. I wanted to yell at him to talk to me, to love me, but I felt like I could fall asleep at any moment.

"Why the fuck did you do that?" he asked, chest heaving. Tears streaked his dirty cheeks, but his hard expression didn't waver.

"I was protecting you," I said in slow motion.

"You were protecting your ego," he spat. Even through my fog, his words cut with perfect clarity.

"I did it for you. I didn't want them to see you." I thought to stand, but my body wouldn't move.

"You lost your temper. You could have been killed, Simón. There was no way you could've handled those guys." His voice frayed like he might disintegrate. "Don't act like you were protecting me. You forced me to fight, too."

My eye throbbed shut, ribs burning. I stared at my bloody hands resting open in my lap like they belonged to someone else. "Of course I lost my temper. They attacked us." These couldn't be my hands.

"You really scared me, Simón." Tears continued streaming down his cheeks. The scowl softened, but his eyebrows stayed tightly bunched, pulling his face into an uneasy cubist composition of angry terror.

"I would never hurt you," I said quickly, trying to stand

but falling back under the pain. I continued, gasping, "Please don't be scared of me."

"I didn't mean I'm scared of you. I was scared to lose you. And if I had stayed hidden while they—" He crouched and put his hand on mine. It was trembling. The contrast of his smooth skin over the blood covering mine unsettled me, so I looked to the ground.

He paused and wiped a tear from my cheek before letting out an exasperated chuckle. "I didn't know you could fight like that."

"I didn't either." I looked up as he cupped the side of my face that wasn't crusted with blood. The swollen, lopsided weight of my head creaked in my neck as I leaned into his warm palm.

"Are you okay? Should we go to the hospital?"

"I don't think I can handle the interrogation." I took a slow, cautious breath. "Just need a shower and some rest. I'll be fine. Promise."

Albi slid his hands under my arms. "Legs in 3, 2, 1 ..." He lifted as I pushed up on shaky legs, pain lancing through my side. The rock had torn a gash across my palm—the perfect place for a nail. I'd read somewhere that in real crucifixions, they drove the nails through the wrists, between ulna and radius, since hands alone would tear apart under the weight. Even battered and bleeding, my brain couldn't help fact-checking the Bible. Albi's hand moved to my back, supporting my weight.

"You look like shit," he said as we started walking.

"And you look like nothing happened."

"Why get these delicate hands dirty when I have you to fight my battles?" The words were meant as a joke, but I noticed the shadow that shame cast under them.

"Albi, I'll fight the whole world for you."

"Please don't." He draped my arm over his shoulder, and we hobbled back toward the apartment.

Three days passed without seeing Albi. He said he wasn't upset with me, but I think my mangled face made him uncomfortable. It never occurred to me that he could be struggling with our relationship itself or how carelessly we'd let our guard down, believing we could live like anyone else in this town. Swimming together, holding each other, pretending we belonged. Maybe he realized how wrong we are. Maybe he realized they were right about people like us after all. I needed to see him. I needed to know that we'd make it through this.

I called Camilo to borrow his car. It would take two hours to reach the next big town, with its different beaches and different people. We could be different people there, too— pretend like we're characters in a new story. After leaving Albi a note at the rectory, I waited for Camilo outside my apartment.

"What the hell happened to you?" Camilo shifted into park, hanging out his window with a mouth so wide a slight breeze might've blown him backward.

"Oh, I forgot I looked like this," I muttered, scratching the back of my head while looking at my dirty shoes.

"How could you forget? You can probably see most of your own face just standing there." He got out of the car and walked over to me, mouth still swinging open. His eyes quickly moved across the lumpy terrain of my face.

"Shut up. It's not that bad." I turned my face away so he'd stop examining me. "Looked worse a few days ago."

"Worse? *Primo* . . . It can't get much worse than this." He grabbed my chin and forced my face forward. He got close to my swollen eye and closed one of his as he inspected the carnage. "Fall down the stairs again?"

I swatted his hand away. "Got into a fight. It's nothing."

"With what? A gorilla?" His eyes moved from the gash above my eye to the bruises peeking out from my tank top.

"Three guys jumped me." I crossed my arms, wincing at my rib.

"For what?" The shock still hadn't left his face.

"Being a faggot."

"Are you serious? Did you hit on one of them or something?"

"Would that have made it okay?"

His shoulders buckled. "I didn't mean it like that. I'm sorry," he said quietly.

"Not as sorry as they are. I bashed one's head with a rock." I showed him my scabbed-over and bruised knuckles like some manly badge of honor. These hands I no longer recognized. The pride I felt suddenly disgusted me. He reached out to touch them, but I shoved them in my pockets and moved away from him. "Anyway, it really shook Albi up. I want to take him out of town for the day. Take our minds off everything. Pretend like it didn't happen."

"I got you, primo. You guys can use the car whenever. You know I'm okay with it, right?" he said, motioning at me and the empty air next to me. "I don't care about that stuff. Hell, I almost let Omar suck my dick once when we were drunk. Came to my senses, though." He snorted violently, sending snot into the back of his throat before launching the glob at the pavement right next to his foot. "When do we get to meet him?"

"No, you didn't. And never." I snatched the keys from his hand and shoved them into my pocket. "He already met Mamá, and you know how that went. I don't need him thinking even less of me after meeting the rest of my barnyard family."

"You sound like your mom," Camilo said. I made three quick signs of the cross, mumbling a mock prayer. He laughed. "She prays more since you left, if you can believe that. She's doing like three rosaries a day or some shit instead of two." He kept tossing an orange in the air, catching and launching it as he spoke. I snatched it mid-descent and started peeling, handing him half of the segments.

"Maybe that's her penance for acting like a psycho," I said around the fruit in my mouth.

"I think she doesn't have anyone to talk to. You know my mom and her don't get along. And she thinks Cari and I are animals, like you said." He picked the white veins from the orange slices and pinched them between his teeth. "Maybe stop by sometime, have coffee with her."

"I'm not taking advice from someone who almost spat on his own foot."

"She misses you, Simo." He tossed a piece of fruit into the air. "I do, too." He caught it in his mouth and gave a toothy grin, secreting juice.

"Shut up." I threw an orange peel at him. He caught it, bent it in half, and squeezed the oil onto his neck.

"Nature's cologne," he said before throwing it back at me and checking his eyebrows in the side mirror. "Have fun, Simón. I'd say don't do anything I would do, but that's a given. You'll be doing other stuff," he added, jerking his fist back and forth in front of his face.

I rolled my eyes and squeezed a piece of orange peel in front of my face, watching the plumes of essence shoot out from the dimpled surface.

"Take better care of yourself, loser," he called over his shoulder as he turned to walk home.

I pulled up to the rectory, and Albi was waiting outside. He looked smaller somehow. His shoulders were narrow, his feet too close together. The car stalled and backfired as I slowed to a stop, startling us both. I let out a small screech, and Albi laughed, eyeing the tin can of a car with obvious doubt. The old yellow Frankenstein machine drove smoothly enough, but its mismatched seats reeked of cigar smoke, the windows were stuck down, and the radio didn't work. Not that it mattered; the engine was so loud it would have drowned out any music anyway.

Albi slid into the passenger seat without saying hi or even glancing at me. There was an edge now where once there had been tender smoothness. A fault line where there had been perfection. Maybe he thought one of those men would recognize him, and word would get back to Father Cordero. I blinked hard a few times and moved it out of my mind.

"Thanks for coming with me. I figured we could both use a little break." I squeezed his knee. His leg gave the slightest twitch, but he didn't pull away.

"Yeah, should be nice," he said, staring out the window. His curly hair whipped in the wind pouring through the open frame.

"I'm really sorry about what happened," I said. My hands gripped the steering wheel, twisting around the leather until it creaked under the pressure. "I won't put you in danger like that again."

"Or yourself." His head didn't move.

"Or myself," I agreed.

Albi kept staring out the window as the buildings thinned around the car. My stomach tightened, tangled up in the fear that some irreparable rift had torn through us. I wanted to force him to look at me. I wanted to force myself onto him. Kiss him. Hold his face and spread his eyes open. But he wasn't in the mood to talk, and I didn't push it. I was just grateful he was there with me, silent or not.

We drove for nearly an hour before he finally turned toward me. He still didn't meet my gaze, but he drew in a breath as if to speak. Then he stopped himself. I waited, but he said nothing. Instead, he placed his hand on my thigh and slowly rubbed his thumb against the fabric of my shorts. My chest fluttered but I held myself steady. We were making progress.

"I'm sorry," he said softly, his voice so delicate it felt like it might break. "I'm sorry for being like this. I don't know how to get over it."

"Hey, it's okay. It'll get better. We'll get better." I placed my hand over his, still resting on my thigh. "The cuts and bruises will heal. I won't be this ugly forever. It'll all be a memory soon."

"Yeah, maybe," he murmured.

"This feels like a trip we could be taking for a honeymoon, right?" I said, trying to lighten the mood, pushing a happier thought into both of our brains. Albi pulled his hand away and turned back to the window.

We drove along the coast, away from our life, away from everything we needed to forget, if only for a day. The next town shimmered in the distance, a new development where a monastery once stood before the church deconsecrated it. The government leased the land to a foreign company, and a resort quickly replaced the holy grounds. The town around it sprang up overnight, its buildings cheap and uninspired. Many were too tall, leaning precariously over the beach, their haphazard placement blocking the ocean breeze that could have cooled the stifling air. I tried to explain this to fill the empty air, but Albi didn't respond to anything I said. We drove on and on, though it felt like we were stuck in place, a stationary car on a movie set, the same backdrop cycling endlessly behind us.

Finally, he spoke. "Do you really think we'd ever be allowed to get married?" His voice hummed low, his eyes fixed on the car floor. My stomach leaped into my throat.

"I don't know," I said, then paused, attempting to keep my tone steady. "I don't think it matters if they allow us to or not. We could do it our way. Our own version of it." The words came out too quickly, too eagerly. I wanted to give him space, but every thread he handed me I was trying to knit into a sweater. Or weave into the lace of a veil.

"I mean a real one," he said softly. "In the church. Something recognized by everyone as a real marriage."

"Anything is possible, I guess. But if I'm being honest, I don't think anyone will do much for people like us. And definitely not the church. We're the easiest ones for them to ignore. We already hide almost everything about our lives . . ." I hesitated, searching for the right words. "But we don't need anyone's approval to love each other, Albi."

"It would make life a lot easier," he said.

"Yeah. It would," I admitted. "But Cordero doesn't disapprove of us. You said it yourself."

"But he doesn't condone what we do either."

"You mean love each other?"

"You know what I mean," Albi said, and the conversation ended.

We pulled into town. The streets were empty, the shops closed, and on a weekday even the resort traffic was nonexistent. I had packed sandwiches and a thermos of coffee, and we parked at the pier, eating with our legs hanging over the water. It felt like we were the only two people alive in the world. Albi seemed to lighten up, and soon we were talking freely again about normal things. Nonviolent things. It felt like we were finding our way back to being us. We sat there and just talked. Eventually, we laughed a bit, and before long Albi was nudging my shoulder with his, playful again. He made jokes at my expense, and I retaliated by attacking his character. It was magical.

At the start of the trip, I had felt like I'd aged a hundred years in the last few days. But just then, as the sun set behind us, painting Albi's face in orange, pink, and gold, I felt like a teenager in love. I placed my pinky over his, gripping the wood of the pier with my other fingers to anchor us, to remind myself it was real. The breeze was soft, carrying the salt off the sea. The beach below was made of pebbles to steer visitors toward the resort's sandy shores at a premium. But I loved the stones. I loved the sound they made as the waves rolled over them, a percussive clatter as the water pushed and retreated. You could close your eyes and listen to the stones and the sea living and moving together. Albi hummed his usual improvisational tune, swaying slightly in place.

A child ran behind us suddenly, stomping down the planks and sending vibrations through our bodies. We clicked back into reality—birds squawking, children yelling, couples laughing, vendors shouting for attention, carnival games dinging and clanging. The clatter of the pebbles was now barely audible beneath the chaos. Where had it all come from? I lifted my head to look around, and Albi snatched his hand away from mine, bending forward with his elbows on knees. His shoulders bunched up to his ears, and his eyes zippered shut. My heart sank under the weight of how steep this uphill battle would be.

"Let's take a walk. I want to stretch my legs," I said, standing and offering him my hand. He ignored it, turning in the opposite direction as he stood. "You have some dirt on your butt," I said quietly near his ear, but his face twisted as if I'd shouted it to the entire pier.

"Be cool, Simón. There are kids around," he hissed.

"What are you even talking about? I wasn't going to wipe it for you. Heaven forbid these strangers—people we'll never see again—think I was admiring another man's ass. Maybe they'll even magically know I've fucked it!" I walked faster, my chest tightening as anger swelled. I wanted to escape it—the helplessness, the sour knot in my stomach whispering that the Albi I knew was gone.

"Please stop it. I can't do this with you right now," Albi said, moving in front of me. He walked backward, trying to catch my eye as I stared past him.

"I'm fine. Are you?" The words came out sharp, hostile, though I'd meant them to sound casual. I knew I needed to try harder, to push past my own frustration and meet him where he was. But I couldn't seem to control myself. Desperation gripped me, dragging me upward by the scalp while my legs scrambled for footing. It felt like the clammy haze of a fever or the salivation just before vomiting.

"Yeah. All good," he said, his tone indifferent, exactly how I'd wanted to sound. The words stung, echoing with the deep, destructive *clung* of a steel beam dropped at a work site.

"I think I need a drink. I'm gonna grab a bottle. Or should I get two so our lips won't touch the same rim?"

"I'll have whatever you're having," he said, rolling his eyes and waving me off as he sank onto a bench.

"Oh right, the booze will kill the cooties," I added, trying to sound playful. I even winked, feeling more confident in my tone. As I headed toward one of the stores lining the boardwalk, I became hyper-aware of my body and how I walked. The motion of my hips, the swing of my arms. I put my shoulders down and back and frowned. I imagined my legs moving without any motion in my butt. Stuck my chest out. Stiff strides. This grotesque, contorted idea of how a "normal" man walks, like a caricature of a bipedal bulldog.

I tried to be quick in the store. I didn't want to leave Albi alone for too long. Visions of him darting away or finding some woman to flirt with flipped through my mind the second he was out of sight. I grabbed a random bottle of whiskey and set it on the counter. As I counted my change, I asked the clerk if there were any other bottles under five dollars. Without looking at me, she reached behind the counter and handed me a bottle of wine. Whiskey and red wine. Most certainly a recipe for indigestion. The whiskey label looked like it belonged on a bottle of cough syrup, and the wine didn't have a label at all. I slapped the money on the counter and practically skipped out of the store, dashing back onto the street.

He was still there. On the same bench. Arms folded across his chest, watching people pass, a resting scowl etched into his angular face. When he saw me, the stone cracked—a brief smile breaking through.

"I did get two bottles, but only because I panicked and wanted to get back quickly," I said, bounding up to him.

"Think I was gonna leave?" He chuckled halfheartedly, reaching for the wine.

"Wine before liquor, never sicker," I said, handing him the whiskey instead.

He tapped the side of his head with a finger. "Smart," he said, before taking a big swig. He winced, his eyes watering as he examined the label. "Is this paint thinner or booze? Jesus Christ."

I grabbed the bottle and took a gulp, holding my breath. Smacking my lips, I sat next to him, leaving a deliberate space between us. "My dad used to make me taste his rum when I was a kid. I think it killed the nerves in my mouth. This tastes like water to me."

"He was a piece of work, huh? Your father?"

"Yeah, he's a huge piece of shit," I said, taking another mouthful of whiskey and holding it under my tongue before swallowing. "The day he left my mom found out he had knocked up my Tía Cachita. She kicked him out, and we haven't seen him since."

"Wait . . . so are Camilo and his sister—?" Albi held out his hand for the bottle. I passed it to him and watched as he drank. His Adam's apple bobbed up and down. The sun had set, but the warm light still lingered, glowing against his cheekbones.

"They were already born by then. But there were rumors about them, too. She miscarried the second pregnancy and accused my mom of cursing her."

"And they still live together? Your mom is something else. The things she will and won't put up with—" He kept staring straight ahead, but I stole as many glances as I could, blinking quickly to capture each one.

"They hate each other, but they're family."

"Hmm." He didn't say more, but I understood everything he meant with that simple grunt.

"Certain things are easier to ignore than others. And certain things are easier to confront, too, I guess." I wanted to cry but masked it with another swig. As the sips kept building, everything felt easier. Or at least less important.

The shadows stretched to their full length and blurred into one another until the street lamps cast softer, amorphous shapes across this little world. Albi didn't say anything more. He leaned back against the bench, stretching his arms across its length. The booze had settled into him, too, and for the first time all evening I felt like I could take a full breath. The crowd had dispersed, off to dinner or the casino. The pier shut down, and we sat watching it all fade, like the final scene of a play. I leaned forward, elbows on my knees, but when I sat back to rest against the bench, my shoulder grazed his hand. I shifted forward again to avoid touching him, but he pulled me back by the shoulder and returned his arm to the bench. His hand rested lightly on me, and I hated how much it affected me. It felt cruel that all the frustrations and pain he'd caused throughout the day could vanish with one small gesture. His thumb rubbed the curve of my shoulder, then moved to the base of my neck. The heat of his hand soaked into my skin. He started humming again, and we sat staring out at the water, listening to the quiet rhythm of the stones rolling under the waves.

The whiskey was gone, and we passed the label-less wine between us, talking into the night. The sandwiches were long gone, but it didn't matter. We talked about everything and nothing. He laughed, and it sounded like heaven. When I made an inappropriate joke, he shoved me, grinning. We were okay, then. Even if we hadn't been before and wouldn't be again, we were us again. Not the us we were at El Palomar or the us we were in our version of home. There was still a darkness behind his eyes, a shadow that had haunted me these last few days. But he was trying. I could tell he was trying even harder than I was.

I can't remember if it was my idea or his to go under the pier, but somehow we ended up there, beneath the planks as if by teleportation. We were kissing, his body a wet, burning heat against mine. He kissed me like he wanted to condense a year's worth of passion into a single moment, like he was trying to press time itself into something smaller.

I pulled back to look at him. He smiled, then kissed me again, softer this time.

"Should we start heading back?" he asked, not moving.

I didn't want to leave. Every inch of me ached to stay. I pulled him close, hugging him tightly in the shadows of the wooden beams above. The rocks beneath our feet shifted constantly, forcing us to fight for balance.

The night was balmy. Stars glittered across the surface of the water a few feet away. His head rested in the crook of my neck as I watched the town's lights blur into the starlight, everything shimmering together in the rippling surface.

Could there be another universe, some other plane of existence, where we were the normal ones? A mirror world where we were the ones who turned up our noses. The world above us was one version of reality. But here, beneath the foot-worn, salt-softened planks, was another. And in the water's reflection, yet another still: a submerged city, identical but reversed, the sea flowing through it like air. We could be different there.

Our bodies pressed together. Albi was still humming, and we swayed slightly. I became giddily aware of his crotch hard against mine. I hadn't thought he'd gone completely cold on me, but I assumed that part of him might stay dormant, at least for now. I swiveled my hips, and our erections slid across each other. He kissed my neck. I rubbed against him again. Another kiss.

Then, at the same instant, we both felt it, the unmistakable sensation of being watched. The awareness hit first, a prickle at the edge of consciousness, followed by the sound of smooth stones shifting in a sudden clatter. A foot turning? A body darting? Our heads whipped toward the noise, but we saw nothing. For five frantic seconds we darted glances into the dark, holding our breath.

I froze, listening for any other movements. My eyes stayed glued to the small rocks. To be a stone. To lose yourself in a pile of stones exactly like you. "Maybe it was a cat. Or a rat or something," I whispered.

"Could've been." Albi cursed under his breath. His forearms coiled, muscles rippling as his fists clenched tight. "Shit." He let out a low grunt of frustration and palmed the side of his head.

"Hey, it's fine. It was probably nothing. Could've even been some guy cruising."

"Simón. Don't." He raised a hand to silence me, and I wanted to slap it down. We both stood still, listening.

"We don't know anyone here. Even if it was a person, what does it matter?" My voice was sharp, every syllable abruptly curving. I was angry not at Albi but at the situation itself. The constant specter of guilt, the shame we could never outrun, the fear after what happened the other night.

Albi stood rigid, his shoulders tight, his posture crooked and defensive. His wide, fearful eyes made him unrecognizable. This couldn't be the same man who found me on the dance floor, the one who swung me around at the beach. The man whose smile told me he loved me without words. This wasn't him. This was someone broken. A scared and troubled boy. "Let's get out of here," he said finally. "We can't run, so let's act like we're walking along the beach. Be casual. Look around, but subtly."

"What are we going to do? Kill the witness?" I said, voice choppy with irritation. "It's fine, Albi." I stepped out from under the pier and bent to pick up a stone. I took off my shoes and waded into the water, tossing the stone and grabbing another just like it. The cold water lapped at my legs while my face burned hot. I splashed water on my face and ran my fingers through my hair.

Albi emerged a moment later, picking up a stone like an understudy mimicking his lead. He slipped off his shoes and turned toward the town. "The buildings here are kinda cool, huh," he said, a little too loudly. His eyes swept over the boardwalk before he tossed the stone and bent to grab another. He froze mid-motion, then straightened and came into the water beside me. His voice dropped to a hiss. "Simón, there's a man up there."

"That doesn't mean he saw us. It's okay. Nothing's going to happen. Let's move down the beach." I spoke as if I were convincing a child there were no monsters in the closet. "He isn't going to say anything. It's okay."

Albi's shoulders stayed taut. "He looks like one of my parishioners, Simón." He turned slowly, pretending to grab another stone. "I think he is. Shit."

"Albi, all old men look the same. Why would one of your parishioners be in this town, lurking around at this hour? Even if he is, you can teach him how sinful eavesdropping is. For all we know he followed us down here to get some himself." I reached to rub his shoulder, and he flinched away. I froze, then took another step forward, and Albi shoved me back.

There was a long, suffocating silence, like a time-lapse of webs being spun between us. His eyes were on fire, crazed almost. Mine were hollow. I felt my mouth open and close. Then, as suddenly as the anger flared, his glare softened. His eyes looked larger, though more distant, more closed off. "I . . . I'm sorry," he said, his voice trembling. "I can't keep doing this, Simón. It's . . . it doesn't feel right." He stepped back, his body coiling inward. "I need space. It's too much. The way you love—it's too much. I feel like I can't breathe sometimes."

I stood there, dumbstruck. Bile bubbled in my gut as the words tore through me. My punctured heart spilled out, bleeding over my other organs. "Where is this coming from? How am I too much?" My voice cracked with disbelief. The stress of the week, the pressure I'd put on this trip, the weight of his paranoia—it all crushed down on me at once. I felt betrayed. I'm "too much." All I'd ever wanted was to be enough.

My rage betrayed my heartbreak, my love twisted into a weapon meant to harm him. "I should've known this was going to happen with you." The first lance. My voice was a sneer. "Why would you know how to be loved? What do you know about love at all? No one has ever loved you before me," I screamed at him.

I realized we were still out in the open, and I dropped my voice to a hiss—not out of shame, but to shield us from further exposure. "Not the real you. And no one ever will. You'd rather bend to these assholes than be true to yourself. To me." I clawed at my hair. "You gotta know what's what, Albi. Fuck. I'm tired of tiptoeing around you. This is crazy." I didn't mean any of it, but I said it anyway. "I don't need you, you know. I don't need any of this bullshit."

"I can't believe you're trying to turn this around right now," he snapped.

"I'm the one who got my ribs cracked and my face beaten in! To protect you!"

"I told you I didn't like doing that stuff in public and look where it got me. I could lose my job, Simón! Don't you get that? The Church won't have a known faggot consecrating the body of the Lord. It's blasphemous." The vein in his throat pulsed.

"I didn't make you do anything you didn't want to do. And by the way, you've always been a faggot, Albi. If it's blasphemous now, what was it before?"

He slapped me across the mouth, sharp and sudden. No anger rose in me. Instead, a cold sense of loss and disappointment plunged in, carving my insides out. Even the most beautiful creature will lash out to protect itself when backed into a corner. We are animals after all.

Albi gnawed the inside of his cheek. "You're a selfish bitch, you know that?" His voice trembled, tears pooling in the corners of his eyes. The thick lines of his brows half-obscured them, forming a tense junction with the bridge of his nose. "I'll be out on the street. I don't have an education like you. Or any other skills. All I have is *you*." This last sentence he said with a serrated edge, and I felt the jagged edges catching on my ribs as the blade slid in.

"You love to say you're alone, that we only have each other, but it's not true. You have a whole family right there." He pointed down the coastline toward the faint glow of our city. "You pretend they're dead because you're a fucking coward. You can't bear to face them as you are. You can't bear to face your mother as this." His strong hands motioned up and down at me. "My mother is dead, Simón. I have no one besides you and the Church. If you leave, where does that leave me? It's been my only home. You're too selfish to see it. It's too much.

I can't do this anymore."

The only sound apart from my heart pounding in my ears was the clatter of stones under the tide. My hands clenched into fists, gripping my hair and tugging hard at my scalp. I was grasping uselessly for something to hold on to, the end of a rope dangling over a cliff.

"What do you mean, you can't do this anymore?" My voice faltered as I struggled for air. "So, you want me to be less? To love you less? It'll always seem like we're going too far to people who are going nowhere. You think you'll be fine— better even—without me. That you can just go back to the Church. Chant the fucking chants, light the fucking candles. Oil the pews. Iron the robes. Bow and kneel, stand and bow, kneel and fucking kneel again. That's no life, Albi. I'm trying to live mine. I'm trying to live it with you."

My voice lost all of its power, and it could barely eke out a whisper. "You're the only one that matters to me. What you say. What you do. What you think of me." The heat drained from my body, and I began to shiver, my bones clattering against each other. "If you think I'm too much . . . that the way I love is too much . . . I don't know what to say to you. I promised you my all, and that's what I'll always give." I realized I was holding my breath, but I couldn't make myself exhale.

After what could have been five seconds or five years, Albi finally spoke. "Your love isn't too much. It's . . . I'm not always equipped to handle it all. You're right. I haven't had someone in my life who loves me like you do. Who knows me inside and out and still loves me." He paused, putting his face in his hands. "When I was hiding in the trees, and you were facing those guys, I felt like I could disappear. I wasn't a man. I wasn't anyone. And you're right. I really am going nowhere. Simón, you still have choices, paths that could change your life, take you to places you've never seen. All I have is the Church. That's all I know. Everything I'll ever do is already decided. I'll probably take over this parish one day, and . . ."

"And be a lonely old bastard like Father Cordero because you threw the only good thing in your life away," I interrupted. "I don't know if I'll go anywhere in particular. I don't care where we go as long as we go together. We'll be happy together, Albi, while everyone else stays stuck where they've always been. We'll walk off into the sunset or whatever fairytale ending you want for us. Just don't push me away. If you do, you might as well shove me off a bridge."

I glanced around to make sure we were alone. The man was gone. I stepped forward and wrapped him in the strongest hug I could muster, despite the exhaustion from everything we'd been through. "It seems to me, when you feel lost and like there's nowhere to turn . . . you close your eyes, spin around, and whatever direction you land on, that's where you'll go." I gripped his shoulders and gave him a reassuring nod. The moment for rage had passed.

He raised his arms, forming a cross, and I pressed my hands to his ribs, spinning him slowly. "Tell me when to stop," he said. I let him turn, picking up speed, until he stumbled slightly.

"Stop in . . . three . . . two . . ." I paused, letting him spin longer.

"You bitch!" Albi laughed, wobbling as he spun himself faster.

"One! Stop!"

Albi came to an abrupt halt, unstable and giggling, facing directly at me. "Guess I know where I'm going now," he said with a hard blink and a nervous grin. He lifted his hand up to take mine and stumbled forward, careening headfirst into my chest. He laughed for a second before bursting into tears. I said nothing. I couldn't. I just held his sobbing head, running my fingers through his curls, sliding them against my palms. His skin grew hot as his breathing staggered and broke. I wrapped one arm around his back. The other roped across his shoulders and neck, anchoring him against me. And I held him.

But the fight didn't end this way. Albi walked away after slapping me. After saying it wasn't right. That I was too much. He walked back to the car and left me standing in the water. He drove away. I know that now. The textures of that other version, the happy one, were only suspended in the growing space between us, like the reflections of the lights in that submerged city, blurring and scattering as I waded through the waves.

I stood there, knee-deep in the water, frozen, shivering as the wind picked up and the waves grew choppier. The water seemed to expand around me—lapping at my knees, then my thighs, rising to my chest, slapping against my head. Some unseen current wrapped its hands around my ankles, and I let it pull me under. My body tumbled and rolled along the ocean floor. I let the fish laugh at me. The crustaceans and sea slugs, too. I'm a bottom-feeder now. I'm the shit you all can eat and shit out again. The waves kept throwing me against smooth stones, my face colliding, teeth clacking in a concussive percussive rattle. Stoned to death in the town center until the sea spat me back onto the shore. I rolled until I remembered I could stand.

Foamy globs rested at the surface as I hacked and spat to clear my lungs. Some converged, but most stayed separate, floating motionless. I hated the way they looked, hated myself for putting them there.

The sound of a car pulling up to the pier swung behind my left ear and then my right.

A door opened but didn't close.

I spat again.

A hand gripped my right shoulder and spun me around.

A voice that sounded like Albi's, but colder, drawled, "C'mon, Simón. Let's get you home."

He waded through the spit, and I wanted to cry. I spat again. It landed on his stomach, and he grabbed my arm to pull me from the water. A hollow tinning rang in my ears as I heard myself tell him that he wasn't what I thought, and that I didn't need him. That the world would keep spinning without us.

Then I was in the passenger seat, aware of the car hurtling forward along the coast. The car was drenched in saltwater. Puddles swelled at our feet. I wanted to turn and look at the man next to me, but I didn't. I wanted to say something, but I couldn't. The confusion in my head twisted into a sharp, all-consuming pain that thumped through my body. It bored down through my guts like nitric acid, dissolving flesh and fatty tissue, pooling with the water on the floor, leaving no trace. All I could see was myself sitting passenger, head and shoulders slumped, body tumbling forward through space.

Albi unraveled, snagged on that moment at the beach. His face seemed alien to me. The map I'd drawn of him was a fairytale land. Our kingdom, built on nothing at all. He sat tall, his posture calm. His white-knuckled grip on the steering wheel. The restless dart of his eyes. My mythological demigod. The shrine I'd built for him. The offerings. The prayers. At that moment he didn't seem as holy to me as he had two hours before, or would again a few hours later.

The wind sliced through the car as it sped toward our town. Albi drove too fast. Desperation clung to the interior, thick and suffocating, like the cigar smoke staining everything yellow.

Yellow like the piss in the water bottle. He'd said he would stop for me. He yelled over the wind, but I ignored him. I threw the bottle out the window, the car swirling with the smells of the sea and my piss, hurtling back to the life we'd left behind.

All I wanted in that moment was to go back. To undo the day, to rewind the week, to stop it all before it could break apart.

When we pulled up to my building, Albi got out first and walked around to open my door. I stepped out and stood there, still silent. I held out my hand for the keys to my cousin's car.

"I'll take it back to Camilo. Don't worry," he said, his voice flat and mechanical, like a robot pretending to be Albi. "You're still too drunk to drive, and I know you promised him it would be back tonight."

I still couldn't bring my eyes to look at him. He stood in front of me for a moment before jerking me into a tight embrace. Too tight. The hug screamed both "I'm sorry" and "I love you" at once, like it was begging to be enough. We stayed locked in that crushing place for what felt like forever, though now I know it wasn't long enough. When he released me, the hollow look in his eyes had deepened, and I felt like I could never have known this man at all.

I stood outside after he drove away, unmoving. I tried to catch his scent lingering in the air, but there was nothing. I listened for the sound of the car circling back, but it never came. Eventually, I slunk into my apartment building, climbed the stairs, and collapsed into bed in my still-soggy clothes. I couldn't make sense of what he'd said earlier, the things that couldn't be unsaid, or of where we could possibly go from there.

Chapter Nine
Flowers on the Dashboard

The percussive clatter of the stones echoes across the shore behind me as the water thrums its retreat to the horizon ahead. Back to where it came from. Where it all began.

The small waves tumble. A brief moment of silence expands. The clatter returns, rumbling along the shoreline.

The earth is breathing. The sea is breathing. I am breathing.

"Wake up, Simón." Lenita's voice reaches me, muffled and distant. My head, cradled. Her soft hand. The rocking of our bodies.

The memory still bubbles in my gut like a sea foam made of whiskey and table wine. Acidic regurgitation burning my throat. I bought the wine with my last five dollars because Albi and I wanted to be so drunk the night would be drowned out of our minds.

Trauma demands rationalization: a thing happens to someone. One plus one. The answer is obvious. It's simple math. A new person emerges; they've been changed.

But when you add one person to another person, the answer becomes something else entirely. You must consider the space between them. The versions of themselves they each carry. Maybe one is losing weight. Maybe the other toggles between a professional voice and a casual one. A third entity forms, fluid and shape-shifting. It has its own distinct needs, its own evolving expectations.

The equation crumbles. What once felt like a simple problem opens into an infinite array of possibilities.

One person plus one person equals infinity.

I told him I didn't need him. That I didn't need us.

I've never hated myself more than when I revisit that lie, that car with its wet seats, that underwater city we left behind. All of it stretching toward infinity.

Lenita calls to me again, but I need to know how the rest plays out. I need to remember the rest, so I will know what to do.

The sensation comes suddenly. Gripping my legs. Wrenching around ankles and hips. Flinging my body flat against the surface like a fishing net. The water curves around every inch of me, holding me in false protection. It should cushion the collision, but instead it slips away, just in time, and my body slams against the bottom. Slamming. Slinking. Skipping me to that upside-down city underwater, where everything could be different.

I fall forward and backward as waves roll me along the ocean floor. My head softly bangs against sand and stone. One side, then the other until I am back in my room, before everything changed irrevocably.

The morning after our fight, I rolled out of bed onto the floor and stared up at the ceiling. My eyes drifted to the window with its mosaic of tiny pieces of colored paper. I wanted to get up and tear it all down. I wanted to shatter the glass.

My head gripped my swollen brain like a fist, and the throbbing in my temples reverberated sharply in my ears. I'd been very drunk, but I remembered everything. I remembered the look in Albi's eyes, how it twisted and distorted so many times in the same conversation. Albi's hands were Albi's hands in my world. But maybe my hands weren't hands at all in his. My hands had reached for his, and then his hands shoved them away. They could have been dogs to shoo, or crumbs to sweep. A fly buzzing.

How could hope shift into terror so quickly? How could terror knot itself into hostility? And how could that hostility aim so easily at me?

I looked at my upside-down sketches taped to the upside-down wall. Had I been seeing the world wrong this whole time? Maybe everything was right-side-up, and I was the one living with the blood rushing to my feet instead of my head. Maybe I was still drunk. I clenched my fists and tried to scream silently. I tried holding my breath until the pressure inside me grew unbearable. All I wanted was to be sure again. To know. I wanted to think of Albi and know that he was thinking of me and that those thoughts were beautiful.

I sat up and looked at the window again. We stood on chairs. We stood on books on chairs. We spat on the window, on our hands, and smeared the spit around before wetting the little pieces of paper. But then we stepped back, and it was all so beautiful. Even if it was difficult or gross at times, the result was breathtaking, and we'd made it together.

The thought clicked, and I jumped up, slipping on my canvas shoes. My clothes resisted the motion, stiff with yesterday's sweat, salt, and shame. These were the clothes he yelled at me in. A shower. Clean clothes. I needed both if I was going to face this. I felt ready to run to him, to tell him

I'd be better. That I wouldn't be so selfish. I'd be everything he needed and nothing more.

Before I knew it, I was tearing through Albi's garden, but he wasn't there. I could've knocked over an old woman or pushed a child out of my way—I had no recollection. I was just running. The jingle of keys caught my attention. The priest was unlocking the door to the church on the other side of the stone wall.

"Hey! Can you tell me where Albi is?" My feet still slapped against the ground as my mouth slapped the words down next to them.

"Hello, Simón. I'm doing just fine. Thank you. And you?" Father Cordero shook his head and clicked his tongue, never once looking at me. His tone was clipped, dismissive like it usually was when we spoke. He'd seen me with Albi countless times but had never voiced any suspicions. He disapproved only when my presence interfered with Albi's work. And since Albi never let that happen, the priest likely saw me as irrelevant. Only some trial for Albi on his path to follow in Christ's footsteps.

"I'm sorry," I said, panting. "I'm doing well. Thanks. Have you seen Albi?" My chest burned, and sweat trickled from under my arms and down my back in slow, irritating streams.

The priest gave me a once-over. "I haven't seen him since yesterday. He might be running errands. But Simón," he said, his tone hardening, "he has no time for whatever exercise you're occupying yourself with right now." He waved vaguely at my heaving, sweat-soaked torso before turning away, signaling the end of the conversation. "Come back later when his workday is done." He made the sign of the cross, kissed his hand quickly—a period at the end of his sentence—and walked back into the rectory.

I decided to check the town. Maybe he was taking robes

to be mended or picking up groceries. The hot pavement crumbled under my feet as I ran. At an intersection, I stopped, glancing around like a character in a cheesy romantic movie, frantic and out of place. A woman swept her stoop with slow, deliberate strokes. A boy counted coins in his palm, eyeing a row of coconut nougat. Across the street, I spotted Lenita haggling with a street vendor, her hands swinging wildly as she argued prices.

"Lenita!" I yelled, darting into traffic. I weaved between two bicyclists and a slow-moving fruit truck, earning a few shouted curses as I scrambled onto the opposite sidewalk.

"You could've been killed! What's wrong with you?!" She smacked my chest as I stumbled forward.

"Have you seen Albi?" I asked, panting and clutching my side. Pain flared under my bruised ribs and in my seizing diaphragm. "He wasn't at the rectory."

"No." Her brows knitted together as she squinted at me. "Was Father Cordero there?" The vendor, sensing the argument was over, whistled cheerfully and turned to rearrange his melons. "Why are you breathing like that? What's going on?" She tugged me away from the busy street, but her eyes kept flicking back to the fruit, already calculating her next counter-offer.

"He didn't know where he'd gone. I need to find him. I need to apologize for being a self-centered prick," I said between gasps, straightening up and pressing my hands into the small of my back.

"Wow," Lenita said, crossing her arms. "Never thought I'd see the day. Start with me."

"What? Why you?" I blinked at her, confused. Had I missed something important? Forgotten her birthday? . . . Twenty-fifth of August . . . No, that wasn't it. My baffled expression made her burst out laughing.

"I'm joking." She slapped my butt lightly, grabbing my arm as she turned to walk. "Want me to tag along? I was about to scam some extra eggs with this fake ration card. Looks real, doesn't it?" She flipped the card in her hand, but I wasn't paying attention. The world continued its maddening routine around us. Two ladies walked by gossiping, a dog tied up and barking, children out-screaming each other.

"This is important, Leni!" I yelled, regretting it as the screech echoed between us. "Sorry. I really need to talk to him. I'm not even sure he wants to see me. It's best if I'm alone." Before she could respond, I grabbed her shoulders, pressed a quick kiss to her cheek, and let go as abruptly. "I'll come see you later!" I shouted, already turning away.

"Simón. Simón!" Her voice sounds too close. Flat and buzzing, like someone speaking through a kazoo. I try to spin around to look at her again, but my vision is completely black. Music rumbles up from El Palomar below.

"Simón, please." Her voice is grave and pressing. A hand presses against my face. "You gotta wake up. We gotta get you home."

Home.

I was home when I closed the door and turned to set the flowers on the table.

A mess of flowers and a crumpled note.

Lenita's arm wrapped around me, but I felt like I was alone. I was at home and alone.

The letter had my name scrawled on it, off-centered, urgent.

My keys hit the table. My wallet followed. It hit me, and suddenly it all felt real.

I remembered him running up to me on the street. I had just turned away from Lenita.

"Simón," he yelled, and my eyes finally focused.

"It's Albi—" Camilo hesitated.

"I found him." His voice wavered, face ashen beneath the midmorning sun. "The police tracked the car to me. He didn't have identification on him." Camilo's eyes lowered, words faltered. "They didn't know who he was, and—"

A distant numbness. The clatter of the stones on the shore. The rhythmic wind moving the palms. Everything blurring into white noise. Jagged edges.

Hours before—just hours, really—Albi had pulled me from the water. He drove me home. Just hours ago.

Camilo stepped closer, hesitant. "They're headed to Father Cordero now. The police. I thought—I thought maybe you should know first."

Lenita grabbed me. "Simón. Look at me. Please." Her words felt far away, muffled underwater. She was shaking. The world was shaking.

My eyes flickered open, then closed again. I didn't remind myself to breathe.

Camilo shuffled toward me. "He'd picked flowers. He wrote something for you. I—I found it on the dashboard. Everything was scattered around him, petals—uh—I thought—" He swallowed hard. "I thought you might still want them, so I gathered up what I could."

The note trembled in Camilo's hand as he held it out to me.

Petals drifted to our feet.

My hands moved on their own. They clutched the note tightly.

The mess of flowers. The infinite equations of love and loss splintering my mind into fragments too scattered to ever reassemble.

"I should've—" I started, but the thought died in my throat. Should've what? Stopped him? Held him longer? Been less selfish? I'd said things I couldn't unsay. He'd walked away. He drove away. The sound of him growing smaller until the silence. And I stayed behind, staring, waiting for him to come back to me. Like he needed to make that move.

Lenita tried to sound solid between sobs. She tried to hold me steady with trembling limbs. "Let's go home, Simón."

Home.

I was at home, and I unfolded the letter. My eyes moved over dizzying letters that formed words my brain refused, like a body rejecting a transplanted organ.

"Where you are is where I thought I needed to be . . ." I sounded each word out slowly. "I can't be this anymore . . ." Each line refused to connect with the following. ". . . kills me to see you hurting . . ." The trembling lines, the dark ink. The uneven spacing. The paper held the pressure from his hand, tremors I could feel through my fingers. My own tears joined his, making watercolor blooms of the ink.

"I can't do this anymore, Simón."

This letter was mine. I hit the floor that was mine.

And I thought then that I would never love a man as much as I loved you. You were mine too. I was sure I should hate you. I hated you so much it hurt. My face, my ribs, my broken body pressing against itself.

I was screaming, but I couldn't tell if I was screaming, and that pain burned away as the letter hit me again, kicked me on the floor, and it flowed.

The letter became you. And you hit me again, Albi.

You hit me, and I was real. Even if real was the last thing I wanted to be.

You hit me, and for that brief moment I was so much more than I'd ever been before. I was you. You were still here. You were hitting me, but at least you're here.

Albi was kicking himself in the gut as I watched him from inside both sets of eyes.

I was that foot flying into that body.

I was the air in your lungs.

I was the blood swelling your face.

I was inside of us.

I imagined our life together. Instead of seeing the past versions, I see a future that I know can never happen. I'm in our house. Our home. I'm cooking. You're cleaning. The radio crackles between stations before settling on our song. And it's just the two of us. I hear your sandals clap against the floor as you move around the bed, folding the laundry. There's saffron in the air. There's garlic sizzling. I look for the spatula you always put away wrong while you fold your clothes and place them on my side of the bed. You fold my clothes and place them on your side. Our coffee cups from earlier that morning leave rings on the windowsill, little halos I'll never clean away.

I stayed on the floor pretending my ears didn't work, that my head wasn't pounding. I tried to become an object. Inanimate. Abiotic. I tried melting into the floor, becoming the room that once held us. I wanted to be walked on. I wanted to be a crack in the wood to collect your dust.

The blows stopped, and you were beside me, your voice

breaking into the quiet as you read the rest of the letter aloud.

"I love you, Simón. More than I love myself.

If you're too much, I know I'll never be enough.

I'm not strong enough to be what you deserve.

I want to be, but I'm not. And I'm not brave enough to change any of it.

I promise I tried.

You're going to make me so proud. I know it.

Please don't be disappointed in me."

The hand strokes my cheek as my eyes slowly open. Lenita's face hovers inches above mine. I'm sprawled across her lap, still outside El Palomar. She kisses my forehead, dropping tears on it as she lifts her head away from mine. My face throbs. I remember her telling me about the baby. I remember careening into the wall.

"There you are," she whispers. Her thumb wipes the tears across my forehead like ashes. "You okay?" She moves her hand gently over my hair as she talks. She's going to be a great mother.

I roll onto my side, turning away from her, though my body remains draped across hers. I cover my face with my hands. Words push against the walls of my throat, but it feels like speaking to them will dissolve me. My chest heaves, lungs failing to pull in air. "I killed him, Lenita," I say slowly, the syllables forcing their way out. "Albi is dead because of me. What is wrong with me?" Hot tears stream down my face, dripping onto her legs.

"That isn't true." Her voice is steady, grounding. "You feel guilty. I get it. It's easy to feel guilty about things we can't control. But Albi couldn't control any of this either. It was an accident."

"He left me, Leni." My chest seizes. "The note. He was going to leave me," I say through an uneasy exhale. "He did."

"Simo. I had no idea."

Lenita sits speechless for a second, but her hand never leaves my hair. "Sometimes love is quick and dirty. Sometimes it sticks." She pauses again.

"But what you had with Albi wasn't just love. It was destiny. You changed each other. You blended together in a way that doesn't happen to normal people. That man knew exactly how to bend the world around you to make sure you were okay, and you opened up his world and made it so much bigger and brighter. Whenever I saw him, I knew if I followed his eyes, they would land on you.

"I don't know how he felt when he wrote that letter, but don't let it turn all those beautiful memories to shit. That's not fair to either of you. We all say shit we regret. We all do shit we regret," she continues, her tone softening but still firm. "But I promise you it wasn't because of something you did or didn't do. There is nothing wrong with you. And there's no one to blame. Not even Albi."

"Don't give me that 'nothing's wrong with you' bullshit. Of course, there is. Everything's wrong. He left me, Leni. I'm so embarrassed. And I'm so angry. I'm lonely. I'm depressed. I drink too much. I eat garbage. I slept for nearly three months straight, Lenita. There is something really wrong with me. Inside of me."

She exhales sharply. "Okay, fine. I won't sugarcoat it. There is a lot wrong, but some of that's on you to deal with." She shifts slightly, her hand steady on my shoulder. "You've gotta decide to face the shit you can change. And yeah, it's gonna suck. It's gonna feel like pulling your own teeth out, but at least it's on you. The rest of it will figure itself out in time."

"I don't understand." I feel like a disembodied voice. I could've left my body behind at the beach this morning. "We did everything together. We talked about everything we were gonna do." I could be a ghost trying to comprehend his own death.

"You weren't with each other every second of the day, Simón. I know he was happy when he was with you. There's no question about that. But those other seconds, the dark and heavy ones. They add up. And sometimes all that bad shit poisons the good." She stops and considers what she has said. "It takes more muscles to frown than it does to smile, right? Imagine how bad shit must have felt for him to choose that path without you rather than smiling." Her hand continues stroking my hair, and we sit in silence.

"I want to go home," I whisper finally, pushing myself up from her lap. A piece of asphalt stays embedded in my palm, and I leave it there.

"How about I stay with you tonight," she offers from the ground, taking the hand I extend to her. She stands and gently pries the stone from my hand and looks up into my eyes. I look back, but I feel disconnected. Like I changed yet again. Like this Simón doesn't know her at all.

She squeezes my hand tighter, and I reflexively pull her into a hug. I know it's what she wants me to do, what she expects me to do. My eyes could close, and my arms could squeeze her a little tighter. They do. She needs to believe everything is okay. I don't know if it is. But sometimes, we do things for the people we care about, even if the meaning is lost on us.

"Thank you, but I'm fine. I promise." A lie. Sometimes, we lie to them too. "Walk me part of the way home. You'll see. I'll be fine."

Her hand still rests in mine, and she tugs me a bit to start walking. I'm a beast of burden—labored steps, heavy blinks, detached rhythmless breaths. She holds my hand as we walk, and I resist the urge to pull away. Walking hand in hand with someone in the street feels strange, like something out of science fiction. Like teleportation or time travel. It's funny how easy it actually is. It's merely a hand holding onto another hand. I chuckle softly, ready to say something about it, but the pain in my face flares.

"You okay?" She nudges her elbow into mine.

"My face hurts," I say quietly.

"You're a mess." She laughs, and I force air out of my nostrils in a laugh-like response.

"This is nice. Just you and me." I hold our intertwined fingers up between our heads. "Too bad I couldn't be straight." Our hands flop back down between us.

"Ha! Who said I'd even wanna date you?" Her laugh cuts through the air, sharp but warm.

"It would've been easier, though, huh? If I were normal?" I'm swaying slightly, and grateful I have her there to steady me.

"Simón, look at your hips when you walk. It wouldn't be that easy for you."

"Do I have you forever, Leni?" I say this, but it feels like something transmitted through the air by radio or telepathy. I knew I would say something like this, but I am not sure I am the one who said it.

"Forever. And you have this one too . . ." Her free hand goes to her belly and does two circles around it. She's still so skinny it's hard to believe she is far enough along to know.

"What will your family say?" I ask, diverting the conversation from my role in this new life budding inside her.

She rolls her eyes. "Mami will cry for exactly three minutes before starting a list of baby names. Papi probably won't look at me, but he'll be the one making *boniato* and *malanga* for the little booger every day and whatever other puree the ladies at the market swear by." She laughed, but it caught in her throat. "Don't tell me right now, but I was wondering—I'd been planning to ask you," she said, then paused with a shake of her head. "If you'd be the *padrino*."

"I don't know if I deserve that," I say quietly. The word hung between us—godfather. Another kind of devotion, another kind of promise.

She takes my hand, her grip fierce. "It's not about deserving, *comemierda*. It's about being there. The way you've always been there for me. The way I'll always be there for you."

"I don't know how to move forward, Leni," I hear myself say.

"Like this. See? We're doing it already. One step at a time. And some steps are gonna feel uphill. Some will be easier. But you've got me here to walk it with you."

"Climbing and climbing until you reach the top of the mountain," I say, more to myself than to her. "And where do you go from there?"

"You admire the view," she says as we reach the intersection where I'll turn left, and she'll turn right. "Are you sure you don't want me to take you all the way home?"

"I'm sure. I feel better now than I have in a while." The words are flat and dry, brittle like dead grass. I pick up her hands and kiss the back of each one before pulling her in for a tight hug. I kiss her forehead, her nose, and then her lips. "I love you, Lenita."

Her eyes glisten with tears, her brow furrowed in a hopeless way. "Please come see me in the morning. When you wake up, okay? We'll get coffee, talk some more. If you're not at my place by noon, I'm sending in the military to drag your drunk ass out of bed." The words are meant to be a joke, but there's no levity behind a single syllable.

"I will." I turn to walk away and listen for her footsteps, expecting them to fade behind me. But they don't. I know she's still standing there, watching me, not moving an inch as I turn the corner and disappear from her view.

Interlude: Cuarenta

Cuarenta's hand rests against the door, feeling its weight as she guides it shut. The mechanism catches with a sound that echoes through the empty house. She stands motionless, her spine straight, breathing measured. The house settles around her with its familiar creaks and sighs. She has lived her entire life in these walls.

Two hours since Simón walked out. She checks her watch. Two hours, seventeen minutes.

She follows her established pattern around the house, the same pattern she has followed every day since her mother died. The familiar routine converted itself into a comfort, a foundation that doesn't shift beneath her feet.

Cuarenta moves through rooms that have no logical reason to be cleaned again. Not a speck of dust exists on any surface, yet her cloth moves with purpose, corners first, left to right, top to bottom.

She pauses at the old French rococo chairs, adjusting one that sits three millimeters off-center from the table. Her hands smooth across the upholstery. It had been reupholstered fifteen years ago, chosen specifically for its durability. A practical choice. At the sideboard, she adjusts a framed photograph of Simón at his high school graduation. Now it lines up precisely with the edge of the wood.

The kitchen bears evidence of the morning's disruption: dishes stacked by the sink, two coffee cups, one with the stain of her red lipstick on the rim, crumbs from pastries scattered across the counter. Black beans cling to the wall from when she had slammed down the wooden spoon. Her eyes fix on the dark streaks, the skins stuck to the ceiling. Evidence of weakness. Evidence of failure. She scrubs them away, the cleaner stinging her nose as she works, ammonia burning her nostrils. She stands back and assesses her own work. All in order. Good.

As she climbs the stairs—right foot, left foot, twenty steps in total—Cuarenta pauses. At the landing, instead of turning right to dust the pictures in the hall, she pivots left. The door to Simón's room stands closed, as it has since the day he left. She has entered only once to make the bed and lightly dust; it simply couldn't be left in that state of disarray. It would have driven her mad. Each day since she has walked past without entering, and this current deviation has taken even her by surprise.

Her fingers hover around the doorknob. Three seconds pass. Then five.

The brass is cold against her palm as she turns it.

The room is precisely as she left it, suspended in time like a photograph. Cuarenta stands at the threshold, allowing her eyes to adjust to the stillness. The bed is still neatly made. Books line the shelves, organized not by author or title, but by some system only Simón understood. A pair of childhood trophies collect dust on the highest shelf, drawings and paintings propped up here and there, curated and considered in that very "Simón" way.

She moves to the closet, opening it fully. His scent,

trapped in the fibers of hanging clothes, escapes all at once—soap, ink, something sweet she can't name. Cuarenta inhales sharply through her nose, holding the scent inside her lungs as if trapping a fly.

His clothes hang in the order she created when he was a little boy, sorted by season, then color, then length. "Another system," she chuckles. "Ay, the things we do." We, she thinks, my son and me. Her fingers touch each item, counting silently. Thirteen shirts. Six pants. Four sweaters, including the one she knit for his sixteenth birthday that he wore on special occasions to please her. At the far end, partially hidden, hangs a white button-down shirt with a small tear at the elbow. She unhooks it and holds it to the light from the window.

"Irresponsible," she murmurs to the empty room, examining the frayed edges. "Always rushing." She had asked him so many times to bring it to her for mending, but he always forgot. Always too busy. Always lost in his head.

Cuarenta sits at the edge of the bed. She removes a small sewing kit she keeps in her pocket. Always prepared, like her mother taught her. She threads the needle, knots the end, positions it at the edge of the tear. The motions are automatic, embedded in her muscles after a lifetime of sewing, but as the needle passes through the fabric, memories surface with every puncture.

Simón at four, standing on a chair beside her at the stove, his small feet pitter-pattering as he shuffled, trying to see what spices she was adding, catching crumbs from her apron.

Simón at seven, tongue caught between teeth as he tried to sew a button, his stitches drunken and wobbly but filled with determination.

Simón at fifteen, crying silently in his room, refusing her comfort but accepting the *croquetas* she placed beside his bed.

She hums as she works, a habit she normally suppresses when others are present. The melody starts low and contained but gradually rises. "*Qué te importa que te ame . . .*" A bolero her mother used to sing about time and love lost.

A drop of moisture hits the white fabric. Then another. Cuarenta stares at the darkening spots, momentarily confused. When she realizes they are tears, her back stiffens.

"No," she whispers, wiping her cheek with efficient movements. "No." The second denial punches, sharper.

The needle continues its path through the fabric, but her stitches begin to waver. Uneven. Imprecise. Each tear that falls makes her hands less steady, her vision less clear. The thread knots unexpectedly.

"*Caramba concho*," she mutters, trying to untangle it. This simple task, something she has done thousands of times, now seems impossible. The thread refuses to behave. The needle slips.

A drop of blood joins the tear stains on the fabric. The dark red spreads and swells over crisp white. She's pricked her finger, a beginner's mistake. As the stain spreads, something breaks inside her. A dam giving way after years of pressure. Her humming and singing that seconds ago filled the room transform into a wail so raw and unfamiliar. She doesn't hear the front door open downstairs. Doesn't register the moment when Cachita's voice fills the house, the twins arguing as they always do. Her world has narrowed to this fabric she cannot mend.

"Cuarenta?" Cachita stands in the doorway, huffing, her purse flopping to the side by her feet. "*¿Pero nena, qué tú haces aquí?*" She looks confused, glancing around the room for Simón.

Cuarenta straightens her back, lifts her chin. Her fingers

move to wipe away tears, smooth her hair, adjust her blouse. The familiar armor sliding back into place. But the half-mended shirt in her lap tells a different story.

"I found a tear," she says, her voice striving for normalcy. "It needed attention."

Cachita's eyes soften. "*Ay, hermana,*" she says softly, and the endearment catches Cuarenta off guard. She steps into the room, crossing a boundary that has stood between them for years.

"He left again," Cuarenta says, fingers gripping the fabric. Her shoulders remain squared, fighting the tremors that threaten to overtake her. "I don't know what happened. I tried to move on. He wouldn't let me."

Cachita approaches slowly, her high heels clicking against the worn wood floor. She sits beside Cuarenta on the bed, the mattress dipping under their combined weight. For a moment, neither speaks.

"For once in your stubborn life," she says, her voice gentler than Cuarenta has heard in years, "let someone else do the mending." Then Cachita's hand, adorned with too many rings, nails painted a bright shade of pink, covers Cuarenta's. She removes the sewing kit and shirt from her sister's lap and wraps her arm around her shoulders.

The walls begin to crack. Cuarenta resists for one final moment, muscles tensed against surrender. Then she breaks. Not dramatically, not completely. But enough to lean into her sister's embrace. Enough to let the tears flow without attempting to stop them. Her sobs come in measured waves. Cachita holds her, rocking slightly, the same motion Cuarenta once used to soothe Simón through fevers and nightmares.

"I've lost him," Cuarenta says between controlled breaths.

Cachita's hand strokes her hair, disrupting its careful arrangement.

"That's not true," she says firmly. "You haven't lost anyone. There's always time."

Outside the window, a pigeon lands on the sill. It watches for a moment, then takes flight, wings cutting through the late evening light.

Part IV

Lamento

Chapter Ten
Benign Masochism

It's dark on the street. A plunging darkness that makes me doubt whether the ground beneath my feet continues at all. It feels darker than it should be. My timid footsteps nudge me forward as my thoughts, submerged, ripple and surge with every breath. A tinking sound floats up the dim street. *Tink. Tink. Tink.* Like ice cubes slowly falling into a tall glass in the kitchen while you sit out on the patio.

I round the corner, expecting each step to devour me, hoping it will. The sound continues, steady as a metronome. *Tink. Tink. Tink.* I picture a loose chain-link fence swaying in the breeze, or maybe a can jostled by a rat bouncing down the sidewalk.

A sickly-sweet rot drifts on the air, rising and dipping in time with that relentless tapping. A man slumps against a wall. His clothes are in tatters, and he's surrounded by heaps of crumpled bags and discarded rags. Through the darkness, I detect a slow undulation in the piles. I quicken my pace, half-wishing the pavement would disappear beneath me, that I could fall through the gap and tumble into nothing. As I get closer, the undulating piles begin to swarm him. They reveal themselves to be dogs. They flinch in chorus with each metallic chime and the wet slurps of their licking.

He stares into emptiness while the mutts clean his filthy legs. I look at his face and see the source of the sound. A glint of serrated metal flashes again and again as he taps a knife against his front tooth. *Tink. Tink. Tink.* I wonder if he's thinking about killing me. Feeding me to the dogs.

I think to offer myself up. Let them have me.

My skin begins to itch. And then, the thought: this man is Albi. Like the beggar Lazarus, surrounded by dogs. They lick his wounds and ready him to walk forward, unsoiled, into heaven, while I remain behind among the rot. I am one of the dogs. I'm licking his feet with the others for the rest of eternity.

I slip off my jacket and walk it over to him. Then I take out my wallet and give him that as well. He clutches them in the same hand that holds the kitchen knife. His face is weathered, caked with grime, but his brown eyes flash in the gloom. In the absence of the tinking, looking into his eyes, I'm ashamed for being revolted by him. I place my hand atop his, unsure if I'm offering comfort or begging forgiveness, and say goodnight.

As I turn toward my building, a tiny squeak sounds from across the street.

Sapo sits on a stoop, paws neatly tucked beneath his body. He tilts his head and blinks slowly as I walk to him. The unease begins to crumble as I slowly blink back. His tail drifts downward, then flicks up again before settling.

"*Mi chispita.* My little angel of beneficence." I cradle his head and press my lips to the ridges between his ears. He purrs, leaning into the kisses, then sniffs my mouth and pushes his wet nose into my nostril. "You've been with me all day, huh? I'm sorry I haven't been paying enough attention." He licks my eyebrow with his scratchy little tongue. I pick him up and he tumbles in my arms, belly up. "You love to be held like a baby, don't you?" Flashes of Leni and her faceless child cross my mind. I see myself holding the little thing, too. Sapo meows and nestles deeper into my arms. "This isn't so hard. See, Sapo? I can hold a baby." My heart lurches at the thought of holding something so small and full of promise. But the thought slips away as quickly as it arrives. Hope like that deserves a future. I'm not sure if, or how, I fit into it.

The glow of my building's doorway pours onto the street ahead. I carry Sapo home. Away from the man and the dogs. Away from the portrait of Albi as Lazarus. I cradle Sapo against my chest, letting the low hum of his purr quiet the shrill noise in my head. It's a fragile calm—one slender thread of grace in the unraveling.

My knees crack and my back groans as I climb the stairs. The steps feel steady beneath me, but my body verges on disintegration. Air moves across my flushed face like water. It flows down my neck, and I imagine it washing me clean. Making me someone new. My bones and skin shift and warp, expanding, contracting, trying to reshape into something less twisted. I let the new body move forward on its own, while Sapo's purr vibrates gently against my sternum.

I reach the top of the stairs and see a slumped shadow just beyond the door to my unit. It's a garbage bag. Or the man from the street with his dogs. Or a sweater draped over a chair in the dead of night. Sapo tenses in my arms as I force myself not to look directly at it. My grip on composure is too tenuous for any deviation from the plan, from the path my body already knows to follow.

I reach for the doorknob, but the garbage bag turns to look at me. The human form it takes resembles my mother, her high-heeled shoes next to her on the floor. My mother would never sit on a floor, most certainly not barefoot.

"Simón." The garbage bag sounds like her.

My head slowly turns to the shadow. It's wearing a pencil skirt hiked up around knees that are clenched to a chest. A mess of hair, lazily done up, balances precariously on the head-like portion of the shadow. As my vision adjusts, my eyes survey the face; it has no makeup on. I haven't seen Mamá without makeup since I was a child, so my doubts double.

The shadow shaped like my mother pats the floor next to her, and my body turns itself and slides down the wall, lowering quickly and clumsily to her level. Sapo jumps from my arms to investigate, but she waves him away. My mother has never had any time for animals.

"You smell awful," she says as I land.

"I had a long day."

"Long day or long night?" she asks.

"Both." I manage a chuckle and stretch my legs out on the floor beside her. Then I move her shoes over, pausing to wipe a scuff mark from one of them.

"It's funny to think back and remember you walking around in those. Look at how big your feet are now. You'd never fit them." She straightens her legs out next to mine, and they seem so short. Such a tiny woman now when she's always been this towering megalith in my life, this all-seeing eye.

Sapo climbs on top of my legs and stretches his body along the length of them, nestling into the divot they make. He turns toward my mother and yawns.

"And this is?" she asks, not bothering to hide her distaste.

"Sapo. He's our—well—my cat."

"What a strange name." She shakes her head and lets out a sharp breath. "The things you think of. I always knew you were different, you know. I knew you would be more than anyone could imagine. So smart. I always told everyone you'd be a doctor or a lawyer, something really important." Her thought trailed off, fading like taillights disappearing into fog.

"And instead, you got me, right?" The words slip out of an unmoving mouth.

"I was blessed with you, Simón. You didn't become the person I dreamed up for you, no, but that doesn't mean I can't still be proud of you." Her voice sounds tired. The spiky edges have all been worn down. "You are exactly who God made you to be. Father Cordero helped me see that. Even if your path isn't the easy one."

"The path isn't what's hard, Mamá. It's the people blocking the way. I'd have a much easier time if everyone would just mind their own business and let me live my life." Sapo stands and looks at me, blinking one eye—the brown one—before lying back down between my legs. "You're mourning the loss of my future because I'm not a doctor, because I can't give you grandchildren. But I'm still here, Ma. I could've still been something important to you."

"You don't let me! You get defensive. You push me away. Every time I try, you snap at me." Her voice pulses as she tries to maintain composure. She takes a breath and straightens the rings on her fingers. "Like today. The way you behaved was inexcusable. That lack of respect you showed me and Father Cordero. I didn't raise you to act like that."

"That's why you're here? To get an apology for yelling at your little boyfriend?"

"No. I want you to apologize for acting like an ungrateful dog—biting hands, nipping at heels. I want you to apologize for making people feel like they weren't worth your time." She wants to yell but keeps that regal poise. "And I don't know where you got this unthinkable idea about me and the Father. You don't know me at all, do you?"

"I saw how you were talking to each other. How often he visits."

"Because I asked him to. I was worried about you." She rubs her temples in defeat. "He'd come by and tell me how you and your friend were doing. I'd make him dinner and ask him about you. That's all. And once Albi passed away, he kept coming for the company. I don't even want to know what—" She cuts herself off, shaking her head. "*Malcriado.*"

"So you had him spying on me. Really, Ma? Instead of talking to me yourself. Instead of trying to fix this." I motion between us. I want to be angry, but I can't feel anything but fatigue. "Well, I refuse to feel bad about any of it. I said what I said and meant every single word."

"You've made that quite clear." She raises her chin, still staring at the wall in front of us.

"I hope you didn't come here to get an apology because you won't get one. Not for that, not for anything, Mamá. It hurts that we haven't been the same in a long time, but this started way before Albi. You changed when Papi left." I feel her tense next to me. She wants to run. She wants to make me run.

"I loved you even when you hurt me, even when you put your sadness over our happiness as a family. But I can't keep loving you and wishing you'd accept me. I can't give my all when nothing is given back in return besides expectations and what-will-The-Family-thinks, and what your priest tells you is right. I am right. Who I am is right." My throat gets tight. I look down at my hands, turning them over in my lap.

"And when Albi died—" I stop. Saying his name stings more than I expected. "You didn't come. You didn't call. Not even a note. I didn't lose only him, Mamá. I lost everything. I was alone."

She flinches as if slapped, then straightens her back. "You think I didn't want to come? You think I wasn't suffering too?"

"I wouldn't know," I say flatly.

"Well, maybe I didn't know how!" Her voice is sharper now, rising. "You think it's easy. To find the right words, to say the right thing to a son who hates you?"

"I never said I hated you," I whisper. "Not once."

She shakes her head and looks away, lashes fluttering, nose sniffling. "I thought I'd only make it worse. I thought you'd slam the door in my face. I didn't know what to say. I didn't know how to talk about it." She clears her throat. "About Albi."

"You're broken. But I am too." I take a breath. "And I wish you could've protected me."

"I did my best, Simón. Even after what your father did, I tried my best. You never went without food; you never went without anything. Don't you think I miss the life we had? Don't you think I miss who I used to be?"

Her voice softens, then cracks. "When you walked out on me that day, it was like watching your father walk out again. After everything he already took from me." She exhales through pursed lips. "I didn't stay away because of the way you are. I stayed away because you left me so easily. Just like him."

She straightens her skirt and smooths her hair, acutely aware now of her disheveled appearance. "And I don't like that you called my religion a cult earlier today. You may not believe in it, but it gives me purpose. It structures my week. It gives me somewhere to put my fears and sadness. It gives me hope.

Is that so terrible, *mijo*?"

"It is when you let it come between us," I say, my voice sharpening. "You and everyone else at that church treat the Bible like it's law, and I'm some kind of criminal. It's ridiculous. That book was written by ordinary men, and rewritten a thousand times over by more ordinary men. It's all fake."

"God wrote it through them, Simón. You think I'm gullible, that it's silly, but without my faith, I have nothing. It's the way I was raised. It's part of our culture. And you'd throw that away for desires you feel inside, desires the Lord doesn't condone."

"The God I was raised with didn't say to change people or expect them to be just like you. The message was love. That's it. Love your neighbor."

"Everything I've ever done, I did out of love for you. Every decision I've made was with you in mind. I fought to give you a better, easier life, and you've thrown it all away." Her voice is thin, stretched tight as though she's holding it between her teeth. "I never wanted you to struggle. And now look at you." She breathes so softly her chest doesn't even move. "I regret so much. I never faced any of it because I was scared to admit I failed. Not because I ever thought you weren't worthy of my love anymore."

"So you don't actually think the way I am is wrong?" I ask.

"*Mijo* . . ." She hesitates, a tentative foot testing a river rock for stability. "That's what I was taught my whole life. Do you expect me to know Chinese if I set foot in China? How could I do that overnight?"

"Ignorance is no excuse," I snap. "You told me how you felt, then told me to leave. You never gave me a chance to prove otherwise." I try to switch gears, be gentle, but it's as if the cables have been cut. "And now I'm independent, and

I don't need to live a lie to appease you. I don't need your approval. I don't need anything from you."

"My worth had an expiration date. Is that what you mean?" Her voice tightens, trembling on the edges of restraint. "I was only useful until you had your own ideas. I was only good enough to raise you, and now that's it?"

The numbness inside me grows roots. My tongue locks behind my teeth. I can't seem to find any words of consequence, so I sit still and let her questions hang there and rattle against each other.

"You really are just like your father," she hisses. "I can't believe how selfish you've become. I don't even recognize you. I ruined my body to bring you into this world. Gave up my life for yours. My identity. And now I'm supposed to sit around until I die? Is that it?" Lava breaks through her frozen surface, spilling out everything built up from my father's betrayal and my own exodus. The Eruption of Mt. Cuarenta.

"When I confronted you that morning, you lashed out. Like I should've known all the right things to say all along. You never gave me a chance to learn, to change. You left me. It was like you died." Her small hands lift, palms upward, then fall back to her lap. "I'm your mother. You should know I'll always love you. I just—I need time, Simón."

"Mamá, I'm twenty-eight years old. That's not enough time? I've been squeezing myself into spaces I don't fit into my whole life, forcing myself into situations that were never meant for me. I'm tired. I can't wait anymore."

"I see." She stands and slips on her shoes. Her face smooths over, and she does the same to her skirt. "Well, I hope it was worth it." Her posture realigns, vulnerability locked away once more. Cuarenta The Impermeable.

She opens her handbag and bends to place something on

the floor next to me. Her jasmine perfume curls through the air as she moves, and I breathe it in, closing my eyes as the clicks of her high heels fade away.

Things are supposed to change. We grow up, and our lives branch off, connecting us to new people. We sever connections we once had—like a root excavated to make way for a sidewalk, a weed pulled so flowers can thrive. Alternate versions of our lives propagate out of self-preservation, planting new versions of ourselves in new places to protect our hearts, our traditions, our devotions.

But when does devotion turn into obsession? Some hostile, blinding mania that takes over our entire identity. Our constant attention and suffocating intentions leave a residue that builds up on the surface, trapping in moisture, warping the thing into something ugly and destructive. It becomes a closed ecosystem, a parasite feeding on itself, self-sustaining until it reduces into vapor. Soon, it's a false idea of what it once was. And suddenly even your loved ones look false. You feed and feed on this devotion until you're nothing. A memory of a memory. And you have to remind yourself how to remember what truly happened, what actually existed.

My hand searches blindly for what my mother left behind, returning to my lap with its prize. A cylinder rests in my disembodied grip. Reckless Rouge is etched around the base. My fingers tighten around the lipstick, and a faint catch escapes my lips.

Bonsai trees are bent and tied when they are young and pliable, shaped to fit the vision of their caretaker. They grow warped, defying their nature, until they match someone else's dream. My ropes are undone, but my branches don't remember how to grow on their own. I want to compensate for the distortion, to stretch toward some invisible symmetry, but my weight tips me off balance. All I want to do is fall. To topple. To uproot myself. To be swept away. I hate what we've become to each other. I hate how she treated me back then, and I hate how I treated her just now. We both thought we knew our roles, but we got it wrong. Being true to myself wasn't the sin, but I was wrong for not being true to her.

I find myself standing in front of my door, though I don't remember getting up. The day floods around me in fragments. How to remember. I know this door is here now, but was it always? I never left this morning. I never walked through it. My heartbeat feels slow, my mind strangely calm.

Doubt seeps in, coloring the edges of the moment. I don't trust these emotions. Nothing feels like mine anymore. I think of Albi telling me about the saint who carried his severed head for miles, still preaching. Today, I was that cephalophoric monster, dragging my headless body through town, spewing my broken thoughts at anyone who came near me.

Mamá has changed, but I couldn't. Lenita is changing, and I doubted her. I see her now, raising her baby to be better than anyone who came before them. Coco, the underground shepherd, glides through El Palomar, welcoming people like me home. The flower vendor kisses her grandchildren. My mother ascends the hill like a stone-faced queen. Everyone is safe in their place.

My hand moves toward the doorknob, the way it's supposed to. The knob turns. The mechanism clicks. My body follows the door's arc, propelled by its motion, forward until I reach the end. And then what?

"You admire the view," Lenita says from somewhere inside

a ridge of brain matter.

I can't bear to look. The view. Home. Whatever waits inside, it all scares me. I close my eyes and step through. Sapo brushes my leg, chirping softly. The tin of cat food still stretches my pocket, metal hot from being carried all day. I hope it hasn't spoiled. His tail wraps around my calf before his footsteps patter ahead. I follow blindly, muscle memory and my obsessive nature guiding me through the apartment's layout, etched in my mind.

At the sink, I feel around the cabinet for a bowl, then another. Water fills one while I fumble with the tin. I'd make a good blind man, I think. The first bowl overflows, and I empty the tin into the second. I lift them both, water spilling over my left hand and clapping against the wood floor as I walk to where I remember the window should be. Albi picked this spot so Sapo could climb in and get right to business. Some routines can survive an apocalypse. He meows, shuffling in place as the bowls reach the floor. I hear his fur brush against the wall before he settles with a low, contented purr.

Sapo's moist lapping fills the silence as I lean against the wall, eyes still sealed shut. Every muscle in my body begs to stay this way—suspended between what was and what is. The darkness behind my lids begins to pulse, like blood rushing to a wound. Red and gold phosphenes dance against the black, a private light show just for me. "Look at everything happening in here," they seem to say. "You don't need anything out there." A desperate deception to keep me blind.

The weight of what I must do presses against my eyelids, relentless as waves pounding a levee. My eyes flutter, an involuntary response like breaking the surface when you thought you wanted to drown. They open, held wide, as everything floods in, rushing to fill the spaces I've spent all day hollowing out.

The room is exactly how I remember it. The mess of it all. The heaviness. The memories. The fly. The bodies. So many bodies. They all look like him. I try to close my eyes again, but they stay open. I try to hold my breath, but I can't breathe in.

I picture myself exploding. My blood splatters across the walls, trying to cover everything. My particles scatter, pulling away from each other so they don't have to belong to me or even be near me. They shimmer, and when I blink fast enough, I see them expanding in slow motion. Stop frames of what I wish were real. An ending. I blink faster, and my body becomes a mosaic of red, black, gold, and white, suspended in the air before it hits the walls.

I've exploded every time I walked through that door. Every time he didn't. I combust. Every second in this room, my fuse detonates, and my particles become air. Hummingbirds blown apart. A rock flying through the air. Jasmine and orange blossoms ripped to shreds. His wet eyelashes. My swollen eye. You. Me. This room I can never seem to fill on my own.

My mother believed I'd become someone important. The idea that I was special came preloaded in my brain. But the bones I thought set me apart are just like anyone else's. Once, they created structures of alien design. Now they've degraded and slumped against each other into something ordinary. The skeleton of any old body. They could have been gilded ivory to the younger me, but now they barely pass for a wet pile of driftwood. My bones, draped with my skin, are propped up here in this damned room again. Like I never left. Like today never happened.

The photographs on my nightstand shine like documents of daylight. Noon at the botanical garden. A cat licking a stubbly cheek. Sunrise over the bay in the clothes from the night before. The candles of a birthday cake illuminating a face. Scorch marks masquerading as brightness. It's a memory of light. It's a scar of life.

I can't remember who I am.

I try to. I really try. But all I can see are versions of myself, mutations shaped for someone else. One for Mamá. One for Lenita. One for Coco. One for The Family. Even one for Albi. Each one crafted to win over, to shield, to make proud. To survive.

But who was I outside of their eyes? Who am I, now that there's no one left to be for?

Maybe that person never existed. Maybe I missed my chance to bring him to life.

Every object, photograph, and sliver of memory looks like it belongs to someone else. Someone who left. Someone who already died. I reach for anything that feels true, but nothing holds. It all slips through. I thought time would help. That I'd step out into a new life. That maybe my old one had been waiting for me all along, ready to continue living again.

The world really did keep spinning without us.

I'm so tired.

I don't want to do this anymore.

My stomach churns, and a dull burning rises in my throat. Bile pools, ready to flow. I dart to the toilet and hold onto the sides of the basin as I retch and spray. Vomit pours over my hands, onto the floor, pooling across the closed lid just inches from my nose. The acidic stench triggers another convulsive explosion. Flecks of blood like constellations orbit each other in the viscous mess.

I strip off my shirt and use it to wipe my hands, the fabric smearing rather than cleaning. Half-collapsed, I struggle to remove my jeans. Socks and underwear follow. Clawing onto the sink like it's a cold, solid friend, I hoist myself up and stumble to the kitchen. I grab a plastic bag from under the sink and shove the soiled shirt inside. Back in the bathroom, I use my jeans to wipe the mess off the toilet lid, then cram them into the bag, too. Socks go over my hands like murdered puppets, and I wipe down the outside of the toilet. An image flicks into frame of my mom showing me how to dust with an old sock that had lost its mate or gained a hole. She said it was given a new purpose. Even if against its will.

What a small life. What a disaster of a life. When you devoted your life to someone, and then they are gone, when you buy a bottle of whiskey, come home, leave the lights off, and drink the entire thing, you wonder where it all fucking went. The vessel has a hole. The holy vessel is empty. An empty vessel is trash.

"Simón, I picked you flowers from my garden. Fill the bottle up with some water and put the flowers in that." His voice is so clear.

I whip my head around at the sound. The room spins around me, blurring in my periphery. Didn't I just touch your hand? Didn't we just love each other?

I can't feel the tears running down my cheeks, but I see them hit my chest.

I can't feel my hands, but I don't need them anymore anyway.

I can't feel my guts wrenching, sitting here, looking into my lap, pleading to be something or someone again.

Turn me into someone you could stick around for. Name it, and I'll be it, Albi. I read once if you name something, you can reject it. We had a name before we ever even spoke, but I never thought rejection was possible. Not when we had the sound of air passing my face as I leaned in to kiss you with my eyes shut. Not when there was bacon sizzling. Billie

Holiday in the "I'll Be Seeing You" kind of way. The sound of you singing, walking to the bathroom. The water hitting the shower tiles in two-second intervals after bouncing off your body, your hands slicking your hair back as you rinse it. Sunday afternoons when the band played on the street below. A guava leaf crinkling in your pocket.

I had two hands once. Two feet that slapped against the pavement. A heart that pumped blood throughout my body. I was me, then "we," and then, in some deliberate yet unnoticed transfiguration, "you" were all that was left. But you're gone now, and that leaves me nowhere. I think of us playing that game where one of us turns the gravity off, and we'd spin slowly and float into things, into each other. Each collision sent us bouncing away until our own pull drew us back together. Now the gravity is gone, but I have nothing to collide with. Nothing to send me spinning in new directions.

Maybe that's the real immaturity of love. We marvel at the wonder and awe woven into everyday life when we're in love, but that innocence is only a cover. Love isn't innocent at all. It's brutal and sneaky. Benign masochism. A trapdoor spider. For all the work, time, and maturity love takes to survive, there's always this predator concealed beneath it, waiting to grab you by the throat and slide your unsuspecting body to its crushing, crunching demise.

It's silent now. The smell of vomit fills the air around me. I look at the pile of garbage on the floor. I squint, but it looks nothing like him. The silence presses against my ears harder than the sound of my own breath in this fucking hole of a room. I think, what if I could escape? What if I could grab this pillow and gently press it over my airways? I imagine myself standing over my body. The sound of flailing extremities against the mattress. The muffled screams. The waning effort.

And then silence again.

We knew silences before, but Albi's silence was beautiful. He'd fall asleep first, and my silence would try to fit into his. Rising and falling with his chest. Rising and falling with his pulse. Rising and falling now with the trembling in my fingertips. The silence is the one holding my head. But it's not his. Nothing can be his anymore because he's dead.

He was being torn in half, tied to horses running in opposite directions. And I couldn't see that I was the horse pulling the hardest. Trampling everything in the way, pulling his body over the debris, shredding his skin, breaking his bones.

The fly slams into the windowpane again and again, watching me kill Albi in its disjointed slamming. Six thousand simple eyes see six thousand different paths, and they all lead me back here to this room. I wanted to be worthy of him, to become him. And now I have my chance.

The silence worms its way in and sits there. It sits in my head till I grow accustomed to it. It metastasizes, spreading through my body. It becomes my identity. I won't even piss standing up for fear of disturbing it. Till I leave the radio off. Till I refuse to answer the door or calls from the street. Till I can't say I love you. Till the word "love" isn't enough.

I hold completely still, close my eyes and breathe in as slowly as possible.

So slowly it hurts my chest.

So slowly I become lightheaded.

So light. I'm headed into the light.

My hands take flight. They've been domesticated and abandoned. They're pigeons that dip and dive around the room. This chair becomes horses. They carry me on their backs. They rollick and kick until they forget they are just horses.

The water has been rising all along. I breathe in, but it doesn't choke me. No pressure builds behind my eyes. No desperate struggle for the surface. The serenity wraps around my head like a plastic bag.

The horses hold me up against the door.

The pigeons fly around my head. They circle my neck.

Are they underwater, too? Are we all swimming?

It'll be morning. Everything will be better tomorrow.

The pigeons settle on my neck. They're nesting closer and closer. Too close.

The horses buck and kick. They run and run until their legs collapse beneath their own weight. They throw me off their backs and leave my body knocking against the door. One moment I heard the singing, and the next I couldn't remember if I was the one doing it. I breathe in, and the burning moves down my throat. My body struggles as I take in the water. The sweet melody surrounds me as I gasp and claw.

A loud pop.

Bright lights.

And now even the pigeons have become birds of prey. I spin until I can't open my eyes, and I say I don't want to open them anyway. The pigeons devour whatever they please, descending to peck at my eyes, my cheeks, my hair. They say they've learned to love the reasons they're feasting on me, this dead carcass. You'll say you love that reason, too, and this carcass loves it the same. Then the pigeons take flight, crashing into windows covered with tissue paper. Everything I thought I knew lies there on the floor. And it looks nothing like the memories.

The horses stop breathing eventually, but I can't stop breathing.

The pigeons bleed from twisted eyes, their necks contorted.

And those things I knew shift and writhe. I can't help but stare across the room, now completely submerged, and see them hold guns to each other's temples. I can't help but see them give each other the world and then take it all back. I keep falling to the floor while the pigeons tear at my skin, and the horses lie dead around me. Their decay fills my lungs with your scent. It smells like your hair, Albi.

I keep hurling my body through the air, hoping I will hit bottom, but I slap against the surface of the water like a skipping stone.

And the people are all lined up. They wait eagerly. Their eyes are salivating as they wait for me to finish choking and kicking.

To die for your religion, you become a martyr, possibly a saint if you check a few other boxes before and after the big finish. But you die for love, and you're a fool, chewed up and spit out. You were my religion, Albi, and in my devotion to you, I became both martyr and fool.

The Hanged Man. The Fool. The Lovers.

The water slips its arms around me. As it swirls, it shapes itself into Albi's curls, my mother's waves, their translucent grip spinning me and then letting go. I swim to the mirror and pick up my mother's lipstick. Reckless Rouge. I delicately slide the crimson stain up and across, down and over. A little spritz of perfume. One last check of my hair.

I could've been beautiful. I could've been happy.

Interlude: Coco

The procession for San Lázaro wound through narrow streets still damp from afternoon rain. Incense cut through the salt air, and drums vibrated against colonial walls that had witnessed centuries of this very ritual. The humidity pressed against windows, slipped under doors, made paper curl and wood swell. Nothing was ever truly dry here. Coco stood with Simón in the shelter of a doorway as Albi passed with Father Cordero and the statue of the sore-laden man surrounded by dogs, his face composed into appropriate reverence.

"Uff. *Ese hombre!* He gets me all wound up," a young woman whispered to her friend, gesturing toward Albi with a subtle chin lift, fanning herself with a floppy hand. "What a waste."

Coco caught Simón's jaw tightening, his fingers digging into his palms. She nudged him with her hip. "Calm down, *papo.* They're not talking about *that.*"

A muscle in his cheek twitched, and he smiled. Obviously, the waste was that he was serving God and not them. Simón knew that, but his feelings were too strong sometimes. "What a waste indeed," he said, laughing. "I wish I could lean over and tell them exactly what they're missing." The humor loosened something in Simón's face. Coco had noticed this about him, how he needed to be pulled from his own intensity before it consumed him. It was like watching a younger version of herself, so tightly strung the strings might snap.

"You'd send the whole procession off a cliff if you gave them even a fraction of that scandal." Coco raised her eyebrows as a short sweaty man and his even sweatier wife passed in front of them and gave her an icy look.

"They celebrate a leper while excluding *us* from the very healing they talk about all the damn time," she said loud enough for them to hear.

"They can't exclude us. Not really. This is our home as much as theirs," Simón said quietly.

Something in his voice, that desperate claiming of space, stirred a memory so visceral Coco could taste it: a single egg with white rice, the flavor of her first night alone.

"You know when I first came here?" she asked, watching the crowd slip and swarm. "I had three dresses, my mother's gold earrings, and this body that didn't feel like mine yet."

"After your family—" Simón trailed off.

"After my father held scissors to my throat and told me if I didn't want to act like a man, he'd help me finish the job." She felt rather than saw Simón flinch. "Sorry, *papito*. Not exactly procession talk."

"No, tell me." His voice softened. "You never talk about before."

"Because before is dead and buried, that's why." Coco adjusted her bracelets, letting them clang together, a sound that had become her signature, a warning bell announcing her approach. "That scared boy died so I could live. What's the point in digging him up?"

The procession turned a corner, drums fading. People dispersed like water finding cracks in stone. Coco touched Simón's elbow, and they began walking, falling into step in the familiar rhythm they'd developed over the years.

"I used to map this town by fear," she continued after a while. "This street: men with wandering hands. That corner: cops who'd want to see what's under your skirt. Here: kids with rocks and nothing better to do. You learn to navigate, to plot the safest course from one point to another."

"Like sailing," Simón offered.

"Like surviving." Coco's heels clicked a staccato melody against the damp pavement. "You know what saved me? Finding that house and that basement."

She remembered it vividly, stumbling down those worn wooden steps by accident, running from a group of men who'd followed her six blocks, their slurs echoing off stone. The stairs had creaked beneath her, bowing like the soft wood might snap. She'd descended, expecting only momentary shelter, but found something else entirely.

"It was empty storage space back then. Water damage and rats." She smiled at the memory. "But the minute I walked in, I knew."

"Knew what?" Simón asked.

"That I could be reborn there." Coco's voice dropped to a whisper. "Not like the church talks about. All that baptism bullshit. Real rebirth, bloody and raw. Cracking yourself open and climbing out inch by inch."

The night she'd signed the lease to the house using the name she was trying to leave behind, she'd stood alone in that empty concrete box. She'd brought white rose petals for peace, pennies for new beginnings, and a single red candle for transformation. In the flickering light, she'd watched her shadow stretch across the wall, no longer fractured but whole, a silhouette that finally matched the shape she felt inside.

"The first night we opened, three people showed up," she

told Simón. "Couldn't have been more than sixteen years old, kicked out by their parents. One of them slept behind the bar for a month before I found him an apartment."

"Isabel?"

"With the Tina Turner wigs, yes." Coco grinned. "Look at her now, stealing the show every Saturday."

"And sometimes people's drinks," Simón said. Coco laughed and pushed him.

They'd reached the corner where El Palomar's entrance waited, the fence posts with their chicken bones clacking in the evening breeze.

"You know what I realized that first night?" Coco paused, turning to Simón. "That this wasn't about me anymore. My rebirth wasn't complete until I helped others be reborn, too."

Simón's face reflected a confusion Coco recognized, the look of someone who couldn't imagine survival, let alone transformation. It was the same face she'd seen in the mirror all those years ago.

"Listen to Mama Coco Tazo," she said, gripping his shoulders. "Resurrection happens when you're still breathing. When you take all those pieces they tried to kill, and you make something true and beautiful they never could have imagined."

Simón's eyes glistened. "I don't know if I can."

"That's because you're still in the tomb, baby." She pressed a red-nailed finger into his chest. "The stone hasn't rolled away yet. But it will."

"How do you know?"

"Because I've seen it. Every single person who walks down those stairs is dying in some way. And every single one of them has the chance to be reborn." She gestured to the entrance. "That's why I named it El Palomar. We're all little birdies looking for somewhere to land."

As they approached the entrance, she glanced back at the distant spire of the church, then down at the worn steps leading to her creation. Music swelled from below as someone opened the door, a heat and vibration that felt like a heartbeat. Coco smoothed her hands over her dress, preparing to descend. These stairs had been her altar, this basement her sanctuary. Tonight, like every night, she would watch her many children walk down these steps and transform themselves into who they were meant to be.

"When he's done with work, you'll dance with him under those lights," she said, gesturing to the strings of bulbs she'd hung herself, climbing a ladder in heels because no one else would do it right. "And I'll watch over you, over all of you." She touched the gold hoops swinging from her ears. "It's what mothers do."

Behind her, Simón followed, step by tentative step, into the warm cacophony below. Into the home she'd built. Into the place where he, too, would learn how to be resurrected.

Part V
The Beloved Disciple

Chapter Eleven
Dura Mater

"There's this figure in the Bible called the 'Beloved Disciple.' Have you heard about this before?"

"Nope, but I'm sure you're going to make me hear about it right now." I was sketching Albi on scrap paper while he sat cross-legged on the bed, reviewing notes for Father Cordero's next sermon. Late afternoon light filtered through the windows, catching his black curls and setting them ablaze, copper and gold at the edges like a Byzantine icon.

Subdural hematoma.
Beep.
Tracheal rupture.
Beep.
Swelling of the dura mater.

"Supposedly there was a disciple that Jesus loved above all others. He kept him near at all times, confided in him, traveled with him." The bottoms of Albi's feet were bare and soft. I reached out to touch them, but he intercepted my hand, holding it gently without looking up from his papers. "There's even a passage where the Beloved Disciple lies on Jesus's chest while the other disciples are there with them. Just resting there, like it was the most natural thing in the world."

"Wait, really?" I laughed softly, offering him my other hand. He took it, turning both palms upward, pressing his thumbs into them in slow, thoughtful circles. "Are you saying Jesus was like us? And they were all fine with it?" I almost shouted. "What bullshit. Why do we get shit on now?"

"I'm just telling you the story as it exists in the Bible, Simón." His voice carried that gentle patience I'd come to know so well.

*More words pass through me. Sterile, clinical. I can't
hold them, but I feel their shapes.
Cold fingers press my wrist.
The scent of antiseptic.
The dry scrape of hospital linen.
A nurse hums beneath her breath—faint, off-key,
familiar now.*

"So which one was his beloved? Peter? The three denials definitely seem a little sketchier to me right now." I tilted my head and watched his face, that beautiful face.

He chuckled and set his notes aside. "Most scholars think it was John." He repositioned himself so we were facing each other, his knees brushing mine.

"The Baptist?"

"No, thank God. That was Jesus's cousin. This was John the Apostle."

"Hmm. I don't remember that one."

"He stayed with Mary during the crucifixion." His hands drifted to my thighs. "Jesus told Mary that John would now be his son, and to John he said that Mary was now his mother." His fingers traced absent patterns, swirling and swooping in the hairs of my legs.

"That sounds a lot like wedding vows." My heart thrummed in my ribcage, the rhythm aligning itself to the rise and fall of his chest.

"It kind of does, huh?" A smile played at the corners of his mouth.

Somewhere close by someone is crying.
"Your son is very lucky," a voice says. "He should make a full recovery."
"He's strong," says another, softer, motherly. "We'll take our time with him."
A hand in mine.
Then silence.

"Would you ever get married, Simo?" he asked me.

"Yeah. To you." The words came quickly, as honest as breathing.

Albi leaned over, crushing his notes and my sketches, and kissed me. I felt his lips against mine. I felt that static electric tingle. I felt different, like every moment between us somehow changed me. Sometimes, something crosses your path, and a piece of it stays with you. Sometimes the whole of it folds itself up and inserts itself into some corner of your body—under your arm, between your teeth. It becomes a part of you. You remember you can fold yourself up, too. You remember you can give yourself over entirely.

Another beep. Another night.
I speak. Just once.

"Am I your beloved disciple, Albi?" I whispered against his lips. "Do you love me above all others?"

"There are no others, stupid."

He kissed me again, and in that moment, there was only his hands on me, my breath in his lungs, and the weight of knowing what it felt like to be chosen. To be beloved, not to any god or saint, but by another person who saw you completely and chose you anyway.

The light caught his curls once more as he pulled away, and I blinked really hard a few times, tracing the copper-gold edges into my memory, the precise way they spiraled against his skin. I didn't know then that this perfect moment could keep me tethered to life or cut me loose from it. But if I had known, I would have chosen this exact snapshot to remember him always: sunlit and sacred, completely and irrevocably mine.

The smell of jasmine perfume wafts around me, and I don't need to open my eyes to know I am not alone. Down the hall, Tía Cachita yells into the telephone about a pair of *chancletas* she scored on clearance downtown. One of the twins slams doors; the other sings off-key about getting a tooth pulled.

"Well, I know this isn't heaven . . ." I mumble through the gravel lining my throat.

My mother laughs, her hand resting on my chest. Her laughter sounds like a wind chime in a light breeze, so natural you'd think she'd done it every day of her life. She lifts a glass of water to my lips. I take a small sip.

It burns to talk, to swallow. Even breathing stings. But it's the stillness of my body that terrifies me most. Panic sets in. I try to wiggle my toes, then my fingers. I can't raise my head to see if they move, but it feels like they might. Could be phantom sensations. I've read about amputees who feel limbs that are no longer there.

Mamá sees the turmoil creeping across my face. "*Mijo*, don't worry," she whispers. "It will all be fine. The doctor said you don't have any permanent damage. *Y mira, ven acá.* Your friends left you flowers. Look there, on the table." Her hand moves over my legs, and a soft rumble vibrates against my shins. "Coco has visited you every day. She is marvelous, that Coco. The most beautiful woman I've ever met. And Lenita, too! She's barely left your side. Even with the morning sickness. Stubborn girl."

"She told me she needs me," I whisper. The words feel foreign in my mouth after weeks of believing I needed no one, that no one needed me.

"Yes," my mother says simply. Her eyes look sunken. Her clothes, wrinkled. "And you need her, too. That's how we survive, *mijo*. Not alone. Together, as a family."

She rises to show me the flowers. Her hair flows freely, waves crashing around her proud, square shoulders. She lifts them and inhales, then turns to me, vase in hand, smiling a tired smile. "You're lucky to have people like that. I told them both to come back for dinner tonight. They should be here soon."

I imagine my mother paused just outside my building, sensing something was wrong. If this were a movie, the camera would zoom in on her eyes—scanning, understanding, replaying our last exchange and my refusal to reconcile. Lenita sprinting up the street, Coco trailing behind. Realization dawning. Lenita bursting into El Palomar while Coco sang *El Amor* by Massiel or some other ballad about being crushed under love.

And of course it would be the women in my life who saved me. Of course I had to burden them with this after life had already piled everything else on their shoulders. They must've knocked the door down, or maybe it wasn't even closed. My mother falling to her knees. Coco holding my body. Lenita pushing the bathroom door open. The belt falling loose as the door swung a fraction of an inch. All three of them rushing to undo the loop around my neck.

The rumble on my legs stops. Sapo's head pops up over the ridge of sheets near my chin. "My little creature," I whisper. "Did you go find my mom to save me?" His tongue rasps against my skin. He settles back down and starts to purr again.

My mother moves around the room, rearranging flowers and smoothing sheets, her anxious energy channeled into care, not control. No matter what's been said, no matter what remains unresolved, a mother doesn't abandon her son. She looks at my broken body. Her eyes are tired, but she smiles and keeps fussing about my comfort.

My heart is barely beating, but I feel it.

I could look down at my hands, but I know they're there. I could listen for the water pooling beneath me, but I know it's gone.

There's a cruelty we reserve for ourselves. Things we'd never wish on another soul, we inflict freely on our own. Heinous thoughts. Physical harm. Dysmorphic spirals. We let grief consume our identity until loss becomes a punishment we welcome—a hole we refuse to fill because we've made a home of the fall.

Loss is not the absence of something. Loss is being drowned. It is being buried under something piling on top of you, bodies falling, cascading like a waterfall of dead weight.

Loss is an extra limb that people stare at, a malignant growth differentiating you in other people's eyes. Only when you realize others don't carry this weight do you understand its magnitude—the rubble in the crater, the trees and buildings felled in the blast zone.

It's more than memory. It's anatomical. A sadness so foundational it becomes your skull, your cartilage, your skin, the jelly in your eyes. And people will tell you to move on, not realizing they're asking you to live without a head. Like a freshly slaughtered chicken, tripping over pebbles, flinging its body around the yard.

But for the first time in a long time, I'm no longer drowning.

"Sapito! *Vente a comer!*" Mamá calls from the kitchen.

Sapo stretches, his fur rippling in waves. He jumps down and trots toward her. He glances back and slowly blinks. His brown eyes twinkle, warm molasses and honey. Maybe he winked. Maybe I'm still crazy. I hear Mamá singing as a fork scrapes a bowl, "Sapo Verde to yooou." He chirps in reply.

I breathe in. The big blue house surrounds me. I'm at the center of the world again. My heart beats. Capillaries and arteries.

When I was a child, my mother told me bedtime stories. One, in particular, shaped what I allowed myself in life. It was about two people who lived in a time that didn't understand them. They thought they missed their chance at happiness, but found their way, in their own time. Maybe I misunderstood the moral. Maybe the happy ending comes after the sad one.

Maybe every ending is the start of another story.

I told you that story the night we met, beneath the same stars she described. I pointed out which ones belonged to my ghosts. You listened. The trees were singing. Clouds tumbled across the sky. I could try to recall every second, but only one thing mattered: you. It was always you. And, boy, were you beautiful.

Life had been happening like a baroque painting. Dark and distorted, pain streaked across heavy faces. But now I imagine a different canvas.

Two sets of clothes are lying side by side on the sand. It's bright. A brightness that welcomes the back of your hand to shield your eyes from it. The kind of brightness that seeps into your bones. Air escapes the sand in that microscopic way it does after a wave retreats. I breathe it in.

A whistling in the air draws closer and closer. I'm lying on one set of clothes, my hand lifted to the sun. You are living in the imperceptible line that separates my hand from the sky. You are living in the grains of sand stuck to my shoulder. I can feel your body heat inside of me, and I know you're near.

I turn to the other set of clothes beside me. My body, faded and flaking, begins to reappear in color, stroke by stroke, as I look into your eyes. A masterful restoration. I paint your hand across my face. Your hair rolling in the breeze. The shadows your shoulders cast. A bead of sweat trailing down your neck.

You pull me against your body, and I remember all of the dreams I invented for us, the fears that don't matter anymore. You sing in the voice of the trees, "*Te amo mucho*, Simón," and the song bounces off the sea while the stars behind the sun and sky sing back, "*Más que mucho.*"

The start happened at one point, and maybe I don't

remember the beginning exactly as it happened, but I remember your face. And your eyes looking back at mine. You. It was always You. And, as I remember it now, you were the only thing in the world at that moment.

"I will never not be like this again, Albi," I say aloud as Mamá enters with Lenita and Coco.

I try to sit up, scrambling against the pillows, but the pain flares in my neck. Seeing me conscious shocks them. Coco leans against the door frame, exhaling hard, wiping her forehead. Lenita screams, drops what she's holding, and gently lies beside me, resting her head on my chest.

"How are you feeling?" I rasp. "Ma told me you've been getting sick."

"How am *I* feeling?" she snaps, sitting up to meet my eyes. "What the fuck, dude. How are *you* feeling?" Her hair seems fuller. She has a glow about her.

"We missed you, Simo," Coco says, settling on the bed's edge. "How does it feel to be back in the land of the living?"

"Been better. Been worse." My voice is raw. "Can I feel your stomach, Leni?"

Coco and my mother laugh. "It's basically still a gummy bear," Lenita says, but takes my hand and places it gently over her belly. "You'll be in its life, then?" she asks. Her voice is careful. She's worried I might disappear again.

"Every day," I promise. "I'm going to teach them everything."

Lenita smiles and slumps against me. "Ugh. They're gonna be so spoiled."

"They're gonna be so loved," I say.

My mother moves my hair from my forehead. Coco rubs my leg. They surround me, and I feel like I am home. Not the kind of home where you forgot if you turned the stove off. Not the kind of home where you feel like you need a vacation. Just home. My home.

When my mother is happy, she can make everything feel right in the world. She smiles at me and laughs, and I feel like maybe I could be okay again. That everything might actually be fine in the morning.

It will be golden. It will be beautiful. Just as it's supposed to be. My heart. My Albi.

Epilogue
Five Years Later

"Did you paint this one?" a small voice pipes up beside me, clear and bright as a bell above the din in the gallery.

I glance down, startled, and there he is—standing no taller than my hip, dark hair a glistening riot of untamed waves, eyes wide with a searching kind of intensity. Something in his face stops me, tugs at me like a thread I didn't remember was loose.

"I did," I answer, and crouch down beside him, smoothing my hands over my knees. "I painted all of them. Do you like it?"

He sets his small hand on my knee, his eyes narrowing as he studies the painting. He's serious about it in a way that makes me smile, the way a child can be when they sense something important without yet having the words for it. The colors layered thickly on the canvas, the shapes moving in subtle currents, tangled and graceful. "Who is it?" he asks, seeing through the abstraction.

I smile faintly. "Someone I knew once. Someone I carry with me."

He tilts his head. "I like it," he decides, turning to me and placing his hands on my cheeks. He leans even closer, nose inches from mine. "I can see your painting in your eyeball. It looks like it's moving," he whispers.

"I suppose it is," I say softly, focusing on the warped reflection of the painting curving around the dome of his eye as well. The shapes seem more concrete at this scale. The abstraction is smoothed over, and the image is clear and controlled. It's a dance, a fleeting swirl of life.

"Who taught you how to paint?" he asks while watching my mouth for the answer to emerge.

"Well, my grandmother taught me how to paint," I say, pausing to consider the moment, "but someone named Albi taught me how to just *be*. How to remember. How to feel." He touches my bottom lip while I answer him. "That's what this piece is about."

"Alberto," Lenita calls from a few feet away, her tone gently scolding, loving. "Don't bother your *padrino*. He needs to talk to the people here with money."

He turns his head slightly but keeps his hands on my cheeks, speaking low in that kid version of seriousness. "My name isn't Alberto."

I raise a brow. "No?"

He grins mischievously and whispers, "It's just Albi."

The words catch in my chest, heart folding over itself. "I know. Don't worry," I say quietly, smiling at him as Lenita approaches.

She places her hand on my shoulder, squeezing gently, and I rise. I kiss her cheek, and she slaps my ass. "Look at all of this, Simo."

"It's only a small show." The room is packed, but I feel like she and I could disappear. Las Locas cackle and caw on the other side of the gallery. Another bottle of champagne pops.

"You didn't sell a single piece, did you?" Lenita teases, nudging me.

I shrug. "Not yet. But they showed up. That's something."

She grins. "That's everything."

"Beloved Disciples," she says, leaning her shoulder against mine.

"Beloved Disciples," I say back. "Think Albi would've blushed at the sacrilege?"

She turns and hugs me tightly. "I think he would've been so proud."

"I think so too," I say into her hair.

Then, a familiar voice joins the chorus. "*Y mi ahijado?* Where is my handsome godson?" I turn to see Coco walking up to us, wine swirling in her glass.

"Nina! My *padrino* made this!" Albi bolts forward and hugs her long legs.

"I think he made all of them, *mijo*. Isn't he talented? Our very own Picasso."

"Picasso was a womanizing asshole," I say.

"Fine. Which ones were gay?" Coco asks, rolling her eyes.

"Pretty much everyone else."

"Leonardo?"

"Very gay."

"*Tenemos un verdadero Da Vinci aquí, muchachos!*" She theatrically looks around and raises her glass before drinking the rest of its contents.

The click of kitten heels announces my mother's approach. Her gold earrings glint in the low light. Her hair bounces around her shoulders. "See, Simón? I told you the space would fill up. He was nervous no one was going to show," she says past me to Coco and Lenita. "*Ven acá*, Albi. *Mi tesoro.*"

He sees my mother, and a huge smile spreads across his face before he takes off running. "No lipstick, Tía! No kisses!"

"Te *voy a comer a besos!*" My mother playfully growls and

whips around to catch him in her arms. She kisses him and leaves a perfect set of red lips on his cheek. Reckless Rouge.

Albi leaves the kiss mark in place and, laughing, slithers between the legs of the guests, disappearing out of sight.

She takes a sip from her glass. "It's a beautiful show, *mijo*," she says.

"Thank you, Mamá." I nod, swallowing past the sudden tightness in my throat. "For everything."

"I recognize him," she continues, nodding her head toward the painting. "He's in all of them."

I blink. "You think so?"

She hums, considering. "Mhmm. You can tell when someone does anything with love. It bleeds through everything. Fills the whole thing up. Why do you think I sing to my *sofrito* when I make it? Love adds another dimension." She kisses her fingers and releases them into the air. "*La chispa de la vida, mi niño!*"

"You always used to tell me I was too romantic," I say. "Always lost in the details."

She tilts her head. "Maybe I was wrong."

I let out a breath of laughter, and she takes my hand briefly, squeezing it once before letting go. The gesture is small, but it is enough.

"You're right. He is in all of them," I say after a moment. "But so are you."

Albi tugs on my hand. "Nino," he says. "Can I paint something next?"

"You can paint whatever you want." I look at him, his face sticky with cupcake frosting. "I'll get you your very own set of brushes."

"I can just use yours," he says.

"Your Nino likes things a certain way," my mother replies.

I wink, and he nods solemnly, like it's a contract.

The gallery hums softly around us, filled with murmurs and laughter, and I feel the warmth of the bodies gathered in the room surrounding me. Like we're all in the kitchen on a Sunday evening. Garlic sizzling. *Chisme* flowing. Mamá rubs my back. Lenita and Coco stomp and laugh.

Albi slips his hand into mine, and it's small and warm and full of life.

Acknowledgments

I began writing this book at a very low point in my life. Putting the grief, loss, and dissociation I was experiencing onto Simón (who is like me in more ways than I'd care to admit) helped me work through those emotions and see the immense community of love and support that surrounded me the whole time I felt so alone. This novel would not have made it past its tear-and-whiskey-soaked first draft without some phenomenal people (and animals) in my life.

Joni was curled up next to me for every draft of this novel. No matter the early mornings or late nights. She kept Henry out when his cat-like ways were too crazy, and allowed Lula in when she thought another pup's cuddles might help get me through the chapter. She's on my foot now while writing this! And I'm not crying, I swear.

I thank my family, given and chosen, for putting up with me talking about this book for five years. The patience you showed is beyond words. There are far too many of you to name (listing my cousins alone would take ten pages), but if you endured my rants, I am forever in your debt.

This is my first foray into traditional publishing, and I had industry champions who helped make it all happen. Thank you to Orlando Ortega-Medina for believing in this story and guiding it across the finish line. To Salem West and everyone at Amble Press for giving *Beloved Disciples* a home—you took a chance on a new voice, and I don't take that trust lightly. To Amelia Possanza at Lavender Literary, for cheering me on and constantly finding ways for me to show the world who I am and why it might matter. To Samuel Hodder for urging me to see the value in levity (Sapo thanks you for opening that window). To Rose Tomaszewska for forcing me out of my head and onto the page—your advice has forever changed how I write. And to Dominic Wakeford, for your gentle and thorough edits.

A few people deserve special mention. Saleem Haddad, my literary guardian angel, gave me the confidence to just *write*. I can never express how much your guidance and mentorship through the first draft meant to me, or how much your continued support still means. Lexi, you read the first sentence I wrote when this idea came to me, and you've read every rewritten sentence since. Your love for these characters kept pushing me through even when I thought there was no point in finishing. Maria, my Lenita, we've been through so much since kindergarten, and all these years later I've never met anyone so beautiful and smart who can fart on command. Thank you for letting me create this character to complement Simón, and for always being there no matter what. James, you helped me work through so many ideas and roadblocks while we painted murals around the country. Working with you is always a dream, but your faith in me and all my creative endeavors will never cease to astound me. Ezra Benisty, you made me consider what I want to say and why. Your handwritten edits and notes on that early draft are hanging in my office next to your poetry. Noor, your words helped me see the true value in the mother-son aspect of this story, and your check-ins have continued to sustain me. Andrew Salgado, I'm so excited to continue this book-writing journey with you.

And Courtney, thank you for being my biggest cheerleader. You always made me feel like writing this story was important, and you never let me listen to my inner dialogue telling me how garbage I am.

Finally, to Mike, for supporting me every step of the way—talking me off every prose-cluttered ledge, wiping tears from my blue-lit face, and buying me chocolate ice cream and Thai food to make it all bearable. I don't know where I'd be in life without you. And luckily, I don't need to worry about that! I'm beyond thankful for your support, your ideas, and most importantly, your love. You make my life golden and beautiful, just as it's supposed to be. My heart, my Mikey.

Glossary

A mimir	Cutesy way of saying "to sleep."
Abuela/o	Grandparent.
Ahijado	Godson.
Amiguito	Diminutive form of "friend."
Apeste	A stench.
Arroz con leche	Rice pudding.
Baboso	Idiot, fool. Literally "drooling person."
Basta ya	"Enough already" or "Stop it now."
Boniato	Cuban variety of sweet potato.
Bruja	Witch.
Brujería	Witchcraft.
Buñuelo	Fried dough pastry, often made for holidays, accompanied by a syrup made with cinnamon and anise.
Cachifloja	Run-on word that combines Cachete and Flojo, meaning "loose cheek."
Cachita	"Sweetheart" or "dear."
Cafecito/Café	Coffee.
Cafetera	Coffee percolator.
Cagalitroso/Viejo/Cagalitroso	Crude insult meaning "shitty old man."
Cara de fuchi	Stank face.
Caramba Concho	Mild curse expressing frustration, like "damn it."
Cariño	Darling, sweetheart, affection.
Chancleta	Flip-flop or sandal. Often used to

threaten discipline.

Chicharrones   Fried pork rinds or crispy pork belly.

Chisme   Gossip.

Chispa/Chispita   Spark/little spark.

Cochino   Pig.

Cocotazo   A smack to the back of the head.

Comemierda   Shit eater.

Coño   Catch-all exclamation. Can be used to communicate surprise, pain, anger, frustration, or any other extreme emotion.

Croquetas   Breaded and fried croquettes, usually ham or chicken.

Cuarenta   Forty.

Dígame   "Tell me." This is also used as a greeting when answering the phone.

El Palomar   "The Pigeon House." This is a loaded name, as "Palomo" is a word that can be used to refer to an effeminate gay man. "El palomar," was also historically used as the name given to prison sections specifically designated for homosexuals as it was still a crime to engage in homosexual behavior.

Encantada   "Delighted to meet you."

Enta albi. Enta hayati.   Arabic for "You are my heart. You are my life."

Ese hombre   That man.

Gran Varón   "Great Man." Reference to the Willie

	Colón song about a trans woman.
Guapo	Handsome.
Habibi	"My love," in Arabic.
Hermana	Sister.
Isabel Panocha	Invented drag queen name referencing Isabel Pantoja, a Spanish singer who gained popularity in the 80's. The word "panocha," is often used as slang for "vulva."
Lindo	Cute, pretty or beautiful.
Machista	Male chauvinist, sexist man.
Madrina/Nina	Godmother, Nina for short.
Maduros	Sweet fried plantains.
Malanga	Starchy root vegetable, similar to taro.
Malcriado	Badly raised, spoiled brat.
Malecón	Stone or concrete seawall that runs along the coast, often serving as both flood protection and a public walkway.
Mamón	Jerk, asshole. Literally, "sucker."
Maricón/Marica	Faggot.
Más que mucho	"More than a lot."
Media Mitad	"Other half," or soulmate.
Mijo/Mijito	My son.
Milagro	Miracle.
Mocoso	Snotty kid, brat.
Nena	Baby girl, sweetheart. A term of endearment.
Noche Buena	Christmas Eve.
Novela	Short for 'telenovela,' meaning soap opera.

Oye	Listen.
Padrino/Nino	Godfather. Nino for short.
Papa Diosito	Name used to describe God to children.
Pastelito	Small pastry, often filled with guava paste and cheese.
Pata de Palo	Wooden leg.
Pelona	Bald.
Pernil	Roasted pork shoulder, traditional holiday dish.
Perra	Bitch.
Picadillo	Ground meat dish with sofrito, olives, and other ingredients depending on the chef.
Pobrecita/o	Poor thing.
Precioso	Precious, beautiful.
Prima/o	Cousin.
Puñalito	"Little gay boy." Derogatory.
Qué locura	"How crazy!"
Qué te calles ya	"Shut up already."
Qué te importa que te ame	"What does it matter if I love you?"
Qué tú haces	"What are you doing?"
Ropa Vieja	Shredded beef dish. Literally, "old clothes."
Sana, sana, colita de rana …	"Heal, heal, little frog's tail …" Traditional healing chant recited by caregivers while gently rubbing a child's injury. The full rhyme continues, "si no sanas hoy, sanarás mañana" (if you don't heal today, you'll heal tomorrow).

Sapo Verde	"Green frog." This is a linguistic adaptation produced by a purposful mispronunciation by Spanish speaers singing "Happy Birthday to You" in English, resulting in "Sapo Verde to you." Often sung with comple seriousness and joy, it embodies the creativity and resilience of code-switching culture.
Semana Santa	Holy Week, the week leading up to Easter Sunday.
Si Dios quiere	"If God wills it."
Sin Bemba	"Without lips"
Sofrito	Cooking base consisting of chopped or blended aromatic vegetables, herbs and spices. Every family typically has their own recipe.
Solito	Alone.
Sucia/o	Dirty/filthy.
Suelta las nalgas	"Loosen your butt cheeks." A crude way to say relax.
Te amo	"I love you." More profound than the more casual "Te quiero."
Te quiero mucho	"I love you a lot."
Te voy a comer a besos	"I'm going to smother you with kisses." Literally, "I'm going to eat you with kisses."
Te voy a decir una cosa	"I'm going to tell you one thing." This phrase is often delivered very dryly and

used as preface to a reprimand. If this is said to you, you'd better listen well.

Tesoro — Treasure.

Tía/o — Aunt or Uncle.

Tú verás — "You'll see."

Una limpieza así de fácil — "An easy cleaning." Limpieza can also refer to a spiritual cleansing or removal of the evil eye.

Ven acá — "Come here." But can also mean to pay attention to what is being said.

Vente a comer — "Come eat."

About the Author

Mario Elías is a multidisciplinary artist of Cuban and Syrian descent based in Chicago. Working across fiction, nonfiction, photography, painting, and printmaking, his practice centers themes of identity, memory, and cultural inheritance. His visual work has appeared in *Vogue*, *San Francisco Magazine*, *Dazed*, and more.

His self-published collection *Queering the Male Gaze*—a series of essays and self-portraits reimagining classical and modern masterpieces through a queer lens—sold out multiple printings and reached readers in over twenty-five countries. The project reclaimed space for the often-overlooked queer and female figures behind the canon.

Elías is also the founder of *The KindaSuper Project*, a philanthropic initiative offering free photo and video services to underserved communities. It has partnered with wildfire survivors, immigrant families, women-of-color-led businesses, and wildlife rescue groups, using visual storytelling as a tool for resilience, advocacy, and joy.

He studied photography and art history at Columbia College Chicago, bringing a richly visual sensibility to his literary voice.

Instagram & Threads: @kindasupermario

Amble Press, an imprint of Bywater Books, publishes fiction and narrative nonfiction by LGBTQ writers, with a primary, though not exclusive, focus on LGBTQ writers of color. For more information on our titles, authors, and mission, please visit our website.

https://amblepressbooks.com

www.ingramcontent.com/pod-product-compliance
Lightning Source LLC
Jackson TN
JSHW020326040426
100314JS00001B/2